Sydney Thompson Dobell

Poetical Works

Vol. II

Sydney Thompson Dobell

Poetical Works
Vol. II

ISBN/EAN: 9783337094027

Printed in Europe, USA, Canada, Australia, Japan

Cover: Foto ©Andreas Hilbeck / pixelio.de

More available books at **www.hansebooks.com**

Sydney Thompson Dobell

Poetical Works
Vol. II

ISBN/EAN: 9783337094027

Printed in Europe, USA, Canada, Australia, Japan

Cover: Foto ©Andreas Hilbeck / pixelio.de

More available books at **www.hansebooks.com**

THE

POETICAL WORKS

OF

SYDNEY DOBELL.

' The flashes of the fire
Are fire, that which was soul is spirit still,
And shall not die.'

WITH INTRODUCTORY NOTICE AND MEMOIR

BY

JOHN NICHOL, M.A. Oxon. LL.D.

PROFESSOR OF ENGLISH LITERATURE IN
THE UNIVERSITY OF GLASGOW.

VOL. II.

LONDON:

SMITH, ELDER, & CO., 15 WATERLOO PLACE.

1875.

CONTENTS

OF

THE SECOND VOLUME.

BALDER.

PART THE FIRST.

B

AUTHOR'S PREFATORY NOTE

TO

THE SECOND EDITION.*

———◆———

IF the Poetry of this book had met with critical censure, I hope and believe I should have received the verdict in silence.   Not from any disrespect towards the organs of public opinion, but from certain convictions on the subject of Poetry, which it is not needful here to set forth Convictions, however, which might be expressed by the author of a book so well received as 'The Roman,' without provoking those suspicions that usually, and often justly, attend a depreciation or deprecation of applause.

But I find that many reviewers have mistaken the moral purpose and import of 'Balder,' and I therefore prefix to my Second Edition these few explanatory lines. The present book is the first part of a work, which I hope to complete in three Parts.   I intend as the principal subject of that work the Progress of a Human Being from

* Published in 1854.

Doubt to Faith, from Chaos to Order. Not of Doubt incarnate to Faith incarnate, but of a doubtful mind to a faithful mind. In selecting the type and conditions of humanity to be represented, I chose, for several important reasons, the poetic type and the conditions of modern civilisation.

And in treating the first and sadder portion of my subject I felt that justice to Nature required me to avoid all conventional portraits of the doubter, and—since in these days his malady is more often negative than positive— to indicate the absence of faith rather by the states and proportions of the other qualities than by a more distinct and formal statement of the differential defect.

I understand that the public press have described my hero to be egoistic, self-contained, and sophistical, imperfect in morality, and destitute of recognised religion, mistaken in his estimate of his own powers and productions, and sacrificing to visionary hopes and dreamy distant philanthropies the blessing that lay in his embrace, and 'the duty which was nearest.'

This is precisely the impression which I wished the readers of this volume to receive, and I owe some acknowledgment for such loud and emphatic testimony that exactly what I desired to attain has been attained. I have reason, however, to blame some of these powerful witnesses for the indecorous haste and uncharitable dogmatism with which, as I have seen and am informed, they have taken for granted that I must personally admire the character I think fit to delineate, and that I present as a model what, in truth, I expose as a warning. That I, in common with many of my critics, am not altogether free from some of the sins of my hero is probable on the general principle that 'Balderism' in one form or another is a predominant intellectual misfortune of our day. But that I have no theoretical approbation of such errors, may, I think, be naturally inferred from the history of failure and sorrow which I have herein attached to them.

That the author of 'The Roman,' a book of faith, patriotism, and self-sacrifice, must be personified in Balder, the egoistic hero of isolation and doubt, is a theory which, I think, contains its own refutation. Its serious maintenance might transfer to our modern critics a satire of Ben Jonson's which we have now no women who deserve :

'Did I not tell thee, Dauphine? Why all their actions are governed by crude opinions without reason or cause : they know not why they do anything, but as they are informed, believe, judge, praise, condemn, love, hate ; and in emulation one of another do all these things alike. *Only they have a natural inclination sways 'em generally to the worst when they are left to themselves.*'

I am told, however, that some important critical authorities, while recognising that 'Balder,' in 'part the first,' is by no means my notion of

——— 'Exemplar Dei,'

have loudly questioned the propriety of his creation, and have demanded by what public want or social necessity the author was directed to this portion of his subject.

Perhaps it would be considered too general a reference if I were to remit my demandants to the whole History of Intellect; and I will therefore indicate some special and recent chapters. In so indicating, I prefer—and can afford—to pass over those which would popularly vindicate this volume of my work, and to direct the really earnest inquirer to the materials of a wider and more philosophic reply. To the elements of my hero as they exist, uncombined or undeveloped, in the much-observed and well-recorded characters of men who have been, and have more or less deserved to be, praised, loved, followed and revered. To such suggestive monuments as the Autobiography of Haydon; to memorable passages in the letters of Keats; to many lessons from the life of David Scott; to sundry incidents in the history of Goethe; to several schools of English, French, and German Philosophy.

I might add—if I had not already confined myself to History—to the secret consciousness of the rising genius —perhaps the rising youth—of our strong, great, ambitious, but perplexed and disconcerted time.

It will be perceived, by the tone of these remarks, that I treat the misrepresentations to which this book has been subject as solely the result of unwilling misconstruction. If at any time or in any place, they have had a less pardonable origin, I am not inclined to be severe on the offender.

Poetry, by whatsoever other qualities it be distinguished, has this common characteristic—that it will live. Whether, therefore, this work be Poetry or not, I think its assailant may equally claim our condolence. On the one hand he assaults it to no detriment but his own ; on the other, I have imposed on him the labour of killing what, if it can die, should never have been born.

My personal relation to either case may be briefly and tritely expressed :

'A modest, sensible, and well-bred man
Will not affront me,—*and no other can.*'

PERSONS.

BALDER (*a Poet*).

AMY (*his wife*).

DOCTOR PAUL.

AN ARTIST.

A SERVANT.

BALDER.

SCENE I.

A STUDY, WITH BOOKS, MSS. AND STATUES. A WIN-
DOW LOOKS OVER A COUNTRY VALLEY TO THE NEIGH-
BOURING MOUNTAINS. A DOOR IN THE STUDY
COMMUNICATES WITH AN ADJOINING ROOM.

Balder (musing). To-morrow I count thirty years, save
    one.
Ye grey stones
Of this old tower gloomy and ruinous,
Wherein I make mine eyrie as an eagle
Among the rocks ; stones, valley, mountains, trees,
In which I dwell content as in a nest
Of Beauty,—comprehended less by more—
Or above which I rise, as a great ghost
Out of its mortal hull ; vale, mountains, trees,
And stones of home, which, as in some old tale
O' the east keep interchange of prodigies

With me, and now contain me and anon
Are stomached by mine hunger, unappeased
That sucks Creation˙down, and o'er the void
Still gapes for more; ye whom I love and fear
And worship, or i' the hollow of my hand
Throw like a grain of incense up to Heaven,
Tell me your secrets! That ye have a heart
I know; but can it beat for such as I?
Or do I unbeheld behold the fair
And answering mystery of your countenance
Passionate with rains and sunshine, and, unheard,
Have audience of your voices, but as one
Who in a temple passes unrespect
Between the kneeling suppliant and the saint,
Meeting the uplifted face and the rapt eyes
That look beyond? Am I but as a fly
Touching the vestal beauties of a maid
Unchidden; intimate but by how much
Inferior? Do ye speak over my head
Even as we pray aloud before a child?
You trees that I have loved so well, ye flowers
Unto whom, by so much as ye are more
In beauty, hath befallen a better love
Than mine, being HER chosen who to me
Is as your airy fragrance and mere hues
To your unblushed substantial; thou sweet vale
In which my soul, calm lying like a lake,
Reflects the stars, or, stirred, upon the shores

Of mountains maketh music, or more loud,
Rising in sudden flood, and breaking up
That firmament to heaped and scattered stars,
Chaotic to and fro from hill to hill
Defiesthe rounding elements, and rolls
Reverberating thunder ; have I lived
Not unbeloved, and shall I pass away
Not all unwept?
                    You floors, in whose black oak
The straitened hamadryad lives and groans,
Ye creaking dark and antiquated floors,
Who know so well in what sad note to join
The weary lullaby what time SHE rocks
Her babe, and murmurs music sad and low,
So sad and low as if this tower did keep
The murmur of the years as a sea-shell
The sea, or in these legendary halls
The mere air stirred, and with some old unknown
Sufficient conscience moved upon itself,
Whispering and sighing ; ruined castle-wall
Whereby she groweth like some delicate flower
In a deserted garden, thou grim wall
Hemming her in with thine unmannered rock
Wherein I set her as a wandering clown
Who, in a fairy-ring, by night doth seize
Some elfin taper, and would have it burn
In his gaunt lanthorn wrought by human hands
Uncouth, yet art so passing bright with her—

So fragrant! little window in the wall,
Eye-lashed with balmy sprays of honeysuckle,
Sweet jessamine, and ivy ever sad,
Wherein like a most melancholy eye,
All day she sits and looks forth on a world
Less fair than she, and as a living soul
Informs the rugged face of the old tower
With beauty; when the soul hath left the face
The sad eye looks no longer from the lid,
The sweet light is put out in the long rain,
The flower is withered on the wall, the voice
Will never murmur any more, and ye,
Ye, that both spake and saw, are dumb and blind,
—Blind save when midnight bolt from your death's-head
Starts like a bloody eyeball, or your rot
Glimmers in corse-lights on the shuddering dark——
And dumb, but for such noise as dumb men make,
When winds are moaning in your empty jaws—
Will there be aught to tell of what has been?
Where for so many nights and days she wept,
Shall not sweet colours in the slanting sun
Cross and recross, and floor the empty space
With rainbows? Will the lingering swallow stay
Within, as conscious of an influence
Like summer? Will an earlier primrose shine
On a peculiar season whereabout
The winds beat idly? Shall the winter thrush
Alight upon your dreary round and sing

As to a nestling? Shall the village school
Know the low turret where all stricken birds
Do shelter? Or the curious traveller note
The lonely tower where evermore the dew
Hangs on the herbs of ruin?

Sun and moon
Rising and setting, but now face to face
In equal Heaven, remember us! O ye
Celestial lovers, you at least should make
A love immortal! On this final eve
Methinks that ye look down on me with eyes
Of human contemplation. Lady Moon,
Casting as yet no shade, thy shade dissolved
In daylight of thy lord, O royal Sun,
Who though at last thou sink beneath the tides
She raiseth, unsubdued shalt glorify
The fatal waters, and still shine on her
With undiminished love, to you I leave
Our memories. Oh consecrate these stones
And point with mindful shadow day and night,
Where we lie dust below.

SCENE II.

Amy. The years they come, and the years they go
Like winds that blow from sea to sea;
From dark to dark they come and go,
All in the dew-fall and the rain.
Down by the stream there be two sweet willows,
—Hush thee, babe, while the wild winds blow,—
One hale, one blighted, two wedded willows
All in the dew-fall and the rain.

She is blighted, the fair young willow,
—Hush thee, babe, while the wild winds blow,—
She hears the spring-blood beat in the bark;
She hears the spring-leaf bud on the bough;
But she bends blighted, the wan weeping willow,
All in the dew-fall and the rain.

The stream runs sparkling under the willow,
—Hush thee, babe, while the wild winds blow,—
The summer rose-leaves drop in the stream;
The winter oak-leaves drop in the stream;
But she bends blighted, the wan weeping willow,
All in the dew-fall and the rain.

Sometimes the wind lifts the bright stream to her,
—Hush thee, babe, while the wild winds blow,—
The false stream sinks, and her tears fall faster ;
Because she touched it her tears fall faster ;
Over the stream her tears fall faster,
All in the sunshine or the rain.

The years they come, and the years they go ;
Sing well-away, sing well-away !
And under mine eyes shines the bright life-river ;
Sing well away, sing well-away !
Sweet sounds the spring in the hale green willow,
The goodly green willow, the green waving willow ;
Sweet in the willow, the wind-whispering willow ;
Sing well-away, sing well-away !
But I bend blighted, the wan weeping willow,
All in the sun, and the dew, and the rain.

SCENE III.

THE SAME. A TABLE COVERED WITH MSS. AND BOOKS.

BALDER, *solus.*

Balder. Looking upon the lives of other men,
I see them move in apt and duteous signs,
That look like cause and consequent, through type
And antitype, day after equal day,

Year after answering year, from sire to son.
But life hath been to me a strange wild dream,
Wherein the prodigies that haunt and home
Within a human bosom have been brought
Marvel by marvel, as to Adam once
The monsters of the Earth, that I might name them,
And know them, and be friends with them.

                                       A youth

In years, I hold the weft and woof of age,
And wheresoever Time may cut the web,
Can find no novel texture.   One sole thread
Thou owest me, Lachesis ! but I will trust thee,
Oh thou unfailing debtor !   Upon Earth
All sights I have beheld but one ; all sorrows
Either in type or kind endured but one.
Death, careful of my learning, hath withstayed
His final presence, lest his shade allay
My wounds, and, as before the King of Beasts,
The lesser horrors of the wilderness
Flee at his great approach.   I have not seen him,
In cause or in effect.   But he will come !
For till he come my perfect manhood lacks,
And this that I was born to do is done
By nothing less than man.

                           That I should do it,
And be the King of men, and on the inform
And perishable substance of the Time
Beget a better world, I have believed

Up thro' my mystic years, since in that hour
Of young and unforgotten exstacy
I put my question to the universe,
And overhead the beech-trees murmured ' Yes.'
Therefore I grew up calm like a young god,
Having in well-assured serenity
No haste to reach and no surprise to wear
The inevitable stature ; nor thought strange
To feel me not as others, to pursue
Amid the crowd a solitary way,
And take my own in the o'er-peopled world,
And find it no man's else.   When at the first,
Because I was no higher than mankind,
All men went past, and no man looked on me,
I felt no humbler.   When this ample frame
Expanded into majesty, and they
Who saw fell back admiring, I beheld
Their change, not mine ; for the unconscious child,
Tho' for his childhead he be special child,
Is universal man, and in his thoughts
Doth glass the future.   The thin sapling oak,
Hid in the annual herbage of the field,
Hath oaken members, and can boast no more
When they defy the storms of heaven, and roost
The weary-winged Ages.   One alone,
Early and late,—faithful as she who knows
And keeps the secret of the foundling heir—
Did bear me witness.   Nature from my birth

Confessed me, as who in a multitude
Confesseth her beloved and makes no sign ;
Or as one all unzoned in her deep haunts,
If her true-love come on her unaware,
Hastes not to hide her breast, nor is afraid ;
Or as a mother 'mid her sons displays
The arms their glorious father wore, and, kind,
In silence with discerning love commits
Some lesser danger to each younger hand,
But to the conscious eldest of the house
The naked sword; or as a sage amid
His pupils in the peopled portico,
Where all stand equal, gives no precedence,
But by intercalated look and word
Of equal seeming, wise but to the wise,
Denotes the favoured scholar from the crowd ;
Or as the keeper of the palace gate
Denies the gorgeous stranger and his pomp
Of gold, but at a glance, although he come
In fashion as a commoner, unstarred,
Lets the prince pass.

      I think my hour is nigh.
I am almost equipped ; and earth and air
Are full of signs. The uncommanded host
Of living nations, swaying to and fro
Like waves of a great sea that in mid-shock
Confound each other, white with foam and fear,
Roar for a leader. All this last strange year

The clouds seemed higher, and each bird of wing
Doubled his usual flight, and the blue arch
Opened above, expansive ; even as tho'
The labouring world drew in a deeper breath,
And raised her swelling bosom nearer Heaven
With expectation. My prophetic heart
Confirmed the omen, and, as ere the crash
Of earthquake the dull sun stands clothed upon
With sackcloth, and as to his golden head
Shorn, I am troubled with the fate not yet
Accomplished ; an unreasoning melancholy
Directs me ; I have lingered by the Past
As by a death-bed, with unwonted love
And such forgiveness as we bring to those
Who can offend no more. The very stones
Of old memorial have been dear to me,
Sitting long days on ancient stiles worm-worn,
And gazing thro' green trees o'er grassy graves
Upon the living village and the dead,
The early and the latter tryst that all
Have kept so long and well ; or to the pile
Reared by those English whose ancestral feet
Trod the same path their children's children keep
Still hallowed, where the beauty of the vale,
The blushing girl of yonder bridal train,
Walks in her love and joy, and passing slow
Salutes unconscious with her wedding skirt
The gable end, no greyer than of yore,

When by the same dark yew for ever old,
The same grey Time did hold his scythe above
Her grandame's head, whose silk of long ago
. So rustled on the wall when she went by
A happy bride, and heard perchance that day
Tales from wan lips of the far morning when
Her mother's mother passed as fair as she.
Or on the leafy and live-long repose
Of country labour, and the unhasted life
That plods with equal step the wonted way,
A-field at morn and homeward slow at eve,
And slow with eve and morn through drowsy day
Doth toil and feed and sleep and feed and toil.
Or on lone homesteads and the untrespassed rest
Of immemorial pastures, and the tread
Of dreamful herds in verdant peace unvexed
And taskless thro' the round of sauntering day,
And all the dewy leisure of the meads.
As though the coming din of war should scare
The tenants of the field, and wildered fear
Distract the rural motion, and repeat
In bleating folds and trampled harvests loud
With dread, the desperate and delirious pulse
Of man ; and knowing I did look my last
Of pastoral quiet, and the passive gait
Of ease that is the step of all their world,
Their world at pace with solemn things above,
With tardy-footed twilight, and all powers

Eterne that tread time with celestial wont
Immortal, with the seasons of the earth,
And with the calm procession of the stars.
'Tis well that on the landmark of to-day
I lean awhile, and with clear eyes look back
Upon the way I came, ere once again .
I set forth on my journey to the goal
Which I have sworn to win.
                    That bard who lies
Like the old knight i' the picture, at the root
Of our hereditary tree, (first sire
Of the long line where Shakspeare is not last)
And by his posture measures height with none,
Beheld a ' House of Fame.'   For me, I seek
A sterner architecture and a dome
More like the heavens, upon that hill which he
Who climbs is strongest among living men,
The seat of templed Power.   Not Fame but Power.
Or Fame but as the noise of Power, a voice
That in the face is wind, but in the ear
Truth, Knowledge, Wisdom, Question, Speculation,
Hope, Fear, Love, Hate, Belief, Doubt, Faith, Despair,
Every strong gust that shifts the sails of man,
And so far worth the utterance; Fame the paid
Muezzin on the minaret of Power,
Calling the world to worship; Fame the pied
And gilded following of the royal house,
Whose function is without, to spread the awe

Of Power among the common herd, and hand
External homage to the chaste convoy
Of them who serve in presence ; or at best,
An argent herald running on before,
Nor daring once to turn his menial mouth
To tell me what I know, and whose great trump
Tho' it blow Regnarok and wake the graves,
Is but a sounding brass.   Not Fame but Power.
Power like a god's and wielded as a god !
I would have been the wind, and unbeheld
Rase the tall roaring forest, not the flash
That cannot move unseen ; the influence
Unnamed that finds a city and leaves a tomb,
But not the conflagration to flame wide
A rabble holiday, round which the Town
Gapes, and whereof all men have leave to speak,
Cried in the civic streets and parodied
In pictures ; and for which, at last put out,
No. hand so base but had availed to do
The final deed, nor urchin but hath spat
Enough extinction.   Whatsoe'er attains
In solitude, and out of sight doth sling
The stone of practice where no vulgar tongue
May cry unskilled applause on the wide throw
Of strong attempt, nor ever in men's eyes
Hath eminence so young that the kind hand
Of popular approval dare be laid
Upon its head, I love.   The Victory

Which hath no mortal opposite to try
Conclusions and assess my over-match,
I covet.   I could wish that the good Powers,
Which watched over my making had denied
The gifts that quell mankind.   I would have gone
Into the wilderness, and in some cell
Of task severe and exercise divine,
Grown god-like till perforce the vigilant gods
Seeing me there made me their deputy
As being next to them.   I would have sat
And blessed creation, seeing in calm joy
The thankless welfare, and content to know,
That from their far thrones, Potentates of Heaven,
When a new glory flushed this planet earth
Did look to me on mine.   Whatever rules
By its mere nature and that native place
Holding of nought below it, from below
Receives nor of accession or decess,
Nay by its sovereign essence, is beyond
The praise and subject homage of the ruled,
I would have been ; up from the viewless air
That feeds the unconscious world, or this rare life
Full in these throbbing veins that moves unfelt
The beating heart I feel, to the supreme
And central force that sways the universe
Unknown, and, being absolute, well pleased
Resigns the weight of glory, and permits
To shining suns and stars the gorgeous crown,

And golden signs of empire.

                              I do think
My throne is set.   If this next year might bring
My one delayed experience!   And, that past,
End, as with harvest, in some genial close
Of happier fortunes!   For the fruit of sorrow,
Tho' it do grow in the shade ere it be ripe,
Asks light and heat, and I am now as when
Oblivious Nature holds the time o' year,
Brimfull in a dead level of dull days,
Till, reaching forth a hand, the sudden sun
Touches the cup, and spills upon the earth ·
The mantling season.
(*Taking up a Manuscript.*)   Oh thou first, last, work!
Thou tardy-growing oak that art to be
My club of war, my staff, my sceptre!   Thou
Hast well nigh gained thine height.   My early planned,
Long meditate, and slowly-written epic!
Turning thy leaves, dear labour of my life,
Almost I seem to turn my life in thee.
Thy many books my many votive years,
And thy full pages numbered with my days.
I could look back on all that I have built
As on some Memphian monument wherein
The kings do lie in glory, every one
Each in his house, and forward to thy blank
Fair future, as one gazes into depths
Of necromantic crystal, and beholds

The heavens come down.

                      I think I have struck off

One from the weary score of human tasks.

Having so told my story in a tongue

So common to the ages, that no man

In after times shall tell it, but the fact   .

To which I have given voice shall be laid by,

And this my sterling with mine image on,

Present the ponderous bulk ; and I shall leave

This history my autograph, wherein

The hand that writes is part of what is writ,

And I, like the steeped roses of the east,

Become the necessary element

Of that which doth preserve me.

                    Howsoe'er

This be, and whether I attain or fail

To add another to those lights of heaven

That rule our day and night,—to set a sun

Of joy above us, or some saddest moon

Whose pale reflected rays, from their first aim

And primal course bent back and contravert

Like some Apollo's golden shaft returned

From an opposing bow, shall still bespeak

The splendour of their quiver—I do feel

I have deserved to win. Thought, Labour, Patience,

And a strong Will, that being set to boil

The broth of Hecate would shred his flesh

Into the cauldron, and stir deep with arms

Flayed to the seething bone ere there default
One tittle from the spell—these should not strive
In vain! No. I have lived what I have sung,
And it shall live. The flashes of the fire
Are fire, that which was soul is spirit still,
And shall not die. I sat above my work
As God above the new unpeopled world
Sat and foresaw our days, and sun and cloud
Of good and ill passed o'er the countenance
Ineffable, and filled the plains below;
Smiled all a floral kingdom thro' the world,
Or frowned a race of lions.

       With the year
That ended yesterday, I close the book
Of mortal contest, and begin to sing
Record of the aërial tournaments
Whereof we are but shadows, on the fields
Where spirit meets with spirit, and god with god.
And first thee, Death,——

    Enter SERVANT, *with post-bag.*

       Letters! (*Opens and reads.*)
  Balder (*after a long pause*). Oh men, oh men,
What are ye that I yearn to you, and ye
To me, but that no grasp of mortal love
Against the strong enribbed heart can break
The mystic band that limits each from each,
Nor sternest edifice of separate life
Can wholly shut ye out? If nought can make

Us one, why can we not be twain in peace?
Why do you touch me, why do your kind eyes,
Unasked, look into mine? Why does your breath
Fall warm upon me, and infect my veins
With strange commotion? Is it to be borne,
That ye will neither enter into me,
Nor leave me? that men look upon my face,
And take me for another; that I know
Your wants before you tell them, feel the pains
You feel; give language to your secret bliss
Better than you who know it? That ye cure
My bodily ailments with the selfsame drug
That heals the fool; that he who should cut off
This right hand with nice science, that foreknows
Each sequent vein and muscle, learned his skill
Upon a felon? That my last death-sob
Will be much like what any hangman hears,
And that the very meanest lips alive
Do speak some word of mine?

                Thou happy God,
That hast no likeness, wherefore hast Thou made
Me thus? Have I not gone into unknown
Unentered lands, and heard in alien tongue
Strange man unto strange man unload his heart,
And started in my soul, and said, ' Eh ghost !
Art thou I?'

          Am I one and every one,
Either and all? The innumerable race,

My Past; these myriad-faced men my hours?
What! have I filled the earth, and knew it not?
Why not? How other? Am I not immortal?
And if immortal now, immortal then;
And if immortal then, existent now;
But where? Thou living moving neighbour, Man,
Art thou my former self—me and not me?
Did I begin, and shall I end? Was I .
The first, and shall I one day, as the last,
Stand in the front of the long file of man,
And looking back, behold it winding out,
Far thro' the unsearched void, and measuring time
Upon eternity, and know myself .
Sufficient, and, that like a comet, I
Passed thro' my heaven, and fill'd it?

[*Through the door are heard the rocking of a cradle,
and the voice of* AMY.]

Amy (*singing*). The cuckoo-lamb is merry on the lea,
The daisied lea; I would I were the lamb!
While that the lark will pipe, the lamb will dance,
And when the lark is mute he danceth still;
Up springs the lark, and pipes again for joy!
He, more by birth, than we by toil and skill,
Is happy with no labour but to live;
He leapeth early, and he leapeth late;
He leapeth in the sunshine and the rain,
Nor fears the hour that will not find him blest,
And milky plenty sauntering by his side.

Also the lamb that doth not toil nor spin,
Lies where he will, and where he lieth sleeps.
Sleeps on the hill-top like a cloud o' the hill,
Sleeps where the trembling Lily of the Vale,
Albeit she is so spotless, sleepeth not,
But like a naked fairy fears all night
The wind that for her beauty cannot sleep.
Sleeps on the nettle or the violet:
Or where the sun doth warm his trance with light,
Or where the runnel murmureth cool dreams,
Or where the eglantine not yet in bloom,
Like a sweet girl full of her sweeter thought,
Reveals unheard the sweetness still to be.
Or where the darnel nods, and, as they tell
Of beauty nursed upon a savage dug,
Sucks grace from the harsh bosom of the waste.
Sleeps in the meadow buttercups at noon,
—A babe a-slumber in a golden crib—
Or like a daisy by the way-side white,
And like a daisy quieteth the way.
The lamb, the lamb, I would I were the lamb!
    Balder (*musing*).   Thou most pure
And guileless voice, I never breathed thee! No,
Thou meek misfortune, thou art not my past.
My Amy, my own Amy, whom of old
I found as a wild sailor of the sea
Comes on some happy isle of Love and Peace,
Some isle where joys that in all other climes,

Sweet flying thro' the night of his dark way,
A moment rest upon his sail, pass on,
And are beheld no more, in equal haunts
And bright assured communion ever dwell,
Day without night, and native, brood and sing!
Thou who thro' the stern ordeal of this life
Didst cling beside me, while I showed my power,
And turned the dust and ashes where I stood,
To gold and ruby, so that the great throng
Cried out for envy, and with murderous shout
Demanded the pure jewel I had not,
And when I trembled, knowing that mine art
Was ended, and the clamorous people saw,
Unseen didst slide thy wealth into my hand
And save me, so that I, serene, unclosed
My palm before the Judge, and lo! a pearl;
My first Love and my last, so far so near,
So strong, so weak, so comprehensible
In these encircling arms, so undescribed
In any thought that shapes thee; so divine,
So softly human that to either stretch,
Extreme and farthest tether of desire
It finds thee still; my ministering saint,
Attendant sprite, enshrined Egeria!
My ornament, my crown, my Indian gem
And incommunicable amulet
Upon my breast, not me but warm with me! (*pauses.*)
You heavens! how far a little breath may blow

The unstable bubble of inflated thought!
O voice, O little voice, what power of thine
Disbands my hosts, which, as a crowd of shades
That scatter at a word, in sudden rout
Like the four winds unloosed have sprung apart
And vanished into distance, until I,
Whose royal and innumerable train
Out-trooped the legioned gods, 'am left alone
As one uncounted?   How those charmèd walls,
And airy castles, that we rear to hold
The powers that plague us, and do well contain
Imprisoned fiends, are pervious to the touch
Of any human hand!   That we should build them,
And a mere child should put his vital finger
Thro' the main bulwark !   That the head should write,
And, with a gush of living blood, the heart
Should blot it !   As one proves there is no God
And falls upon his knees.   Right sapient sage !
Supreme intelligence !   Sole substantive !
Lord of the empty dark !   True Prince of Nil
And Nihilo ! a royal argument ;
But ere thou sign triumphant demonstration
Be blest and let a benefit refute thee !
My little Amy !   [*Exit.*

SCENE IV.

THE EMPTY STUDY.

Through the half-open Door is heard the voice of AMY.

Amy.   My lord, that walkest thro' the universe,
Did I not go beside thee, as a child,
With humble step and looking to thy face?

My king, who reignest wheresoe'er thou art!
All do thy hest, my King! but who as I?
Hast thou not all thy subjects here in me?

My husband, who hast loved me like a god,
And blessed me, surely I did well to love
Thee as a god?—but can a god forget?

Wherein have I offended? Nay, thy brow
Is sweet and cloudless—I have done no ill.

My husband, have I not been still thy bird,
Thy dove, thy snow-white dove, upon thy wrist,
Or in thy breast, or feeding from thy lips,
Or round thine head, or fluttering with fond feint
Before thy footsteps—with mine eyes on thee?

Was I not as a lamb around thy feet,
That loved thee? For my neck thou didst entwine

Sweet garlands and I followed thee, nor knew
The inexorable sadness, till a door
Opened, and thou art among men, and I
Am but a lamb, and bleat about the gate.

My husband, I have been an orphan fawn
That ran beside the cubless lioness ;
Who spared her, and did make with her what sport
Befits the offspring of the forest king.
And the poor fawn still gambolled in her blood.

Have I not been a moth about thy light
Scorched, scorched ; but, husband ! when the wound was
    worst,
Winging with madder passion still to thee !

   Wert thou not always as a crescent moon,
And I thy star within thee, till the time
Came, and the lengthening distance, and I knew
My rising and my setting were not thine.

   Oh was I not a floweret in thine hand
When thou didst stand upon the peak of thought
Gazing to heaven, which with a thunder-shock
Rolled back, and angels came to thee, and thou
Didst stretch to them thine open hands uplift
In welcome, and I fell to where I am.

VOL. II.   D

I think they touched thine eyes, and that thenceforth
Thou seest all things clearly, and me here,
Nor knowest. it is very far from thee.
Oh husband ! it is night here in the vale,
And I lie on the rugged earth who had
Thy bosom ; moreover I cannot hear
Thy voice, nor tho' thou seest me can I see
Thy face.   It is not with me as with thee ;
The shadows here are always long and deep,
Also the night comes sooner than to thee.

SCENE V.

THE STUDY.

Balder, at his writing-table.

Balder.   Death, thou must stand aside !   The mood
      is not
Upon me, and my gold is only dug
I' the vein.   The microcosmos, like its twin,
Hath climates and their seasonable fruits.
My brain is warm, and I behold the sun ;
Clear as a pulsing wave of hyaline,
And I cry ' Light ;' tender and beautiful
As the west waiting for the evening star,
And loveliness, like a fair girl, comes forth
Into the dewy silence.   As I throb

The sense responds, and, like a courtier's eyes,
Finds for each royal folly of my soul
Portentous reason.   The disordered fact
Outruns its antecedent, and so much
Eternity within doth set at nought
The wont of time, that I am stirred yet ere
Disturbance, and do suffer by the ill
Not yet admitted to the sum of things.
I will await what figure now unseen
Is to rise up and lay his charmed hand
Upon this inner harp, from string to string
Already trembling, and arrive, tho' late,
To give a name to that foredone effect
Which else had lacked a father.

　　　　　[*He meditates, writes, and reads aloud.*
'Then saw I Genius, blind, with upturned face,
As one who hears, and to the struggling sense
(Tottering beneath accomplishment, and faint
In touch of the inestimable prize)
Each from his office brings her conscript powers
Auxiliar, and in strained conflux sustains
The sole perception ; happy so to gain
The one sufficient knowledge, and therein
Utterly blessed.   Like a listening saint
Lifting her wrapt brow to the audible Heaven.
Nor sightless by defect, but that her lids
Closed o'er the needless eyes.   Her moving lips
Perfunctory incessant murmur made,

And thus she held her unrespective way,
Following the upper sound which no man heard,
Summer and winter, day and night; but more
Like a sweet madness in those dearer times
Wherein the hornèd seasons fill and wáne,
Spring, autumn. morn, and eve; o'er hill and alp,
Forest and city, steep and battlement,
Or wrought or native; through vales, gulphs, and ca
And midnight solitudes, and martial plains,
And sun, and storm, and frost, and flood, and fire.'

Bah, is this Genius who should rule the world
And be incarnate God? Rather, methinks,
Some maimed celestial, feeling back her way
To the lost heavens, or that fair Eve whom once
Genius, what time she ' listened to the voice,'
Caught in his arms in Eden.
(*Turning to a statue.*)   Listening Eve !
What marvel that my spell-bound fancy drew
The captive, not the captor? As the earth
Revolves, and we behold the vanished stars
Of yesterday, that, being fixed, remain
To gladden lands beyond us, so in thee,
Immortal! this our Present, wondering, comes
Round to the sight of long lost Paradise,
And all the primal act. And we go down
To death, but thou, fast held, remainest to rise
On other times, and, orient by our fall,

Shalt light the orb of ages.

                   Thou rare power,
Sluggard, ungrateful, wayward, false, and vain,
Whom men call Muse !   I cannot fetter thee,
But I can punish.   Back into the void,
And bring me what I seek?   ⌊*He writes.*

                Now what art thou,
Genius? (*reads.*) 'There came a chariot o'er the earth,
Swift on strange wheels, such as eye hath not seen,
Nor can see, in the speed of their great course
Viewless, but leaving tracks which nations ran
To wonder at.   Whether o'er rugged rocks
Passing, and turning all their streams to tears
Sad down the channelled visage of the hills ;
Or o'er the level sea, whirling strange dews
And rainbows to a luminous mist, wherein
Mermaids in sportive companies made play
Beneath their dark hair, till the heaving sea
Blushed like a cloudy morn, and dolphins leaped,
And Triton mounted on a foaming wave
Sounded pursuit ; or o'er the beaten road
Of daily use raising a dust that fell
Upon the things that were, and made them new.
(The clime cleared, and on either hand the path
Arcadian did spontaneous holiday
Prankt with its herbs of grace.   Fair sun and moon,
From signs of fortune with consenting stars
In sweet succession, or conjunctions rare

Shone festal round the car, while Time himself
Grew young, and ran before.   Fierce beasts that shun
The common sunshine, rose, and each subdued,
Moved to the genial light, from his dark den
Approaching tame by every forest glade,
Where Una led the lion.   Nor rude race
Of daily men, that like a city flood,
Came headlong heedless mixed in civic din,
Escaped the spell ; nor touched the enchanted ground
But sudden as to music in the air,
Grave measured step and custom of the gods
O'ertook them—Salian and Œnoplian dance
Heroic, and the front of golden days.)
Or whether over Alpine solitudes
Ploughing such record as nor mountain storms
That rage midway, nor high above the thunder
The ceaseless snows of silent centuries
Efface ; or crossing immemorial plains
Indentured where the furrows fill with flowers
As with a Tyrian rain ; where'er on earth
It found the barren wilderness, and left
Eden—if Eden was the rosy prime,
The master passion, and first ecstasy
Of this our world.   Nor drawn by steed, nor steered
By human hand, it came an empty car
To the embattled people as of will,
And took its martial station in the van,
And post of honour.   Then the mighty men

Climbed, venturous, its crystal sides wherein
The changing tumult of the mirrored field
Shone, like opposing armies.   But behold
A marvel ! for the empty car was full,
And none could enter.   Therefore moved with fear
And jealous doubt, they called the legions round
To thrust it forth, which passive in the midst
Stood stirless—tho' still wheeled the wheeling wheels
Invisible with motion.   But when spears
Were couched and charging, sudden from the ground
Wingless it rose ! and all the baffled host
Fell with deceived expectance.   As it rose
Slow thro' the day, the wondrous wheels being still
Hung in the air, and the great multitude
With upturned eyes amazed at once cried out
Their likeness, and of countless voices each
Belied its neighbour.   But the car sublime
Above the round horizons, each on each
Widening like circles in the stagnant sea
Of space disturbed, showed like a lesser world
Dyed with the coloured earth, and as it went
Heavenward, and we astonished still beheld,
Lo ! we were ware as of a countenance
Unspeakable, and as of burning hands
Waving farewells, and somewhat of a form
Sitting within the brightness.   Then convulsed
With shame, both of their tardy eyes obscure
And lost revenge, from instant bows and slings,

Artillery and every loud offence,
Sudden the universal host upsent
Impotent rage.   As tho' the earth that lay
A sleeping beast, sprang up, and with a roar
Shaking his shaggy hide, with thickest dust
Darkened the air.

         Then the mysterious wheels
Whirled in the sky; the burning hands uplift
Pointed to Heaven ; and the tremendous car
Launched thro' the seas of light, and passed the noon
As the mere yellow strand whence it set sail
To sea ; careering as to reach the goal
Of all things, and come back.   And, as it passed,
He whom we saw threw out a golden chain,
And linked the sun, and led him from his lair
Obedient, while night fell on earth ; and He
Shot thro' the darkness and was lost.   But soon,
—Himself unseen—I knew his viewless way,
Thro' the stirred Heavens where I saw the stars
Leaving their spheres, till as it were a host
Of meteors shone across the streaming sky.
Nor him victorious long the toil delayed,
But on a time thro' all the flaming air
Rose the large dawn of his far-off return,
And as it rose and rose embraced the earth
Into a breast of glory; such great day
Began the morning as if life had changed
Its metre, heaving nature had attained

To grander issues, and a rounded year
Came up the ampler east.   And Him I saw
Rushing upon the Orient ; in his train,
Fierce as reluctant lions dragged at speed
Behind a victor,—all their forest-brood
Roaring around and leaping—captive suns
Attend him, and their wild and scattered moons
Whiten the air.   Then the pale nations cast
Dust on their heads, and hid their dazzled eyes,
And over all a great sound, full of death,
Shrieked like a plague-wind from a battle-field,
Noisome with mortal horror thro' the land.
" Woe, woe, we cast him from us in his day,
And now he will return to take the world
And burn it in his fury !" '
(*Throws the MS. to the ground.*)   Lie thou there !
Genius is yet unwritten.

       [*Through the door is heard the voice of* AMY.
Happy eve, happy eve !
But the mavis singing in the eve,
Singeth for the silence of the eve.

Happy flower, happy flower,
But the golden secret of the flower,
Hidden honey sweeter than the flower.

Happy moon, happy moon,
But the loving moonlight of the moon,
Tender wonder fairer than the moon.

Little child, little child,
As the evening mavis unto me,
As the twilight mavis unto me.

Little child, little child,
As the hidden honey unto me,
As the golden honey unto me.

Little child, little child,
As the wondrous moonlight unto me,
As the better moonlight unto me.

SCENE VI.

THE VACANT STUDY.

Through the open Door the voice of AMY.

Amy. Sleep thee, my child, altho' when thou didst
      sleep
And shut thine eyes methought the world was blind.
Sleep thee, my child, altho' thy mother wakes,
Sleep, happy babe, upon a woeful breast.

Oh, babe, I can endure to live ; oh babe,
I see thee thro' the anguish of my years
Like a star rising thro' the smoke of hell.

Oh babe, I have escaped to thee beyond,
Beyond the present torture, calm and sweet ;
A moment, and I reck not of the fiends.

And I am bathed in dews, and in thy sphere
Thou bearest me naked of all my woes
Which burn upon me, babe, but are not me.

My vesture is on fire ; all all in vain,
In vain I tear it, knotted strong and deep
With chains more cruel than the flames, in vain
I run and fan them in the wind of life.
A moment I am free beyond the years !
Thou risest, oh my star, and I to thee !
A moment, and the flesh must needs be here,
And the fierce anguish knotted to the flesh,
And I am like a spirit in thine urn,
Cool thro' the balmy shades of painless heaven.

Sleep, sleep, my babe, thou shalt not cry me nay ;
Sleep, sleep, my babe, my babe, while it is night,
Ah, who shall say the morn may not be fair ?
Sleep, little babe, and let my terror sleep !
Oh sleep awhile, and stop the wheels of fate.
I think that there is privilege in woe,
And sorrow may not seize us everywhere,
And havoc doth not hunt where'er he list,
And sleep is halcyon time when griefs are still.

Sleep, sleep, my babe, and let me clasp thee fast
And know a little space thou canst not die,   ⎰
Nor earth nor heaven or plots or works thine ill.
Sleep, sleep, my babe, my babe, and let me hold
My destiny a moment in mine arms,
Nor find it heavier than can rise and fall
Harmless as thou upon my heaving breast.

Alas ! alas ! the vision of my youth !
When that I lifted not mine eyes to pray,
But I beheld HIM thro' the cloudless air,
Walking as on a morning mountain-top
Transfigured, with the azure clothed about,
Nor on a higher earth, but lower heaven !
Sleep, sleep, my babe, and dream thy mother's dream,
That all her joy may be contained in thee.

He stood in light, he stood in blinding light !
I loved, I climbed to reach him where he stood,
I the weak woman, I the child of clay !
I fell ; to see him, from the beetling brink,
Stretching for ever unavailing arms
To her who, as in dreams, for ever falls.

Oh hapless, hapless heart, too proud to fall !
Oh hapless, hapless limbs, too frail to climb !
Heart of these limbs, how couldst thou be so proud ?
Oh limbs, how could ye mate so proud a heart ?

Sleep, sleep, my babe, and dream thy mother's dream,
And if to wake like her, oh wake no more !

If thou couldst grow what once I prayed to be,
If I could see a daughter at his side,
And he might look upon himself more fair,
And all her mother with a kinder fate !

'Tho' I have failed and fallen in the race,
Thou shalt redeem me, and with better limbs
Contend.   And I will kneel and shew my scars,
And make too memorable with my tears
Each treacherous fortune where thy mother fell.
And break with mine own hands her image fair,
And show her to thine eyes so wan and weak,
Crazed with waste life and unavailing days.
And stir thee, blushing with her penitence,
And in the fire of a great love and woe
Become as nought before thee, that thou, Babe,
Inherit from her ashes, and arise
Triumphant from the pyre, and so in death
I load thee with my hopes, and win in thee !

Awake, awake, my babe, my only babe,
Sleep not too deeply, babe, thou art my heart,
And only by its pulse I know I live.

————————

SCENE VII.

THE STUDY.

BALDER, *writing*.

Balder (*reads*). ' I stood and did not dream.
Before me was the great plain, and behind
The long dark mountains over which the sun
Held noon ; and as I stood the earth till now
All summer trembled, and beyond the ridge
A pulsing murmur as of coming seas
On echoing shores from out a further void,
Grew in the far dim distance, as once more
Old ocean made invasion, and advanced
With all his waves.   And as a dreamer hears
What sounding on her fleeing track pursues
The frantic soul that in the panic dies,
In louder progress, strepitous, so came
The great approach.   Whereat the agued earth
With deadly fear did shiver to her core.
And the sound rose, and her great dread became
Convulsion, and the rampant uproar beat
Wilder alarum on the battered ear,
Swift waxing to the tumult of a host
Charging to battle all on serried steeds
That stepped as one.   I strained to the event
With eye-balled sight as to a cry i' the dark,

And all the unseen pursuit more near enraged,
—The panting terror and the throbbing chase,—
Wilder as if the beating heart o' the world
In palpitation mad and moribund
Huge in its quaking tenement did shake
Th' enribbed rocks.   And—as me, utterless,
Strong tumult choked, and sick expectance pale,
And horror of the end—a louder blast
Rush'd o'er, and sudden at a thunder peal,
As tho' the loaded sound did with a roar
Discharge its cause, while the great herd that grazed
The summits parted like a scattered flock
Beneath a lion, somewhat leaped the hills,
The awful hills, and on the shattered plain
Came like the crash of doom !   Riderless he,
Who can bestride him ?   Tho' his reeking flanks
Sonorous clang with loud caparison
Of sounding war.   A moment, and he stands
Heightened with pride, dilate at haughty gaze,
His swelling frame to half the horizon round
Breathing defiance ; fierce his levelled head
Equals the clouds ; his eye is as a hot
And bloody star ; his nostrils as the red
Round throat of fiery ordnance, and his snort
Ten thousand clarions.   Such a steed, so wild,
Left, in some ancient battle of the gods,
Great Mars unhorsed.

     And now as one who sees

His foe beyond the river, with a plunge
Divides the waters, he with sudden spring
From the recoiling fields that reeled and broke,
Breasted the big spent clouds that, faint with flight,
Each upon each lay cumulous, and thro'
That sundered sea, tremendous, a mile hence,
Swift as a bolt and heavy as a hill,
Shocked the rent plain, and in as wild rebound,
Leaped in mere strength a thousand fathoms high,
Lashing new winds, and, wanton in descent,
Spurning far heaven with upslung vehemence
Of impious heels ; and gnashing rooted oaks,
Wilful did fling them into either sky
Like loathed grass.   Then sudden in career
He stretched across the flats.   His mighty limbs
Resulting in the plunge from rest to speed
Caverned whereon he stood, and left his place
Mixed in tumultuous ruin.   As he went
His hot hoofs thundering filled the fatal air
Recalcitrant, and scattered rocks and stones,
Crushed hall and hamlet, trampled tower and town,
Aye peaceful earth, and sods that nursed the lamb,
Red with the trodden flocks, in hurtled death
Swept the disastrous land.   As when some mine,
Dark filled with sulphurous slaughter, at a nod
Belching its storm, o'erwhelms in sudden wreck
The startled siege.   O'er all the wide expanse
The wondrous swift concussion of his course

Sped desolation ; far and near I saw
How dust-clouds, hovering like the pestilence,
Marked fallen cities, that on either hand
Confessed the unseen commotion where he passed.
And round the extremest verge dim rocks were rent,
And him in distance lost a sound betrayed,
The loud world groaned within as the great cry
Of crushed mankind proclaimed the track of " WAR." '

SCENE VIII.

THE VACANT STUDY.

Through the open door the voice of AMY.

Amy.   Is there no hostel by the way of life?
My wayfare was from far as I can see ;
As far my toil is hot and white before ;
I stagger with my load, and halt midway,
And trembling turn beseeching eyes and vain
Backward and forward from my pitiless place.
The weary miles lie infinite beyond,
And each might be the future and the past.
I would lay down my burden lest I die.
Is there no hostel by the way of life?

SCENE IX.

THE STUDY.

BALDER, *at his writing-table.*

Balder.　This very morn
Thro' her green island home the laughing spring
Drove, flinging joy, her blossom-laden car.
Forth from the polar cavern of the snows,
Dripping with winter, leaped a northern storm,
And shook himself ; and she lay buried white
Beneath an avalanche.　At that dread sight
Up rose the West, and such a wind went by
As stunned the isle with voices, like a chief
Rushing to battle with a sounding host
In shouting ranks wide on the echoing hills.
At first a roar of warning, 'to the north !'
Then like the shriek of all a ravished land,
'O Europe, Europe, Europe, Europe, Europe !'
And then like the world's trumpet blown to war,
'The North, the North, the North, the North, the North !'

Enter, under the window, wandering SAILORS, *singing.*

Sailors.

'How many ?' said our good Captain.
'Twenty sail and more.'
We were homeward bound,
Scudding in a gale with our jib towards the Nore.

Right athwart our tack,
The foe came thick and black,
Like Hell-birds and foul weather—you might count them
    by the score.

The Betsy Jane did slack
To see the game in view.
They knew the Union-Jack,
And the tyrant's flag we knew !
Our Captain shouted ' clear the decks ! ' and the Bo'sun's
    whistle blew.

Then our gallant Captain,
With his hand he seized the wheel,
And pointed with his stump to the middle of the foe.
' Hurrah, lads, in we go ! '
(You should hear the British cheer,
Fore and aft.)

' There are twenty sail,' sang he,
' But little Betsy Jane bobs to nothing on the sea ! '
(You should hear the British cheer,
Fore and aft.)

' See yon ugly craft
With the pennon at her main !
Hurrah, my merry boys,
There goes the Betsy Jane ! '

(You should hear the British cheer,
Fore and aft.)

The foe, he beats to quarters, and the Russian bugles
      sound;
  And the little Betsy Jane she leaps upon the sea.
  '.Port and starboard!' cried our Captain;
  'Pay it in, my hearts!' sang he.
  'We're old England's sons,
  And we'll fight for her to-day!'
  (You should hear the British cheer,
  Fore and aft.)
    'Fire away!'
  In she runs,
  And her guns
  Thunder round.   [*Exeunt* SAILORS.

Balder.   As he who turns
From the full-shining and white orb of noon
Sees a black sun in air, this chant of Freedom
Leaves in my soul its hideous contrary.   [*Pauses.*
Be patient, Death, for if not thee I paint,
None but thine immemorial minister,
Thy dear abortion whom thy craft sent here
That by his side thou mayst look good and fair,
Prevents thine honours.

                My poor goosequill!   Bah!
Had I a pen plucked where Celæno flies

Uncleanest !

        My old ink-horn !—why thou drop

Of rheum ! thou milk-pot !—   [*Writes and then reads.*

Lo Tyranny ! a Juggernaut than he

Who makes an Indian Bacchanal blush blood

At his unuttered hideousness more foul.

Nor on a car of India, but upborne

Upon a monstrous shape for which the brood

Of creeping reptiles, or the noisome plagues

Egyptian found no type, nor Hydra old,

Nor fell Chimæra.   High the idol sat,

Gore-stained, nor arm to seize, nor leg to stand

Had he, but from his beast his branchless trunk

Rose festerous thro' the morning.   What he rode

Headless came onward, manifold and one

As a dishevelled legion, and far off

Showed like a galley of ten thousand oars

In numberless commotion, nor in stroke

Ordered, but with division infinite

Beating the air ; for round its dreadful length

Such moving arms innumerous like a fry

Of twining fiery Pythons plied the earth

Incessant, and, alternate feet and hands,

Bore the black bulk, or with contentious haste

Incredible, before, beside, behind,

In manifold appearance all too slow

To feed consumption, filled the ghastly maw

Of him who sat above, and eyes had none,

Nor human front, nor but a mouth obscene,
Abominable, that for ever yawned
Insatiate, drivelling from its carrion sides
Infernal ichor.   Wide the cavern gaped,
Still straining wider, and thro' gurgling weight
Of seething full corruption night and day
His craving bowels, famished in his fill,
Bellowed for more.   Which, when the creature heard
That bore him, dread, like a great shock of life,
Convulsed it, and the myriad frantic hands ˙
Sprang like the dances of a madman's dream.
And so he came ; and o'er his head a sweat
Hung like a sulphurous vapour, and beneath
Fetid and thunderous as from belching hell, .
The hot and hideous torrent of his dung
Roared down explosive, and the earth, befouled
And blackened by the stercorous pestilence,
Wasted below him, and where'er he passed
The people stank.

SCENE X.

The Vacant Study.

Through the open door the voice of Amy.

Amy.   Neither gold nor silver, oh ye heavens !
Only a little sunshine and sweet air,
The sunshine and the air of the old days !

Only to be a feather on the stream,
A thistle-plume upon the changing wind
Hither and thither'; to go to and fro
And up and down the joyance of the world,
The happy world, and be a part of all.

Ye are now unto me, oh ye bright heavens,
As one who should misuse the deaf and blind
In secret, but full loud when men are by
Speaketh rich words of love into the ears
That hear not, and before the sightless eyes
Makes vain ado of all they cannot see.

I pray ye ope the lattice of my soul
And let the wind blow on me ere I die,
And let me hold my forehead to the light,
And let me feel the falling of the dews,
And know the holy blessing of the rain !

SCENE XI.

THE VACANT STUDY.

Through the open door the voice of AMY.

Amy. My babe, my babe, when thou art grown to age,
What will thy speech avail thee among men ?
Thy father-land speaks not thy mother-tongue.

For loving me, and thou wilt love me, babe,
I shall be still thy book, and all thy words
Of love and gladness thou shalt spell in me.

And loving me—and thou wilt love me, babe,
Shall I not be thy beauty and thy good?
And thou wilt seek mine image in the earth,
And make thy world of all things likest me.

Thou wilt not make day night, nor night thy day,
But dwell in the unvalued parts of day.
Shadow shall be thy light, and light thy shade.
What men forget, thou wilt remember well,
And all they know and love thou wilt forget.

Also, poor babe, thou wilt not hear the birds
Of morning, but if any night fowl wail
Far in the lonely hills, thou wilt awake,
And I shall see thee listen in my breast !

Nor shall thine eye pursue the butterflies,
Nor joy in shining beetle, nor humming bee ;
But thou wilt clap thine hands to feel the bat
Stirring the twilight ; and at hoot of owl
Shalt laugh and leap as at a mother's voice.

Also when thou shalt go upon thy feet,
Thy tiny feet beside me, well I know
Thou wilt not bring me daisies, nor sweet cups
Of gold and pearl, nor ever-ringing bells.

But we shall pass the flowery banks and braes,
Unheeded as a winter—thou and I.
Thy little footstep will be old and staid,
And thou wilt gaze upon the ground like me.

And I shall see thee stoop for withered straws,
And every joyless waif the wind lets fall.
I think thou wilt not pass a blighted leaf
Dead in the dust: and I shall lead thee by
The churchyard yew with lingering gaze and long
Reluctant; I shall sit me down and weep,
And thou wilt climb my lap, and deck my head
With garlands, till I tremble at thy glee,
And lift my hands to find—hemlock and rue.

Also, poor babe, these walks that once I loved
And tended shall have nought for thee in spring
Or summer, but thy childish eye shall light
With knowledge when in any plot unseen
December brings the thorn that flowers in vain,
Or hellebore, like a girl-murderess,
Green-eyed and sick with jealousy, and white
With wintry thoughts of poison.   All the year
Thou wilt be doleful in the planted beds
And bowers, but a strange sense shall draw thee where
Whatever nook that never saw the sun
Is dark and cold, with undescended dews
And saddest moss, and mildew of the wood

And wall, and livelong orpine that cannot die.
Moist ivy, and inglorious moschatel
Like a blind beggar 'neath a upas-tree
Sickening below the nightshade.   And thine heart
Shall fill thee, and thou shalt be rich and glad
As at a garden!

          Oh my babe, my babe,
That wert to be his glory and his joy,
The flower of women and the star of men.
Latest of mortal daughters, and the best.
The final Eve to sum up once for all
The loveliness of woman, and touch lips
With her who first began us ; the born theme
Of all the poets since the world was new,
Who singing as they could still sang of her,
And knowing only she must be, knew not
Or,when or where.   She, she, that was to come
In the whole image of the Beautiful,
Between the attending Loves, and bear aloft
Wisdom and knowledge as a wreathèd lyre
That sounds but with her going, trembling sweet
In trembling garlands ; or with bolder hand
Run o'er all noble arts as one runs o'er
A nine-stringed harp, and at her changing will,
Equal in each, be every Muse in turn,
And multiply the Graces as she moved !
His words are on my lips, my babe, my babe,
He sang them to me, child, in olden days,

Till I sprang up before him, full of pride,
And reeled, and fell, and mourned until thou camest,
And ever since have sung his song to thee.
And thou wilt grow like me, my babe, my babe,
And he shall seek and seek thro' all the earth,
Nor see his heart's desire until he die!
Will no one snatch thee from my bosom, babe,
And save thee from thy mother? Do not love me,
No, do not love me, no, no, do not love me,
No, do not love me; 'tis the lullaby
I'll sing all day. No, do not love me, no,
No, do not love me.

     Dost thou waken, babe?
Hush, hush, rebellious! Is my breast so hard
A pillow? Nay, what ails thy mother's milk?
Ah, dost thou turn from me, my little babe?
Does the spell work already? Love me, love me!
Love me, my babe, lest I go mad with fear!

SCENE XII.

THE STUDY.

BALDER, *at his writing-table.*

Balder. The great array is marshalled; on the right
Freedom, Truth, Justice, Mercy, Love, and Peace
Captained by Genius, stand under the broad

Standard of day held by the east and west
With sanguine hands and high.

                              In horrid rank
Sinister, front to hostile front opposed
Beneath a banner dark as if black winds
Of chaos rose in tempest and did blow
The billowy verge of everlasting night
O'er the celestial border, glare the host
That follow the blind Power whose headless beast
Some evil god directs.   Above his crest
Driven in the inevitable storm behind,
Like lambent flames of darkness licking far
The middle air, his terrible ensign
Roars to the coming war.

                              They stand at gaze,
Expecting till the equal voice of Death
Midway between the fierce and serried vans
Give signal of advance.   But his great place
Is empty, and the crowded action waits.

        Through the door comes the voice of AMY.
        Amy (sings).
Up went the jaunty jay,
Bough by bough, bough by bough,
Up went the jaunty jay,
Up the tall tree.

Up the tall tree where a happy bird was singing,
By his mossy home was singing,

To his callow brood was singing
In the green tree ;
In the tall tree-top, in the merry tree-top,
—Alas, so merry !
In the brave tree-top,
Waving to and fro.

As a gay gallant up the stairs of pleasure,
By leaps the jaunty jay went up the tree.
Thou knowest, O mother bird ! for thou wert by,
O mother-bird, thy young, thy callow young !
When he stood o'er them as one stands at meat,
Did they not lift their heads up as to thee ?
And like a fruit he plucked them one by one,
—The jay, the shining jay, the jocund jay ;—
In the tall tree-top, in the merry tree-top,
—Alas, so merry !—
In the brave tree-top,
Waving to and fro.

Like a gay gallant from a ruined maiden,
The painted jay came smirking down the tree.
Oh bird, oh crying bird, oh mother bird,
Oh childless bird, could I not die for thee ?
Yes, I could die for thee !

SCENE XIII.

The Study.

Balder, *at his writing-table.*

Balder.   Had it been my portion here
With these obedient limbs and iron aid
Of some unconscious instrument to dig
The unquestionable soil, so that this hand
Thus armed should with no further cost than throes
Of definite volition—as to grasp,
To sink, to raise,—complete the stated dues
Of daily labour!

              Were I born to plough,
While the lark drops upon his meal, the long
Material black and measurable furrow,
Whereof the brute sense of returning steer,
Treading the line, observant, testifies
That it is made indeed, and grossest clown
Who holds two eyes in use is a critic
Superfluously endowed!

              Happier to drive
The patient ass along the beaten way,
Laden with humble fruits to the set mart
Of fixed reward, and back to certain rest,
And sweet assured possession, than like me
Bound helpless on the fury of the winds,

To scour the plains I seek not, scale the height
Where my brain swims, and leap, as in a dream,
Down into the unfathomable void,
While from the fall—like my back-streaming hair—
Fear-blown in all my veins the blood streams back,
And faints with horror.

     I that am called proud,
Lying most humbly weary and abject
On the immoveable earth that doth so please
This mortal frame, and seeing my dull race
Doing their easy pleasures to and fro,
Self-ordinate, could sometimes sell my birth-right
For any pottage that would feed the flesh
Of other men upon me.

     Death, Death, Death!
I have seen every face but thine to-day!
And to behold thee, from sunrise till now,
How have I strained these eyeballs!   [*Exit.*

Through the open door comes the voice of AMY.

 Amy.   A pool in a deep valley at dead noon,
Lidless and shadeless like a burning eye,
Low lieth looking at the summer sun :
So in my bosom, oh my babe, my babe,
Thou liest low, and lookest up to me.

SCENE XIV.

The Study.

Balder (*solus*) *at his writing-table.*

Balder. My heart is heavy.   This it is to speak
On Alpine heights, and with the profane breath
Of innocent words, to bring the avalanche
Upon my human head.   I might have known
That he who treads these altitudes must walk
As from the mansions of eternal snow
I have beheld two customary stars
Go forth in sovereign converse, like to gods,
But seen to speak, not heard.

      A dread is on me
As in a mortal illness, when the flesh
Knows in the air the coming dart, and shakes
With terror.   I have called so loud and long
Into the twilight cave of Mystery ;
And now at length, when thro' the cavernous dark
I hear far answering feet, my stout heart sinks.
That Dream !   As some wild legendary rhyme
Heard on a grandame's knee, that being at end
Is still again begun, while at each turn
O' the winding tale the listener, cowering low,
Whispers the wonted question, to receive
More cold and pale the expected old reply

That lifts another hair, I ponder o'er
My strange adventure, and do press and wring
The mirk and husk of memory.   Once again
I'll fill the cup to the enchanted brim
And drink it slowly.   Yesterday I sat
From early morn till dark and strove in vain
To see the face of Death.   And in the night
I dreamed.   Methought I stood within this room,
As on the day when first I saw it grey
And empty; o'er my head a single branch
Of ivy threaded the high wall and hung
In green possession.   And medreamed I stood
Robed like a necromancer, and with spells
Called on the name of Death.   The wizard's store
Hung at my girdle, and on this last prize
I spent it sternly with the desperate hand
Of him who will be Prince or Beggar—each
New spell was more tremendous than the last.
At first there was great silence thro' the cell,
And then the cell was moved, tho' nothing stirred,
But under the gross visible I knew
An inner perturbation, as the crowd
Before the curtain feel the viewless scene
Inscrutable which heaves the swaying folds
That roll the mystery from stage to roof,
And roof to stage.   And then a hush like death;
And thro' the hush a somewhat in the air
Twisting and falling; and I looked and saw

The ivy-branch, and all the branch was bare,
And the broad leaves lay shrivelled on the ground.
The fourth time the strong silence in the cell
Was as the straining silence of the rack,
When the still-tightening torture wrenches him
Who will not speak.   The great veins in my brow
Throbbed with suppression, and such consciousness
I had of coming uproar, rising up
Thro' the containing stillness—as the fire
Of Ætna swells under her dark blind hill
And bursts in desolation—that my lips
Cried out.   As if the sudden whip of Hell
Flashed on a pack of demons caught asleep,
The place brake silence, and a naked shriek
Came thro' the right-hand wall and, shrieking, passed
Out on the left, and when I called, returned,
Still shrieking, and so out upon the right,
And to and fro until my deafened brain
Reeled, and I fell down flat and slept as dead.
Then to me, sleeping, in my ear, these words,
Not as from outer nature, yet in voice
Not mine, tho' nearer to me than the ear
That heard it, as if in my head the blood
Along the intricate deep veins did hiss
A whisper and fled shivering to the heart.
' Bring me the inflated skin thou callest Life,
And I will turn the wind-bag inside out
And clothe me.'

I am not the fool of dreams,
Yet hold it not incredible that things
Are seen before their time, and,—as to-night
In this strange vision, where, while all was still
I felt the undelivered silence swell—
Somewhat to be lies in the womb of Now,
And eyes unstayed by mortal obscuration
Behold at once the Mother and the Child.
A white skin and the sweet fair-seeming flesh
Shut back the common eye-sight ; but there be
Who looking fast on the unblushed repose
Òf Beauty—where she lieth bright and still
As some spent angel, dead-asleep in light
On the most heavenward top of all this world,
Wing-weary,—seized with sudden trance and strong
Thro' the decorous continent and all
The charmed defence of Nature can behold
The circling health beneath them, the red haste
Of the quick heart, and of her heaving breast
The cavernous and windy mysteries ;
Yea, all the creeping secrets of her maw,
The busy rot within her, and the worm
That preys upon her vitals.   So perchance
I see the Future in the Present.   Or
If in the smoothest hour of patent nature
That overhanging weight of Destiny
Which loads the heavy air do brood on us,
What wonder that our tenderer substance take

Impress divine, and show the awful stamp
And parody of Fate?

                  One can be brave
At noon, and with triumphant logic clear
The demonstrable air, but ne'ertheless,
Sometimes at Hallowe'en when, legends say,
The things that stir among the rustling trees
Are not all mortal, and the sick white moon
Wanes o'er the season of the sheeted dead,
We grow unreasonable and do quake
With more than the cold wind.   The very soul,
Sick as the moon, suspects her sentinels,
And thro' her fortress of the body peers
Shivering abroad ; our heart-strings over-strung,
Scare us with strange involuntary notes
Quivering and quaking, and the creeping flesh
Knows all the starting horrors of surprise
But that which makes them, and for that, half-wild,
Quickens the winking lids, and glances out
From side to side, as if some sudden chance
Of vision, some unused slant of the eye,
Some accidental focus of the sight
O' th' instant might reveal a peopled world
Crowding about us, and the empty light
Alive with phantoms.   Doubtless there are no ghosts ;
Yet somehow it is better not to move
Lest cold hands seize upon us from behind,
Or forward thro' the dim uncertain time

Face close with paly face.   My ominous Dream
Leaves me in shuddering incredulity
As logically white.

SCENE XV.

The Vacant Study.

Through the door the voice of Amy.

Amy. Out of the dungeon comes the captive's cry,
Whose no man knoweth, nor shall ever know.
The cry ! the cry ! out of the sealèd cell
That no man may look into, comes a cry !

Up thro' the dumb sod of a churchyard green,
One of the undistinguishable dead
Below the many many graves complains.

The Beloved and Unbeloved are lying there,
The stifling earth on them.   The cry is dull,
Whose no man knoweth, nor shall ever know.

Thy cry, thy feeble cry, my little babe !
All the long day and all the weary night !
I bend me down over the sealèd cell,
And strain my ears against the sodden grave,
And weep and know not, nor shall ever know.

SCENE XVI.

The Study.

BALDER (*solus*) *at his writing-table.*

Balder. Yesterday I said
That as the lion at the water-brooks
Prints his dread feet, to-morrow's great event
Fording our sleep to his appointed place
Beyond that Rubicon perchance may leave
His footsteps in the sand.

                    'Twas but a fancy,
But in a sleepless night seeking those steps
Thro' all the inner wilderness, I came
On other scars and traces, real as rock,
Familiar too, and terribly historic
As the carved walls whereon a martyr leaves
His storied wrongs.

                    I see the Poet's heart
Is but a gem whereon his woe doth cut
Her image, and he turns upon the world
And sets his signet there in high wild shapes
The necessary convex of a wound
As miserably deep.

                    I cannot stamp
The face of Death upon the universe
Till Death hath graven the scal.   I wait that one

Last dreadful blazon to fulfil a shield
Persèan; that being held up to the day
Shall make mankind my marble.

                                    Yet how long?
Proud Death, thou keepest not the company
Of lowlier pains and griefs.   It may require
A greater light than I have known to cast
Thine awful shadow.   Whom thou visitest
With thy best pomp, and all the circumstance
Of special love, are not of those who house
The common brood of sorrow; but they seem
Set up in shine of great prosperity
Upon the dial of Time, with one sole shade
To point the final hour.   Yet peradventure
We who stand out of the sweet sun perceive
No shadow, not because the shade is less
But more.   Aye, in this twilight atmosphere
Thou mayest approach unseen as air in air,
And strike me unaware.   But near or far
I need thee, and in all the strange sad past
Of my predestined life to say ' I need,'
Hath been to move the universal wheels
In answering motion, which in act I knew
When the concluding cause and last result
Of thousands dropped into my open want
The supplementary fruit.   Whether my will
Hath power on nature, or this heart of mine
Is so compacted in the frame and work

Of all things that in various kind they keep
Attuned performance, I know not.   Perhaps
There comes to each man in his day some word
Whereto the tacit Visible without
Is the foregone conclusion.   As amid
The silent summer eve of violet air
That which thou seest hath no superscription
Or title written; when we speak of it
'Tis with a finger pointed to the sky,
' Behold ! ' as in despair of human speech.
But lo, if in that moment and the hap
Of other descant one say ' Holiness,'
A pulse of sweet emotions thro' the dark,
As tho' that somewhat in the mystery
Responded to a name !
                              Such moments make
My hours, such hours my days, such days my years.

(*A long pause.*)   Who is to die?   It is not credible
That this I have begun should come to end
For lack of human lives, or that a pang
Not mortal should fly wide of me ; of me
Who had I the round earth within my hand
O'er-populous as a green water-drop,
Would swallow it to taste a novel savour.

(*Another pause.*)   If I could give up
This seasoned body to the advance of death,

And from my vantage-post within survey
The slow assault, and mark the victor, held
In view before the garrisoned approach
And each well-fought obstruction, and so write
The story of the siege—ay, while he climbed
The mound I sat on, till the pen fell, struck
From mine untrembling hand ! But who shall bear
To the externe and living world, that last
Convicting record ? What strong sign convey
Safe thro' the taken barriers, and the close
Opposing ranks of Death the lineaments
Which end his long disguise? No. The same key
Which let him thro' the circle of the sense
Would close the gate behind him, and secure
The first last secret all men hear, and none
Betray.
　　　　If but to me the privilege
To know and to declare ! To suffer all
That in our common nature doth fulfil
And end perception, with a sense exempt
From that benign conclusion ! In the arms
Of health to hold each form of mortal ill,
Till death should die upon my conscious breast,
And I by superhuman strength complete
The sum of human sorrow—God to see,
And man to suffer ! The unchanged gold
On the charred bones of the Pompeian bride,
Tho' it survive the murderous fire, hath felt

A deadly heat.   If I could seize a soul
And part to part adjust my qualities
Upon it, so that like to like consort
Might form a whole whereof the half could die
And the remainder watch it !
(*Starting up.*)   You just gods,
Is it not thus already—you good gods—   .

     [*He walks in great agitation.*

(*Sits again.*)   A thought stood at the threshold of my
  heart
And shut the light out.   It has past, and I
Have not yet half beheld it.   But I know
That as its shadow came along the way
I looked up, and the valley and the hills
A moment swerved and failed, and as a smoke
Rolled over in a wind of coming death.

   Through the door is heard the voice of AMY.

 Amy.   If thou wouldst sleep, my babe, if thou wouldst
  sleep
And weary of the never-ending day !
Thou hast not milked me of my sorrow, babe,
Why must thou moan and watch and wake like me ?

My babe, my babe, is it not well with thee ?
And if not well, the end is come indeed.

My place was dark, and o'er a darker place   ,
A great hand held me that I could not see.

Below us the dark gulph, for ever deep,
Above us, thro' the dark, a light of day,
And thou wert as a jewel on my breast,
Sweet shining in the light that lit not me.
The hand is weary with upholding me !
If ill hath touched thee, babe, we are given o'er,
Given o'er and dropt, a pillage and a prey !
Ah ! in the dark gulph what shall not seize thee !

If thou wouldst sleep, my babe, if thou wouldst sleep,
Nor scare me with the mystery of thine eyes.

Alas, thy parted lips, my babe, my babe !
Alas, the hot breath from the cankered rose !
Alas, the little limbs !   Alas, the heart
That beateth like a wounded butterfly !
My babe, my babe, what hath befallen thee?

I see it all; I see, I see it all !
How couldst thou lie upon my breast and live?
The doom has run its date, the hour is here !
Not enough, babe, oh ! not enough, my babe,
That I who was the favourite and the flower,
Bruised and beaten by a thousand ills,
As to the utter shelter and mere shed
Of this great gilded palace-world did creep
With thee, not wholly lost since thou wert not,
Nor in my desolation desolate,

Because the glory could not give thee more
Than me, or the bare walls of sorrow less.
My babe, it was too good for thee and me.
God hath abandoned us, and from His home
Is driving forth the mother and her child.

My child, my child, the wolf is in the way,
And what if he doth choose the suckling lamb?
Hush babe, my little babe, my only babe,
That I might die for thee, my babe, my babe.

    Balder (*sinking his head into his hands*).　So soon, so
        soon!　My lamb, my lily-bud,
My little babe!　My daughter, oh my daughter!　(*A long
        pause.*)
(*Looking up.*)　Yes, I redeem the mother with the child!
Fate, take thy price!　If this hand shakes to pay it,
'Tis with the trembling eagerness of him
Who buys an Indian kingdom with a bead.
'Tis past.　I rise up childless, but no less
Than I.　There was one bolt in all the heavens
Which falling on my head had with a touch
Rent me in twain.　This bursting water-spout
Hath left me whole, but naked.　Better so
Than to be cloven in king's raiment.　Ay,
My treasure-house is broken, and I lose
What nothing can restore, and poorer men
Had held to the last drop of desperate blood.

But I, who know the secrets of the place,
Breathe freely when I learn the worst, and find
The felon sought no further.

                      Yet my babe !

My tiny babe !—

SCENE XVII.

THE STUDY.

BALDER, *solus.* *Through the door comes a sound
of weeping.*

Balder. My heart doth beat,
But I am calm, calm as a winter tree
Whereon one dead leaf flutters in the wind.
The waters of my soul that swelled so high,
Broke up my deeps and filled my universe,
Have sunk to such a mirror as reflects
The heaven and earth, and makes whatever face
Bends anew o'er them out of the unknown
A part of all things. Now I cannot weep.
I have climbed out o' the thunder, and most cold
Upon the heights of everlasting snow
Stand with cherubic knowledge.

                    This hot breast
Seems valley deep, and what the wind of Fate
Strikes on that harp strung there to bursting, I,

Descending, mean to catch as one unmoved
In stern notation.   A strange sense of sight,
Fearless that lightning-like finds easiest way
Self-warranted where way is none, makes wide
Mine eyes that could look thro' into the depths
Behind the face of God.

                    'Tis well.   Even so
Would I meet DEATH.

          [*Exit through the door of the adjoining room.*

SCENE XVIII.

THE STUDY.

BALDER, *solus.*

Balder.   If to the long mysterious trance of death
There be immortal waking, he who lifts
His head from the clay pillow, and doth stretch
Eternal life thro' all his quickening limbs,
And conscious on his opening orbs receives
Remembered light, and rises to be sure
He hath revived indeed, tastes in that first
Best moment what the infinite beyond
Can never give again.

              I should awake
On some such resurrection, having lived
Thro' what I feared was mortal, and endured

That most malignant hour which must or close
The perilous adventure, or, being forced,
Admit to happier times.

                   The ground grows firm
Beneath ; the elfin atmosphere of spells
That smit these limbs with palsy, has given place
To vital air.   I smell the native world.
The fortress of the last enchanter yields ;
My life is free before me.   I am strong ;
I shall survive, subdue, surmount, attain !
Thou mystery, which dost attend my voice
Like a tame beast, and goest in and out
Whene'er I will, and liest at my feet,
Come let me paint the picture I have bought
So dearly, but, being painted, will hold cheap,
Ay, tho' I rent it at the yearly cost
Of such an annual tribute !   Here ! Be here !
He comes.   Even now this black environment
Grows cold with his approach ; and as on one
Benighted in the forest dreadful eyes
Shine thro' the dark, and Somewhat unbeheld
Draws nigh, thro' the thick darkness of my night
I see thine eyes, oh Death !

     *[Takes pen and paper, in attitude to write.   The
       voice of* AMY *comes through the door.*

Amy.   That I might die and be at rest, oh God !
That I might die and sleep the sleep of peace ;

That I might die and close these eyes within
That shut not when the outer lids are sealed ;
That I might die and know the balm of death
Cool thro' my loosened limbs ; that I might die,
That I might die and stretch me out unracked,
And feel but as I died what is not pain.
It is dead midnight, and the time to sleep.—
My light has gone out in the dead midnight ;
All things are equal in the utter dark ; ,
I cannot see my way upon the-world.

All in the dark a tempest beateth me,
Black waves out of the north and of the south,
Black waves out of the east and of the west,
Black falling waves that drench me from the sky !

On every side the waters lash me round,
And lift me till I know not where I stood,
And wist not where is earth or where is heaven !
                    [*Listening, he falls into a reverie.*

Balder.   Little babe,
Who wentest out from us two days ago
Not to return, what has become of thee
In this great universe ?   That thou art changed
I know ; for whereas thou hadst lain since birth
On the warm breast that fed thee in a dream
Of peace, and, like a flower, wert given and ta'en

Unconscious, on a morn thou didst awake,
And while we weeping strove to keep thee, thou,
As at some awful voice that called thee hence
On high behest, becamest a man in will,
And ceasing thy babe's cry didst go in haste!
We also went a little way with thee,
As they whose best-beloved doth cross the seas
Attend him to the shore—even to the brink
Of the great deep, and stretch along the sands
Wringing vain hands of sorrow; yet none saith
'Why goest thou?' nor with naked sword of love
Denies; and none doth leap into his fate,
Crying 'I also,' and with desperate clasp
Hang on his neck till breakers far behind
Forbid return.   Spell-bound they stand and dry
On the sea-line, and not a quivering lip
Murmureth 'To-morrow;' but his sire doth seize
The prow that would recede, and with stern will
Holds it, rebellious, to the task, and she
Who bore him, with her tears and trembling hands
Constrains and hastes him lest he lose the tide.

So also in a dream as one who walks
Asleep, and with her sunk eye on a star,
Rising doth take her slumbering babe, and o'er
The snows of midnight to the precipice
Paceth with silent purpose, doubting nought,
And turneth on the brink, with empty hands,

And to her bed unconscious, nor till morn
Beholds the vacant pillow—and, well-known,
Her foot-prints,—passionate ; we went with thee,
And did return alone.   My babe, my babe,
What have we done?   At whose sufficient pledge,
Upon whose testimony, and well-sworn
Assurance have we left thee, and believed? .
Did I go down before thee ?   Did I try
'The unventured way?   With which hand did I smooth
Thy pillow?' Or with what nice care explore
The grave which in my trance I called thy bed?
Thy bed? wert thou so cradled?   Doth the boor
Upon the hungry common save his hide
By such a lodging as thou in thy pomp
Didst enter, while the sable priest gave thanks,
And praised the long home where he would not chain
His dog?   Thy home, poor babe?   Bah! the stone den
Of murder is more human ; the dank keep
Of felon anguish built to house despair
Hath not a cell so rude !   [*Muses.*
                    Was it a door
From this most ordered world into the waste
Of all things?   Have we shut thee forth, poor child,
And wist not of thy journey, nor the end
And exit of that gloomy subterrene
Which thou didst enter, and whose unknown mouth
May be in Chaos?   This, the upper gate,
Was fair, and, hanging o'er, the flowers looked down

After thee going, shedding many dews
That went as falling stars into the gulph,
A moment bright like thee.   But, oh thou babe,
What of the nether port, which thou hast reached
Who wert so swift to go?   We shut thee in
As to a chamber of rest, and did confirm
The outer bars, and on the adit set
The seal of Hermes, and o'er all dispread
The cheerful turf, and sowed it round with spring.
Mad faith !—false father !—customary fool !—
Tool of low instinct and obsequious use !—
Curse thee, blind slave ! why didst thou leave her thus
In her worst need ?   Who, who shall certify
Her rest ?   And thou, oh mother, that didst plunge
So boldly into the vexed flood of life,
Holding thy babe aloft, with thy right hand,
Braving the billows ; what unseen sea-scourge
Had struck thee, that thou too didst bow thine head
A-sudden succourless, and hast gone down
As others ?   Doth no voice out of the ground,
Up thro' the music of the grasshoppers
Smite thee ?   Whence, mother, had thy nursling child
This gift to sleep alone ?   Whence knowest thou,
O mother, who in its long dying swoon
Didst warm it in thy bosom, and forfend
The summer wind, and kiss the tenderness
Of years upon its momentary brow,
And with the wild haste of thy maddened eyes

Course heaven and earth, as to glean anywhere
One help forgotten; and at the last breath
Distraught and bending over it didst break
Thy life upon it, if perchance that balm   ·
Might heal; and ere it died wert as one dead
With dread of ill, whence knowest thou what change
Absolves thy care?   What thunder or what bush
Of burning spake to thee when thou didst rise
And veil thy face, and, unresisting, feel
The child go from thee out into the rains
And dews, and didst kneel silent while we threw
Cold earth upon it, and piled up that wall
Which late compunction and awakening throes,
Pangs of reproach and passion of despair,
And starting eyes mocked by the empty world,
And famished breasts convulsed when nights are
    chill,
And stretched-forth arms that waste with vacancy,
And all the tumult of the desperate heart
That leaps to the impossible desire
And unsurrendered bliss, can pass no more.

SCENE XIX.

The Study.

BALDER, *at his writing-table, preparing to write, when the voice of* AMY *comes through the open door.*

Amy.   My heart is shivered as a fallen cup
And all the golden wine is in the earth.

My heart is stricken, and it cannot heal.
Tho' thou art but a little grave I know,
O little grave, it will bleed into thee
For evermore, and thou wilt not be filled.

The fountains of my fate are dry; my soul
Is dying in the famine of my lot.
I am a dead leaf in a wintry wind;
My stem is broken from the tree of life,
I wither in the sun and in the air,
I wither in the rain and in the dews.

And though the wind doth throw me on the tree,
Oh wind! thou canst not bind what thou didst break;
I wither in the verdure of the leaves.—
Beneath my window built the nightingale;
Ah cruel, who despoiled her happy nest!
And in his wanton gripe he crushed her egg,
Her one lone egg ;—so doth Fate crush my heart.

The spring returns unto the nightingale,
The nightingale shall find a happier tree;
The ravished nest must drift upon the day,
The wind shall toss it as an idle straw,
The rain shall tread its ruins to the earth,
And I am all despoiled for evermore.
                    [*He rises sorrowfully, and shuts the door.*

Balder.   How often our twin passions do exchange
Fraternal uses, and alike in face
But opposite in sex, confound the eye
That reckons on their valour, or makes bold
Upon presumptive weakness, nor descries
The pious counterfeit when manly strength
Presents meek maidenhead, or female parts
Complete the heroic brow, and she who lacks
So much of manhood plights her faith as man,
Or strong Sebastian's virile arm redeems
The gage of virgin Viola.   To-day
My grief—like one who crossed in hapless love
Betakes him to the wars, and tells in blows
His bitter need of kisses—speaks with voice
Of fiery wrath.   [*Writes and then reads.*
                    Lo, Justice! and led in
By History, as by a little child.
She, moving as a goddess, slow drew nigh
Three adverse forms and human to behold,
Each a Colossus; Insolence, and Fraud,

And Malice. These approaching her, advanced
A step, and drew their several weapons. One
With voice like a cracked trumpet, and too loud
For that he said; and one with whisper dire,
Like the great ghost of a great sound, as large
But bodiless; the third as still as death.
They came: then Justice, lifting up her hand,
' Back to your shapes!' The three fell down headlong.
The first a Cur deformed, of monstrous birth,
With head that Parthian-like still looked behind
And fled from what he hurt; the next a Spider,
Gaunt black and lean, full of unnatural eyes
Detestable; the third a reeking Toad.
Bare in the day, these, or with horrid whine
Slunk to the earth, or crouched in dark and foul
Discovery, or swat a cancerous pool
Of poison, and lay hid. But Justice spake:

' Because ye did your will upon the weak,
Because ye had no pity on the poor,
Because your hands were quick to stab the fallen,
Because ye made your pillage of the slain,

Because ye lay in ambush for the brave,
Because ye stole by night upon the good,
Because ye dug a pitfall for the true,

Because ye overcried the voice of Right,
Because ye clapped your hands when strong men lied,

Because ye smote the cheek of innocence,
And spat your fetid spume in Wisdom's face;

Because being bestial, ye bewitched men's eyes
To see my sons as beasts, and ye as men,

Because in all your sins ye knew your sin,
And saw me while ye sware that I was not,
And heard me thro' the clamour of your tongues,
And shouted more lest men should see ye shake;

Because my sons have spoken in mine ears,
And all ye did to them of old I know;

Because, accursed! they shall not defile
Their hands to slay you, since with such as ye
'Twere equal shame to be at peace or war;

Because outcast from heaven, and earth, and hell,
Detect, disowned, detested, and despised,
There is no power to which ye can be true,
And Satan cannot trust ye more than God,
I come!'   She wrenched the bandage from her eyes,
And looked on them :—and—as the summer bolt
Falls in the forest on the gathered leaves
Of winter, and they start into a flame
Out of their empty place,—a kindling fire
Consumed them, and a sudden rolling smoke
Showed they had been.   And lo! from out the smoke

I saw the grim and clanking skeleton
Of the dead dog, licked bare to the white bones,
Run as alive.   With skull revert, and jaws
That may not cease to move, but make no sound,
He flees for ever o'er the startled earth,
A terror and a sign.

SCENE XX.

The Vacant Study.

Through the door the voice of Amy.

Amy. Oh wounded dove, oh dove with broken wing,
Oh dying dove, wert thou not beautiful?
Why didst thou hide thee, trembler, from the day,
And strain into the crevice of the cliff,
And press thy beating breast against the hill,
As if the rock should ope and let thee in?

I took thee to my heart, oh snow-white dove,
I would have kissed and kissed thee o'er and o'er,
But thou wert fierce with fear, and with wild eyes
Didst turn upon me like a frantic maid
That struggles with a lover in the dark,
Bruising the hands that would have cherished her,
And gnashing on the lips that seek her own

Oh dove, I also fall with broken wing,
I also strive and turn upon my fate,
And strike the inevitable hands in vain.
I also strain my bosom to the earth,
The earth that will not ope and let me in.

SCENE XXI.

THE VACANT STUDY.

Through the door the voice of AMY.

Amy.   That I might only die and be at rest,
That I might die and sleep the sleep of peace,
That I might die and close these eyes within,
These eyes that start and stare so hot with life,
And mad-wide while the outer lids are sealed!
That I might die and know the balm of death,
And feel but as I died what is not pain.

The summer is a load upon my sense,
A pile of durance builded over head ;
The battening shadow, and the fattening earth,
And all the thick abundance of the trees !

Fall, Summer ! rend the cerements of my tomb !
If I might know that aught that binds can break !
If I might struggle thro' my choking bands,

And cheat me with the transport that I rise !
Alas, thou fallest, and I am not free !
Alas, alas, thou canst not let me forth !
Alas, alas, the grave-clothes, not the grave !
Alas, alas, the vaulted adamant,
And dolour of inexorable things !

SCENE XXII.

THE VACANT STUDY.

Through the door the voice of AMY.

Amy. Swallow, that yearly art blown round the
world,
What seekest thou that never may be found ?
Whither for ever sailing and to sail ?
I think the gulphs have sucked thine haven down,
And thou still steerest for the vanished strand.
What cheer, what cheer, oh fairy marinere
Of windy billows, sea-mew of the air ?
The viewless oceans wash thee to and fro,
Spout thee to Heaven, and dive thee to the deep.
Swallow ! I also seek and do not find.

SCENE XXIII.

The Court-yard of the Tower.

Balder, *solus*.

Enter Dr. Paul.

Balder. Doctor !

Doctor.   You're well ?   My patient ?

Balder.   Only now

She went to sit beside the little grave.
Prithee, friend, wait awhile.   It were ill-done
So soon to follow.

    Doctor.   Is this pilgrimage
A manner with her ?

    Balder.   Thou may'st even trace
The path her feet have worn across the mead
Straight from our threshold.   Many times a day
She rises up as who should hear a sound
Far off.   I have gone with her hour by hour,
And still she hath the step of expectation,
Kneels by the woful mound and leans her ear
Upon the earth, lifts her wan cheek with flush
And gesture of surprise, feels one by one
The gaps and junctures of the ungrown sod
As 'twere new broken, and anon doth shake
Her piteous head, and look into my face

As if I wronged her; and so home in haste
Unresting.   But she watcheth night and day
To steal unnoticed forth, and then she stays
Till someone lead her homeward.   Drawing nigh
Beneath the twilight I perceive she sits
Upon a neighbouring stone, and by her lips
I think she sings, slow swaying to and fro,
As one who rocks a child.   I give her way,
For fancy,—like the image that our boors
Set by their kine,—doth milk her of her tears,
And loose the terrible unsolved distress
Of tumid Nature.   Under observance
She hath been silent since that mortal hour;
Lying close like a toiled bird, that with wide eyes
Is mute and strange, but, being alone, lets forth
Its sad wild cry.

            Paul, I have heard that cry
Twice lately in the dark, here, where we sit!
How I have been so long both deaf and blind
Confounds invention, but my sense at last
Is opened, and I do perceive this ill
Is not a growth of yesterday.   They tell
In sea tales of deaf men made whole amid
The roar of battle, who go forthwith mad,
Wild with the naked torment of the bruised
Unseasoned function.   I do think my case
Is such a thunderous healing.   What I hear
Strikes through the feeble garment of the flesh,

And stuns the very soul.   My book stands still.
I am no carpet knight, and in my time
Have known hard knocks, but, callous as I am,
This breaks endurance.

                  Since the malady
That racked her, three short summers since, I held
Her sorrows to be no more than the toys
And creatures of a tender melancholy,
The honey-droppings of an atmosphere
So delicate that every mist and whiff
Which sails a grosser sky came down in rain.
But this is hell, and the infernal fall
Of burning snow.

    Doctor.   Poor thing, poor thing, poor
       thing !
How long think you?

    Balder.   An hour ?

    Doctor.   If it must be.
We men of drug and scalpel still are men
And have our feelings.   I call us the gnomes
Of science, miners who scarce see the light
Working within the bowels of the world
Of beauty.

    Balder. But your toil, like theirs, gives wealth
And warmth, and glory, to a fairer sphere,
Brings forth the golden wonder, which in hand
Of prince or clown, of poet or of fool,
Is standard still ; lights up the common hearth

Of household joy familiar, and makes bright
The jewelled front of kings.

  Doctor.   Ah, my good friend,
I was a poet once, and thought strange things,
Very strange things. How I would walk alone
And mutter in my going, dare the heavens
As thus ! clap sudden hand upon my brow,
Hold up a finger and cry hist ! to the air,
Walk you a mile bareheaded in the rain,
Stop, gaze the ground, stamp like a bull, and sigh,
Sigh like a painted Boreas ! or, in fierce
Obstetric frenzy of the labouring Muse,
Collar the astonished wayfarer with ' Sir,
Your tablets ! ' scare the woodman's hut with calls
For pen and paper, or make eloquent
The graphic bark of beech. Ah, those days when
I courted Sophonisba, long ago,
And we two loved the moonlight and wrote verses !
It melts my very heart to think on't !

  Balder.   Love
Makes us all poets. Each man in his turn,
At culmination of one happy hour
Consummate of some sole and topmost day
Hath his apotheosis. Nature thus,
Ere she send forth her mintage to the world
Assays it for eternity, and sets
The stamp of sterling manhood. From the mount
Of high transfiguration you come down

Into your common life-time, as the diver
Breathes upper air a moment ere he plunge,
And, by mere virtue of that moment, lives
In breathless deeps and dark.   We poets dwell
Upon the height, saying, as one of old,
' Let us make tabernacles : it is good
To be here.'

  Doctor. Out of mortal sight !   Ay, you
Live to posterity.

  Balder.   Your pardon ; no !

  Doctor. To the mere present ?

  Balder. No.   I do not scorn
Fame, and those wide and calmer after days
Where Time's thick flood grows quiet, letting down
Its golden grains to be the jealous wealth
Of nations ; but I choose to say, ' I live
To God and to myself.'   Of God I know
Little to satisfy a human heart
So fashioned to adore Him ; of myself
Still less, yet somewhat ; of posterity
This only,—that in circling cycles, come
What will come on the ever-rolling years,
The Ages will not outlive a true man
And his Divine Creator.

  Doctor.   Well, well, poet,
If love makes heroes it makes fools.   And Nature,
If, as you say, fresh from that crucible,
She marks us current, full as often signs

The cap of Momus as the bay of Cæsar.
Were you but where I am, and with my eyes
Saw as I see to what this love can bring
Men down.

  Balder. Not love, but passion, the mere dance
Of this gross body to the soul's sweet singing,
Which you mistake for love, because sometimes
The singer, high and pale, descends to join
(With haughtier step as consciously a god)
The Paphian measure of his mortal twin.
And strange reflection of the glowing flesh
Doth flush the soul.

  Doctor.   I have walked far.

  Balder.   We'll enter—
From the high window in the turret there,
I see the churchyard in the dale.

  Doctor.   Dost spend
The day in watching?

  Balder.   I keep vigil on her
As any star behind his golden face
Spends his great gifts upon his proper world,
And lights us with an idle faculty.

  [*They enter the Tower, and mount to the Study.*

  Doctor A poet's studio! I have often passed
The lintel of your home, but ne'er before
The threshold of its penetralia. I
Long to behold your gods.

  Balder.   Expect none, Paul.

Doctor. How?

Balder. Expect none, my friend, if seeing me
Thou hast seen none. My word on it Æneas
Is godless, or 'Penatiger Æneas.'

    Doctor. Thou Pagan ! why the room is an Olympus !

    Balder. Olympus' top is a long way from heaven.

    Doctor. From heaven say you ? The mason, by my
      count,
Is greater than the house, and I perceive
That old Italian, whose Uranian pride
When his great prince had forfeited the skies,
Built him another heaven, and filled the dome
With angels, like the first.

    Balder.   Ay, dauntless Michael,
Who drew the Judgment, in some daring hope
That, seeing it, the gods could not depart
From so divine a pattern.

    Doctor.   Ah ! thou, too,
Sad Alighieri, like a waning moon
Setting in storm behind a grove of bays !

    Balder. Yes, the great Florentine, who wove his web
And thrust it into hell, and drew it forth
Immortal, having burned all that could burn,
And leaving only what shall still be found
Untouched, nor with the smell of fire upon it,
Under the final ashes of this world.

    Doctor. Shakspeare and Milton !

    Balder.   Switzerland and home.

I ne'er see Milton, but I see the Alps,
As once sole standing on a peak supreme,
To the extremest verge summit and gulph
I saw, height after depth, Alp beyond Alp,
O'er which the rising and the sinking soul
Sails into distance, heaving as a ship
O'er a great sea that sets to strands unseen.
And as the mounting and descending bark
Borne on exulting by the under deep,
Gains of the wild wave something not the wave,
Catches a joy of going, and a will
Resistless, and upon the last lee foam
Leaps into air beyond it, so the soul
Upon the Alpine ocean mountain-tost,
Incessant carried up to heaven, and plunged
To darkness, and still wet with drops of death
Held into light eternal, and again
Cast down, to be again uplift in vast
And infinite succession, cannot stay
The mad momentum, but in frenzied sight
Of horizontal clouds and mists and skies
And the untried Inane, springs on the surge
Of things, and passing matter by a force
Material, thro' vacuity careers,
Rising and falling.

   Doctor.   And my Shakspeare! Call
Milton your Alps, and which is *he* among
The tops of Andes? Keep your Paradise,

Anu Eves, and Adams, but give me the Earth
That Shakspeare drew, and make it grave and gay
With Shakspeare's men and women ; let me laugh
Or weep with them, and you—a wager,—ay,
A wager by my faith—either his muse
Was the recording angel, or that hand
Cherubic which fills up the Book of Life,
Caught what the last relaxing gripe let fall
By a death-bed at Stratford, and henceforth
Holds Shakspeare's pen. Now strain your sinews, poet,
And top your Pelion,—Milton Switzerland,
And English Shakspeare—

  Balder.   This dear English land !
This happy England, loud with brooks and birds,
Shining with harvests, cool with dewy trees,
And bloomed from hill to dell ; but whose best flowers
Are daughters, and Ophelia still more fair
Than any rose she weaves ; whose noblest floods
The pulsing torrent of a nation's heart ;
Whose forests stronger than her native oaks
Are living men ; and whose unfathomed lakes
For ever calm the unforgotten dead
In quiet graveyards willowed seemly round,
O'er which To-day bends sad, and sees his face.
Whose rocks are rights, consolidate of old
Thro' unremembered years, around whose base
The ever-surging peoples roll and roar
Perpetual, as around her cliffs the seas

That only wash them whiter; and whose mountains,
Souls that from this mere footing of the earth
Lift their great virtues thro' all clouds of Fate
Up to the very heavens, and make them rise
To keep the gods above us!

Doctor.   Your hand on it!

Balder.   The wicket swings, how now?

Doctor.   A tattered man.

Balder.   I must go down—

Doctor. •   An aged peasant woman,
A chubby child beside her; by my soul
The rosy blossom and the withered crab,
Both on one bough? who are they?

Balder.   Pensioners.

Doctor.   Your's?

Balder.   Her's.

Doctor.   Some say the illumining sun is dark;
But poor as you are—

Balder.   Is this blossom sweet?

Doctor.   Most fragrant!

Balder.   Yet I plucked it on a rock
Where common grass had died. Learn this, my friend,
The secret that doth make a flower a flower,
So frames it that to bloom is to be sweet,
And to receive to give. The flower can die,
But cannot change its nature; though the earth
Starve it, and the reluctant air defraud,
No soil so sterile and no living lot

So poor but it hath somewhat still to spare
In bounteous odours.   Charitable they
Who, be their having more or less, *so* have
That less is more than need, and more is less
Than the great heart's goodwill.

                            Here are books, here
A picture, still unpacked, from the great city,
Sent by an early college friend, who vows
A pilgrimage to these old hills ; and there
(Arrived this morning from the muse knows where)
That strange sweet mystery, the early scrawl
Of young Ambition.   Genius is born blind ;
See how the nursling fumbles for the dug,
Lipping each barren likeness ; now distent
As limpet on a rock, and sucking hard
The east-wind, and now drawing with a touch
Nectar for gods ; 'twill help the hour on—
(*Going.*)   . Stay !
Paul, thou art somewhat of an antiquary ;
Let these walls entertain thee ; at thy leisure
Spell out these parchments, which my chamberlain,
The spider, deems too bare for such a presence,
And with his orfrays and embroidery
Decks an' I will or no.   To my heart, Paul,
The mouldering stones of this old tottering tower
Are not more ancient ; this, for all I feel,
Might be the dust of centuries !

         Doctor.   What are they ?

Balder. Listen : when we came here, a bridal pair,
Joyous and young and poor, I took this room
For mine, the forge in which to beat my gifts
To the white heat that lights and warms the world ;
And so I left it bare. We had small store,
And that I spent on her's. But still she came,
And sat beside me at her daily tasks
In happy silence ; then I said 'not here !'
But she said 'here !' and kissed me ; oh those days !
She was so fair——

    Doctor.   She *was ?*

    Balder.   She is ; she was
So fair, so delicately bred ; I saw
Her there, and all the strong unseemly place
Disturbed me. 'Oh for cloth of gold,' I cried,
'To make a palace for thee !' But she smiled.
When she came in I felt the cold grey air
Strike her like a stone, and when she walked methought,
Oft as she passed between me and the wall,
The rudeness of the unhewn and jagged rock,
Albeit that bodily it touched her not,
Harried her beauty ; and, whene'er she sat
Looking her sweet content, stern histories
Sank from the dark roof thro' the dungeon day,
And fell upon her face like grinding dust
Upon the apple of mine eye. She knew
My trouble, saying, ' Where thou art, to me
Heaven arches o'er thee, and I dwell in tents

Of azure ; but, my husband ! as thou wilt.
Nevertheless, not silver and not gold,
Silver and gold are not for me or thee ;
But oh, my poet husband ! what thou hast
Give me.'   And so I hung the room with THOUGHT.
Morning and noon, and eve and night, and all
The changing seasons ; scenes, or new or old,
Strange faces and familiar ; forms of men
Or gods in valleys deep, or mountains high ;
And how she loved them !   Tarry till I come. [*Goes.*
  Doctor (*unfolding a scroll*).   What's here ? sad heart !
    some withered primroses !
(*Reads.*) 'Spring, who did scatter all her wealth last year,
Had gone to heaven for more ; and coming back
Flower-laden after three full seasons, found
The Earth, her mother, dead.

                    ' Far off, appalled
With the unwonted pallor of her face,
She flung her garlands down, and caught, distract,
The skirts of passing tempests, and thro' wilds
Of frozen air fled to her, all uncrowned
With haste,—a bunch of snowdrops in her breast,
Her charms dishevelled, and her cheeks as white
As winter with her woe.   She fell upon
The corse, and warmed it.   The maternal earth,
Which was not dead, but slept, unclosed her eyes.
Then Spring, o'erawed at her own miracle,
Fell on her knees ; and then she smiled and wept.

Meanwhile the attendant birds her haste outstripped,
Chasing her voice, crowd round and fill the air
With jocund loyalty ; and eager winds
Her suitors, at full speed with Love and wild,
Hie by her in the lusty cheer of March,
Crying her name.   Laughed Spring to see them pass,
—Laughing in tears.   Then it repented her
To see the old parental limbs of Earth
Lie stark as death ; and fared she forth alone
To where she left her burden in the void
Beyond the south horizon ; her fair hair
Streaming spring clouds among the vernal stars.
Returning, slow with flowers, she dressed the Earth,
Which had sat up, and, being naked, blushed,
And stretched her conscious arms to meet the Spring,
Who breathed upon her face, and made her young.
Then did her mother Earth rejoice in her ;
And she with filial love and joy admired,
Weeping and trembling in the wont of maids.
Meantime her pious fame had filled the skies ;
He that begat her, the almighty Sun,
Passing in regal state, did call her "child,"
And blessed her and her mother where they sat—
Her by the imposition of bright hands,
The Earth with kisses.   Then the Spring would go,
Abashed with bliss, decorous in the face
Of love parental.   But the Earth stood up,
And held her there ; and, them encircling, came

All kind of happy shapes that wander space,.
Brightening the air.   And they two sang like gods
Under the answering heavens.'

   Doctor (*unrolling another scroll*).   Here Summer,
    (*reads.*)   ' Summer,
Mother of gods and men, with equal face
Unchangeable, and such wide eyes divine
As on the Athenian hill-top Phidian Jove
Inherited ; whose universal sense
Seems made with ampler vision to behold
A larger world than ours.   She leans in light
On rose-leaves, as a long and lazy cloud
Leans on the broad bed of the blushing west.
In her right hand a horn of plenty, red
With fragrant fruits exuberant ; in her left
The early harvest ; crowned with oak and ash,
Her hot feet slippered in the calid seas.
Her voice is like the murmur of the floods
Sluggard with noon, or the thick-leaved response
Of sultry forests to the languid winds
Dull with the dog-days.'

         Nay, no more ; one knows
This better out of doors.   Now Autumn ! blow
A windy morning, and a whirr of wings.

     [*Unrolling another scroll, reads.*
' He stands beside a throne of golden hills,
And up the steep steps of the royal throne
The burdened forests climb like countless slaves

Laden with gold.   He stands and heeds them not ;
Meanwhile his hand, with air abstract and wan,
From the abounding tribute of the earth
Scatters imperial largesse.   All her fields
Are his ; they own their lord ; his barns are full,
His rivers run with wine, and his red plains
Shout with the vintage.   Yet he stands beside
His golden throne, and looketh up to heaven,
And sigheth in the melancholy winds,
And smileth sweeter sadness,   He hath learned
The lesson of power ; therefore his locks are sere,
Therefore there is no light in the sunk eyes
Which day and night reproach the sun and stars
With the unsated hunger of a soul
That is no richer tho' the world be won.'

    Too sentimental !   He should take a license
To kill game.—   '
(*Unrolling another scroll.*)   Autumn still ?   Corpo di
    Bacco !
A metamorphosis !   'The Death of Autumn !' [*Reads.*
'Sometimes an aged king upon his bed,
He dieth 'mid the conscious hush of all
His reverent realm, and silent snows him wind.
Or, haply, at midnight a choir of winds
Chanting great anthems, bear him to his rest.
And sometimes doing battle with his fate,
A wreathed wrestler from a gorge of wine,
He falls in pride ; a giant in his blood,

Dashed with the purple feast as to his robes
Of azure triumph and his golden crown
Olympic, while his dying eye on fire
Brings a red glow into the cheeks of Death,
His ghastly foe, and his felled stature shakes
The sounding halls.

    'And sometimes as a maid
Dead and undone, the pale and drowned year
Lies still and silent on the mortal shore,
With dank unmeaning lips and sightless eyes
Ooze-filled, and blanch limbs stark and stiff beyond
The draggled robes soaked with a colder death.
And sometimes as a trusting maid who waits
Her far false lover, and thro' long lone hours
Expects in vain, but as the sun goes down,
Chilled with the bitter day where love is not,
Blighted and mute, astonied beyond speech,
Stands utterless; while all within is changed
From life to death, and under that pale breast
Unheaving and those glittering eyes transacts
The alchemy of ruin. Nor she weeps,
Nor starts, nor shrieks, nor throws her arms to heaven,
But motionless and crimson with her wrong
Dies in her silence, and falls still as leaves
Thro' stiller air.'

    Enough. Shall I try Winter?
     [Unrolling another scroll, reads.

'Who is he

That o'er green pastures of the latter year,
And on the mountain-tops, and through the woods
Passeth amid the pageant of the world
Silent and ceaseless, laying hand on nought?
Not as content, for greed is in his eye,
But patient in the confidence of fate.
Downward in face, and as to his bent head
Covered; by night and day, in sun or rain,
Unlooked for, unforeseen, but ever found,
And keeping ever on an aimless way
With the firm foot of purpose, as in dreams
We walk to airy biddings, and as on
A king's death-day, while all the court stand round
Power unresigned, the inevitable heir
Doth eye the crown and pace the palace floors
Expectant.   But none know him for a king
Nor do him homage.   The too-lusty green
Of the o'er-confident time unawed stands out
Into his path, and the insulting growth
Below retards his unrespected feet.
He sees, and a cold smile comes on his face
As moonlight upon ice; the shivering wind
Starts from his side, and fleeing ominous,
Spreads such a sign as in the latter day
Shall blow from chill Damascus; but no roll
Of answering thunder nor dread bolt of wrath
Smites the roused world that listens and forgets.
Yet some are wise.   With him on hill-tops hoar

The o'erruling spirits and attentive hours
Confer, and seek and take his high behest
In secret, and make peace with things to come.
And failing Autumn, like an aged king,
Talked with him on the field of cloth of gold,
And as he spake fell dead ; and the lush powers,
And pleasures full, which ruled the summer reign
(Like ships on a calm sea, that, sinking slow,
Of all their gallant bulk above the wave
Leave but a naked mast) sank one by one
Into the earth, and in the wonted place
Were found in lesser fashion, daily less.
And now the fields are empty, but He walks
Hale and unminished to and fro and up
And down, and more and more the observance
Of the astonished year is turned and turned
Upon the Solitary, and the leaves
Grow wan with conscience, and a-sudden fall
Liege at his feet, and all the naked trees
Mourn audibly, lifting appealing arms.
Which when he knew, as a pale smoke that grows
Keeping its shape, he rose into the air
And froze it, and the broad land blanched with fear,
And every breathless stream and river stopped,
And thro' him, walking white and like a ghost
With grim unfurnished limbs, the cold light passed
And cast no shade.   Then was he king indeed,
And all the undefended World he saw

Bare at his will.   His brow grew black on her ;
And with a sound that killed her shuddering heart,
He whistled for the North.'

                            Nay, rheumatism

Forbid !   Let's have some sunshine (*unrolling scrolls*)—
     Æschylus—
Thor—Balder—a Viking—a Runic Skald—
Kun-y-a and the Gopees—Seeva-deo—
What next?   Stay, here's some warmth in prospect.
     ' Dawn.'
(*Reads.*)   'See her in naked beauty, calm as snow,
And cradled in a cloud upon the east.
Unblushed, unconscious, with unopened lids,
Fair as the first of women where she lay
Among the asphodels of Paradise
Before God breathed for her the breath of life.'
Too cool, I long for morning.   Here !
(*Opening a scroll, and reading.*)   ' Lo, Morn,
When she stood forth at universal prime,
The angels shouted, and the dews of joy
Stood in the eyes of earth.   While here she reigned
Adam and Eve were full of orisons,
And could not sin.   And so she won of God
That ever when she walketh in the world
It shall be Eden.   And around her come
The happy wonts of early Paradise.
Again the mist ascendeth from the earth
And watereth the ground, and at the sign

Nature, that silent saw our woe, breaks forth
Into her olden singing, near and far
The full and voluntary chorus tune
Spontaneous throats, and the ten thousand strings
That by meridian day, being struck, give out
A muffled answer, peal their notes, and ring
Reverberating music.   Once again
The heavens forget their limits, pinions bright
O'er-passing mix the ethereal bounds with ours,
And winds of morning lead between their wings
Ambrosial odours and celestial airs
Warm with the voices of a better world.
Dews to the early grass, Light to the eyes,
Brooks to the murmuring hills, Spring to the earth,
Sweet winds to opening flowers, MORN to the heart !
But more than dew to grass or light to eyes
Or brooks to murmuring hills or spring to earth
Or winds to opening flowers, MORN to the heart !
Once more to live is to be happy ; Life
With backward-streaming hair and eyes of haste
That look beyond the hills, doth urge no more
Her palpitating feet ; Her wild hair falls
Soft thro' the happy light upon her limbs,
She turns her wondering gaze upon herself,
Sweet saying—" It is good."   Once more the soul
Rises in Eden to immortal gifts,
And by the side of morning,—new from heaven,
Fresh from the stores of all things, and within

Her limpid face still wearing reflex bright
Of joys that shall be,—dances glad with strange
Unutterable Knowledge.   We are healed ;
The curse falls from our eyelids ; all the thorns
And thistles that do plague us, clad in gems
Stand round ; and we behold them as they are,
And call them jewelled friends.   All fetters break ;
From the tremendous girdle that doth round
The globe and keep her, to these heavy bonds
That bind us to her, and whose last stronghold
Is clenched in central fires.   We are not dogs
Nailed to a needful den, but wingèd lions,
And walk the earth from choice,—the fair free earth
That willeth to be here, and cares not yet
To mount up like a coloured cloud to God.
The pulse of Being flows, the ill that ran
Along her veins, the hand of Incubus
Upon her throat, are gone like night !   All things
Do well, and still his function is to each
Consummate welfare.   As the unheeded garb
Upon the rising and the falling breast
Of beauty, that still moveth as she moves,
Breathes with her breath and quivers with her sighs,
So Nature's varied robe lies light on her,
The beautiful broad surface of the world
And all its kingdoms.   Memory that stirred
And murmured thro' the helpless dreamy dark,
Snuffing the eternal air, sinks silent down

To utter sleep, for whereas day that is
Bendeth beneath the golden multitude
Of all the days that have been, each to-morrow
Heavier for yesterday, Morn hath no past.
Primeval, perfect, she, not born to toil,
Steppeth from under the great weight of life,
And stands as at the first.

                'The feast is spread,
And none know wherefore. Wherefore? who shall ask?
Who cannot feast? As a rich bride in smiles
And blushes for her much bliss eateth not,
And seeth that they serve a sacrament
And something more than wine, the poet sits.
While Who stood glorious at the shining head
Of jubilee, where men a light beheld
And he a presence, clad in sounding joy
Moves down the festal aisles. As a true queen,
In whose ennobling eyes her lowliest guests
Are princes, so she slow descends to far
Forgotten places, and with her mere smile
Rights the unequal board. Light shines to light
Down to the earth and upward to the heaven,
And whatsoe'er unknown it is whereof
Our lives default, whatever of divine
Whose all irreparable absence makes
The nameless dolour of a mortal day,
Returns in full. As love, that hath his cell
In the deep secret heart, doth with his breath

Enrich the precincts of his sanctuary
And glorify the brow and tint the cheek ;
As in a summer garden one beloved
Whom roses hide, unseen fills all the place
With happy presence ; as to the void soul
Beggared with famine and with drought, lo God !
And there is great abundance ; so comes MORN,
Plenishes all things and completes the world.'
(*Opening another scroll.*)   Now for the matron sister,
        drowsy Noon,
The lotus-eater, nay, nay, I must keep
My eyes open ; I'll pass her for the next.
This should be evening by its place.   No title !
(*Reads.*) ' And seest thou her who kneeleth clad in gold
And purple, with a flush upon her cheek,
And upturned eyes full of the love and sorrow
Of other worlds ?   'Tis said that when the son
Of God did walk the earth, she loved a star
Which went aloft with God, but, lest she die,
Day after day looks out on her from heaven
At sunset smiling, so she wears her robe
Sad but imperial, as of right a queen.'
        [*Turns to another scroll, unrolls, and reads.*
' And lo the last strange sister, but tho' last
Elder and haught, called Night on earth, in heaven
Nameless, for in her far youth she was given,
Pale as she is, to pride, and did bedeck
Her bosom with innumerable gems,

And God, He said, " Let no man look on her
For ever," and, begirt with this strong spell,
The moon in her wan hand she wanders forth,
Seeking for some one to behold her beauty,
And wheresoe'er she cometh eyelids close,
And the world sleeps.'

                         I'm sleepy too ; Heigho !
Is this a dream?
(*Opens a scroll and reads.*) ' I knew a family
Of fairies.   Thou wouldst hear their history?
But how ?   I cannot speak of them apart ;
Nay, hardly of the matter of this breath
May frame their common story.   Our least word
Too palpable is grosser than the strength
Of all, as one bright water-drop contains
An animalcular people.   Oberon,
Step forth, and let me fit thee with a sound
Wherein from top to toe thou wouldst not stand
Hid as an urchin in his grandsire's coat !
Their dwelling-place was by the water's edge
Under a stone.   The mosses of the brink
Spread ample shade with branching arms at noon,
And there each day they lay at ease, all three
Singing a drowsy chorus like the hum
Of hovering gnat above a bed at night,
Heard when the house is still.   Such needful rest
Concludes the daily feast ;—a grain of grass
In no more honey-dew than loads an ant

Driven like an ass before them.   Once a day
They fed at home, but morn and eve I saw
Where in green ambush under milking kine,
Looking up, all, as to a precipice,
They watched the pail, and when the white plash fell
Cupped in some patent floweret, gathering round,
Climbed the laborious stem, and bending o'er,
Drank deep; which done, they seek the lucid lake,
And sailing forth in pride, the emerald wing
Of summer beetle is a barge of state ;
Her cock-boat, red and black, the painted scale
Of lady-fly aft in the fairy wake
Towed by a film, and tossed perchance in storm,
When airy martlet, sipping of the pool,
Touches it to a ripple that stirs not
The lilies.   Thus I knew the tiny band,
Nor only so, but singly, and of each
The several favour ; yet I can but speak
With organs made to tell of gods and men.
Thou who wouldst know them better *think* the rest,
And with some fine suggestion which has taste
Of a remembered odour, silent sweet,
Or what rare power divides the last result
Of mortal touch, and to the atomy
Gives an unnamed inferior, or what sense
Responds the tremors of the soul and takes
The sound of wings that, unbeheld by eyes,
Mystic and seldom thro' its upper air

Pass as in wandering flight; therewith behold
My vision, and therewith accept the parts
Of the so delicate whole which my strained care
Brought not unminished, nor could bring, but found
As 'twere an elfin draught in faëry cup,
And to be spilled by the mere pulse of hands
Like mine.   Therewith attach each separate grace
Of those thus fair together; know what made
Each brother beauteous, what more subtle charm
The lovelier sister, and what golden hair
Hung over her as sometimes shimmereth light
From smallest dew-drop, else unseen, that crowns
The slimmest grass of all the shaven green
At morning.   Love them by their names, for names
They had, and speech that any word of ours
Would drop between its letters uncontained;
Love them, but hope not for impossible knowledge.
In their small language they are not as we;
Nor could, methinks, deliver with the tongue
Our gravid notions; nor of this our world
They speak, tho' earth-born, but have heritage
From our confines, and property in all
That thro' the net of our humanity
Floats down the stream of things.   Inheriting
Below us even as we below some great
Intelligence, in whose more general eyes
Perchance Mankind is one.   Neither have fear
To scare them, drawing nigh, nor with thy voice

To roll their thunder. Thy wide utterance
Is silence to the ears it enters not,
Raising the attestation of a wind,
No more. As we, being men, nor hear but see
The clamour and the universal tramp
Of stars, and the continual Voice of God
Calling above our heads to all the world.'
I like this better. Shall I try again?
Wheugh! what a roomful; I'm not half-way round.
Courage, Paul! one more venture!
(*Unrolls a scroll, and reads.*) 'Chamouni!'

'If

Thou hast known anywhere amid a storm
Of thunder, when the Heavens and Earth were moved,
A gleam of quiet sunshine that hath saved
Thine heart; Or where the earthquake hath made wreck,
Knowest a stream, that wandereth fair and sweet
As brooks go singing thro' the fields of home;
Or on a sudden when the sea distent
With windy pride, upriseth thro' the clouds
To set his great head equal with the stars
Hast sunk Hell-deep, thy noble ship a straw
Betwixt two billows; Or in any wild
Barbaric, hast, with half-drawn breath, passed by
The sleeping savage, dreadful still in sleep,
Scarred by a thousand combats, by his side
His rugged spouse—in aught but sex a chief—
Their babe between; Or where the stark roof-tree

Of a burnt home blackened and sear lies dark,
Betwixt the gaunt-ribbed ruin, hast thou seen
The rose of peace ; Or in some donjon deep,
Rent by a giant in the blasted rock
And proof against his peers,—hast thou beheld
Prone in the gloom, naked and shining sad
In her own light of loveliness, a fair
Daughter of Eve : Then as thou seest God
In some material likeness, less and more,
Thou hast seen Chamouni, 'mid sternest Alps
The gentlest valley ; bright meandering track
Of summer when she winds among the snows
From Land to Land.   Behold its fairest field
Beneath the bolt-scarred forehead of the hills
Low lying, like a heart of sweet desires,
Pulsing all day a living beauty deep
Into the sullen secrets of the rocks.
Tender as Love amid the Destinies
And Terrors ; whereabout the great heights stand
Down-gazing, like a solemn company
Of gray heads met together to look back
Upon a far fond memory of youth.
Northward and southward of my hut, from heaven
To earth, two gates of ice shut in the scene,
As tho' between twin icebergs a green sea
Had melted, and the summer sun and sky
Shone in the waters.   All the vale is flowers.
Take thy staff shod with iron, gird thy loins

For conflict.   Let us to the northern gate !
Is this a wood of pines ?   Are these but rocks,
Hurled by the winter tempest ?   Did a chance
O'erthrow these trunks—in the stern wont of war
Supine ?   Or was it here the Thunderer smote
The Giants—And the battered remnant stand
Astonied giving glory to the Heavens ?
Aye, these are pines ; but thou shalt turn and break
The hugest on thy knee, having once passed
Out of their umbrage, and in open day
Fronted the everlasting looks of them
Who sit beyond in council ; round whose feet
Are wrapped the shaggy forests, and whose beards,
Down from the great height unapproachable,
Descend upon their breasts.   There, being old,
All days and years they maunder on their thrones
Mountainous mutterings, or thro' the vale
Roll the long roar from startled side to side
When whoso, lifting up his sudden voice,
A moment speaketh of his meditation,
And thinks again.   There shalt thou learn to stand
One in that company, and to commune
With them, saying, " Thou, oh Alp, and thou, and thou
And I."   Nathless, proud equal, look thou take
Heed of thy peer, lest he perceive thee not,—
Lest the wind blow his garment, and the hem
Crush thee, or lest he stir, and the mere dust
In the eternal folds bury thee quick !

The forest now behind thee, at thy feet
The torrent, thrust thine head back as who seeks
The polestar; and above the mountains green,
And o'er the shepherd's shealing,—less than nest
On tree-top—and o'er woods that are as moss,
Black on a ruin,—over the icy sea
—A billowy Sibir of ten thousand hills
As tho' yon white rocks, bending evermore
So potently above the floods, begat
A likeness, and from out their yielding breasts
Compelled a brood of stone—o'er naked crags,—
Aye, above where the shyest roe unseen
Draws the thin breath, and marmot cannot pass
The inexorable famine,—over wilds
For ever dead, and snow, and upper snow,
And wastes above the snow, see nearer heaven
The base of a great pyramid, and rise
Slow to this peak, like a grey pinnacle
Of the towered earth piercing the cloudless skies.
To us how calm and lonely, tenantless
And silent as the still and empty air,
But to that height the seldom mountaineer
Looks from the extremest footing of some ridge
Incredible, three times beyond our ken,
And to his keen and upward-straining eyes
Round it midway the circling eagles sail,
As daws that round some thin and distant spire
On English hill, scarce seen thro' lucent air

Are motes in the evening sun.

                                    ' Now, if thou durst,
Drop from the Alp to lowest vale remote
Breathless ; nor be the first in that great fall.
So yon dark glacier from his native snows
Fell on the narrow valley, which beneath,
Like a poor foundered skiff, when some vast whale
In his unwieldy death-pang leaps and falls,
Is sunk and lost.   Grim with mortality,
War-stained he lies in heavy length, and bleeds,
A hill of death.   Behold aloft the seas
Whence he came down, unmelting seas of snow
Well-named, the ocean of a frozen world.
A marble storm in monumental rage,
Ploughed on the fragment of a shattered moon.
Passion at nought and strength still strong in vain,
A wrestling giant, spell-bound, but not dead.
As tho' the universal deluge passed
These confines, and when forty days were o'er
Knew the set time obedient and arose
In haste : but Winter lifted up his hand
And stayed the everlasting sign which strives
For ever to return.   Cold crested tides
And cataracts more white than wintry foam
Eternally in act of the great leap
That never may be ta'en, these fill the gorge
And rear upon the steep uplifted waves
Immoveable, that proudly feign to go, —

And on the awful ramparts of the rock
Bend forward, as in motion—side by side
Mixed manifold, rank after mingling rank,
In all the throng of multitude, but each
Condign, and in a personality
Confest.   Nor from the valley seen as waves.
But as lone shepherd, on some battle hill,
At setting of a chill moon on the wane,
Beholds his heroes from their unknown graves
Snow-cold, with blades of ice, out of the night,
The peopled peopling night, o'er airy crag
Crowding unstaunched invasion, with consent
Of hands that point advance, and martial gaze
Of helmèd heads, silent, majestical,—
All ghosts !   Or as some great acropolis,
Above the wondering eyes of ancient men,
On sacred feast, a statuary host,
Sent out her idols round the incandent hill,
And all her marble deities went by
In solemn march, tall, white, innumerable,
Each after each divine ; while far beneath,
Lone, like some shattered pillar of the skies,
Half-buried by his fall, headlong and prone,
The broken worship of a ruder race,
A Greater lay.   Or so methinks of old,
Below a mount of Jewry, Dagon fell
Before the Highest ; and in him subdued
From their high seats, fair bowers, dim haunts beloved,

And temples of the abdicated earth,
Upon a day the great mythology
Came forth by legions to behold the sign.
Dethroned, discrowned, divestured ; with bare brows
Paler than men ; proud whispering as they pass,
In murmur of a thousand waterfalls,
While somewhat like the finger of the world
Pointeth above their heads into the heavens,
And crash as of avenging thunderbolts
Pursues them,—nor can haste the step of gods.
Low in the abject earth lies Chamouni,—
Low in the last profound, whose narrow deep
Seems from yon midway and diminished peak—
So hunters say—who, clinging to the rock,
Dizzy look down—a gulph of mountain-mist,
Rainbowed, or if substantial, sunk and lost,
Drowned in the abyss of air, and lapsed below
Terrestrial, hopeless in a void of dreams.
Beheld as one should spy from upper wave
Of seas unsounded fathomless and dark,
Low, thro' mysterious waters infinite,
Illumined by a gleam, some jewelled mine
Emerald and ruby flashing dreamy gold,
Rent in the nether bed of the mid-main.
Nor less above yon midway crag the calm
Unventured summit, than if who descried
The deep-sea gulph, with sudden gaze revert,
Sees from his span of footing on the wave

Far in unearthly ether unassailed,
A great white cloud serene in sacred light
And happy skies.

     ' Here, in the lowest vale,
Sit we beside the torrent, till the goats
Come tinkling home at eve, with pastoral horn
Slow down the winding way, plucking sweet grass
Amid the yellow pansies and harebells blue.

    " The milk is warm,
     The cakes are brown ;
     The flax is spun,
     The kine are dry ;
     The bed is laid,
     The children sleep ;
     Come, husband, come,
     To home and me."

So sings the mother as she milks within
The chalet near thee ; singing so for him
Whom every morn she sendeth forth alone
Into the waste of mountains, to return
At close of day as a returning soul
Out of the infinite ; lost in the whirl
Of clanging systems and the wilderness
Of all things, but to one remembered tryst,
One human heart and unforgotten cell,
True in its ceaseless self, and in its time
Restored. But now the dusk which like a tarn
Lay long since in the hollows of the hills,

Swells from deep caves and tributary glens
Unnumbered, till the lower mountain tops
Are covered, and the dull and dead sea line
Rests tideless on a shore of sacred snow.
And now an unknown trouble has made cold
Those higher Alpine foreheads whence supreme
Over our darkness a serener day
Looked westward and to all that we saw not,
The glory and the loss.   For they do watch
The journey of the setting sun as one
Who when the weaker inmates of the house
Have sunk about his feet in dews and shades
Of sorrow, watches still with brow of light
And manly eye a brother on his way ;
But when the lessening face shines no return
Thro' distance slowly lengthening and sinks slow
Behind the hill-top, nor him. looking back,
The straining sense discerns, nor the far sound
Of wheels, stands fixed in sudden gloom profound,
And thoughts more stern than woe.
                               'Over those heights
Untrod, nor to be trodden, let thy soul
Pass like a fleeting sunshine.   Let it glide
Over the summit, southward, and descend
Where, thro' black mountains, a great river of snow
Banked by two Alps, from the eternal source
Whiter than clouds between the awful shores   .
Shines to the valley.   Meantime we below

Tread the dark vale uplooking; or sit long,
With hopeless upturned eyes, as one let down
Into the abyss of everlasting night,
From the impossible deep should gaze in vain
Up through the silent chaos to the skirts
Of ordered Nature.   What is he, unseen,
Who with the dreadful glacier as a sceptre
Touches the vale, and in his left hand holds
Yon rounded summit as an orb of state?
Thou canst not see them now, but forth to meet
The sovereign symbol, venerable woods
Climb the huge steep where age and pride allow,
And send their lither progeny to scale
The bleaker rock, ambitious.   These, inured,
Attain the lower precipice, nor blench,
Storm-bred : but these fall back aghast in sight
Of everlasting Winter, where, snow-borne,
In his white realm, for ever white, he sits
Invisible to men ; and in his works
Gives argument of that which, seen, makes faint
Aspiring Nature, and his throne a mount
Not to be touched.   On either wilderness
A snow-land spreads along the level skies.
Now from the eastward midnight draweth nigh,
When all things rest from labour.   As she goes
Her vestments floating shut out moon and stars
Mysterious ; and she breathes before her face
Darkness where all is dark.   Mute goeth she,

And silently on either hand unyokes
The willing mountains from beneath their load
Even now dispersing while the valley shakes,
And in his bed the sleeping peasant stirs,
And dreams of thunder.   They, beheld no more,
Leave only to the cataracts, and thee,
The great snow baseless in mid-heaven, self-shown,
Out-stretched and equal, like supporting wings,
Or thro' the windy and tumultuous dark
Down the long glacier sounding to the vale.
There was a legend wild, whispered at eve,
Late round the dying watch-fires to awed men,
In those dead seasons whence our Danish sires,
Of the Great Arctic Ghost, the efficient power
And apparition of the frozen North,
The mystic swan of Norna, the dread bird
Of destiny, world wide, with roaring wings,
Flapping the ice-wind and the avalanche,
And white and terrible as polar snows.
By them unseen behold it ! thro' the night
Swooping from heaven, its head to earth, its neck
Down-streaming from the cloud ; above the cloud
Its great vans thro' a rolling dust of stars
Thunderous descending in the rush of fate.'

After Mont Blanc one may sit down unblamed.
Eh ! this is tempting—these old eyes were dull
Not to see this at room's-length !   A veiled frame !

Reverently set in honour, and once wreathed,
It seems, with living flowers now long, long, dead !
The veil of funeral black, embrowned with dust !
A portrait as I guess—I'll see it.

Enter BALDER.

Balder.   Hold !
'Tis sacred !
    Doctor.   Pardon, friend, you make me nervous,—
I thought these heads said ' Hold.'
    Balder.   They had cried out
If I had held my peace.   A time may come
To raise that veil.   Not now.
    Doctor.   Your invalid ?
    Balder.   Not yet returned.   I'll fetch her.
                         [*Goes to window.*
                    Look here, Paul !
That figure stealing down the linden grove !
'Tis Evening, or 'tis she ! she comes ! she comes !
    Doctor.   'Tis a most happy symptom.   Let her take
Her will.   I'll wait.
    Balder.   Good God ! she turns aside
From the field-path into the winding track
We used in other days.
    Doctor.   Still happier sign !
Nay, I'll not hurry her.
    Balder.   Thanks, thanks.
    Doctor.   But, friend,

Hast thou no song to wear the hour away :
I'm weary.

    Balder.   Paul, thou art an emperor !
Decree.

    Doctor.   Thou hadst of old ' a song of seasons,'
With dainty amours and a fire-side close
Most comfortable.

    Balder.   Ay, an evensong.

                   [Goes to his harp, and sings.
In the spring twilight, in the coloured twilight,
Whereto the latter primroses are stars,
And early nightingale
Letteth her love adown the tender wind,
That thro' the eglantine
In mixed delight the fragrant music bloweth
On to me,
Where in the twilight, in the coloured twilight,
I sit beside the thorn upon the hill.
The mavis sings upon the old oak tree
Sweet and strong,
Strong and sweet,
Soft, sweet, and strong,
And with his voice interpreteth the silence
Of the dim vale when Philomel is mute !
The dew lies like a light upon the grass,
The cloud is as a swan upon the sky,
The mist is as a brideweed on the moon.
The shadows new and sweet

Like maids unwonted in the dues of joy
Play with the meadow flowers,
And give with fearful fancies more and less,
And come, and go, and flit
A brief emotion in the moving air,
And now are stirred to flight, and now are kind,
Unset, uncertain, as the cheek of Love.
As tho' amid the eve
Stood Spring with fluttering breast,
And like a butterfly upon a flower,
Spreading and closing with delight's excess,
A-sudden fanned and shut her tinted wings.
In the spring twilight, in the coloured twilight,
Ere Hesper, eldest child of Night, run forth
On mountain-top to see
If Day hath left the dale,
And hears, well-pleased, the dove
From ancient elm and high
In murmuring dreams still bid the sun good-night,
And sound of lowing kine,
And echoes long and clear,
And herdsman's evening call,
And bells of penning folds,
Sweet and low ;
Oh maid, as fair as thou
Behold the young May moon !
Oh ! happy, happy maid,
With love as young as she

In the spring twil'ght, in the coloured twilight,
Meet, meet me, by the thorn upon the hill.

[Interlude of Music.

At the midsummer, at the high midsummer,
Deep in the darkness let me sit embowered
All alone;
What time the children of the earth and heaven,
As of two houses whom a feud divides,
Meet in the mingling mystery of midnight,
And melting clouds sink low with woers' tears,
Felt but unseen, dropping a balm of joy
Whereto the love-touched leaves
Tremble and whisper thro' the gentle land.
The incense riseth and the incense falleth
And all the stolen hour is stirred with kisses,
And silent loves constrain the passionate time;
Rich loves that as they list
Exchange and take and give
Unmeted mede and debts for ever due.
And sweets are mixed along the languid air
Like balmy breath of lovers warm and near,
And glowing faces meeting thro' the dark.
Hush! for the world stands still
Held in mere joy, as nought on earth would lose
The happy place and moment where it stood.
Hush! o'er a stillness, still as Love's delight,
Hearts gushing, bosoms heaving, moving arms
Winding, unwinding; lips that close and part

And love still ending and beginning; Hush!
Put back the dawn, O Phosphor! Set again!
Fall like a sweet drop from the honeyed heavens!
Go down, and carried by a tender cloud!
The exquisite best moment of the night
Sinks down with thee. This is the ecstasy!
It sheds, it sheds! The night is filled with flowers,
——The viewless night, faint night, the yielding night,
The favouring night,— with flowers and happy rain!
As tho' to-morrow's blossoms spreading odours
As they float
Soft thro' the season, shy thro' the dark season,
Like a warm dew sank murmuring from the skies.

                              [Interlude of Music.

Fall, fall, fall,
Fall, fall, fall,
Oh orchard fruit fall from the fading tree,
Fall fruit of Autumn on the sullen sod,
Heavy and dead as clods into a grave.
Fall, fall, fall,
Fall, fall, fall,
Lone lingering rose thou knowest all must die!
Canst thou convince the breeze of spring, or blush
The summer thro' the cheeks of sallow day?
Thou, sick with solitude, and blanched with tears?
Fall, fall, fall,
Fall, fall, fall,
Sere leaf that quiverest thro' the sad still air,

Sere leaf that waverest down the sluggish wind,
Sere leaf that whirlest on the Autumn gust,
Free in the ghastly anarchy of death.
The sad still air which as a alkahest,
Potent and silent doth dissolve the year;
The sluggish wind that as a red stream slow
With carnage welters dull, and steams with death;
The sudden gust that like a headsman wild,
Uplifteth Beauty by her golden hair,
To show the world that she is dead indeed!
Fall, fall, fall,
Fall, fall, fall,
Fall twilight rain that dost not strive nor cry,
But chillest all the time with silent sorrow;
And not a wind does violence, nor a plaint
Stirs the dank quiet of the latter leaves;
But—as in speechless looks of him who stands,
Withered and wan by the wayside of Fate,
Timeless, unwelcome, all his better lot
Outlived, and the dear fashion of his day
And race forgotten, bended to his ill,
And lifting not the unavailing voice
Which no man heedeth—lorn and stillest tears
Grow in the fade eyes of the relict world.

[*Interlude of Music.*

Trim the lamp,
Pile the fire;
Brim the cup,

Touch the strings ;
Sigh of love,
Sing of joy ;
Trill of maids,
Chant of men !

Oh the young,
And the fair ;
Oh the love,
And the wine ;
Log of Yule,
Log of Yule,
In thy glamour
They shine !

For an hour
We are gods,
And of all
Love hath given
Lacking none
From our world
See the sun
Of our days !

Round the forms
That to-day
Blushed with life
Meet and smile
All the shapes

Of the past
In the light
Glimmer pale.

Early loves,
Friends of yore,
Ancient eyes,
Voices old,
Where the blaze
Charms the air
By our hearth
Come again.

And the sounds
And the dreams
And the quick
And the dead
In spell-dance
Move round me,
In murmur
And maze.

Oh ye Loves !
Oh ye Days !
Oh ye Dead !
Oh ye Dreams !
Bar the door,
Bar the door,
With a shout,
Shut them in !

For all the outer world is rocked in war !
The powers of harm break faith, and in mad might
Yell for the rout and will not be denied !
Even now the hungry sea begins to wreck,
And the impatient storms, eager for ill,
Bide not the expected signal, but blow out
The lingering Light that flickered in the west.
To-day is dead an hour before his time !
Good spells are broken, and the shrieking night,
Down from the haunted and mysterious hills,
Comes black and shuddering, wrapped about with snows,
Like a starved Ethiop sheeted from the grave.

SCENE XXIV.

THE STUDY.

BALDER, *solus, writing.   Enter* AMY.

Amy.   I have somewhat to say : let me come close,
Close to thine ear ; my husband, I am well !
Balder.   Thy pain ?——
Amy.   Gone ! I am well ; speak very low ;
The butterfly fresh from his living grave
Feels not so frail and new.   Hist, not a word,
'Tis resurrection morning ; I am free.
Balder.   My poor child——
Amy.   Nay, I know ; I am not mad ;

Hush! for I think a whisper would disturb
This footing; I am well, so well! I feel
I have slipped through the chains that held me down;
I could move like a mote thro' the warm air
Up to the hills. Let us go to the hills.
Hush, do not answer. I have spoken now.
I thought it would not last while I could tell thee. [*Exit.*
Balder (going to his harp and touching a solemn sweet air).
I praise thee, mother earth! oh earth, my mother!
Oh earth, sweet mother! gentle mother earth!
Whence thou receivest what thou givest I
Ask not as a child asketh not his mother,
Oh earth, my mother! [AMY *reappears, habited.*
   Balder. And thy lute, Amy? I will bring thy lute.
Nay, my poor nightingale, and art thou dumb
By day? But thou wilt be the lark, my child,
So near heaven's gate. Look to the morning hills,
With such a golden tumult over them
As if the everlasting port above
For the imperial Sun did ope and close
With clangor. Well, well, I'll not let thee sing,
But thou shalt murmur to me as the dove
When she alit upon the mountain-top
And found the leaf of peace. And I will make
Thy lute-strings shimmer as the sunshine shook
About her as she murmured. [*Takes up his hat and staff.*
               My Alp stick!
I think thou art King Edward's staff to-day,

For I feel more than king and half confessor. ·

      [They pass side by side into the fields.

 Amy. The hay, the new-mown hay! the birds, the
  birds !

 Balder. The audible soul of the warm balmy wind
That moves in music. Yonder pensive thrush
Singing his rhythmic cadence, and, below,
The blackbird, earnest in the flowering thorn,
Chanting his mellow prose as tho' he told
A wonted story, ever old and new !
The fitful chaffinch, like a bashful youth
That hurries forth his love in sudden speech
And blushing pause, the loud and cheerful wren,
The sparrow's chirp, the swallow on the wall—
The swallow that pours out her liquid joy
Upon the morning flood of happiness,
Wherein it falls with silver sound and sweet
As water into water ; these, and all
The warbling voices breathing of the South,
The slender treble of the tuneful year
With throbbing throats that chorus sunshine thro'
The vocal world, dainty, and soft, and low !
And high o'er all a languid noise of rooks,
Lost in bright air, circling in sunny calm,
Or cawing from the haunt of oaken green
The leafy rest of June !

      [They enter a meadow of flowers.

 Amy.   See !

Balder.   Seems it not,
My Amy, that this prattling Babe, the Earth,
Sole sitting at the footstool of the Heaven,
Strives to repeat her stars?

    Amy.   Yes.

    Balder.   Thy small feet
May tread the pathway careless of the dews:
We mortals are contemned of Nature,—she
Casts not her pearls before us.   But look, Amy,
This blade of grass from the untrodden field,
This green perfection of abundant health,
Complete with dew.   Herein behold why Nature
Is the one Teacher whom the Poet needs,
For she alone can show him in her works
Consummate art, and that supreme excess
Which fashions her fair work until the bound
Of possible performance, and the verge
Of the wrapt heart's belief; and while we say,
' Behold the final good!' sprinkles a dew,
And with divine complacence, passeth both.
Or having wrought her statue from a block
Infallible, with an unfailing hand
Quickens the faultless whole, and with a touch
Makes cold Perfection live.   With her he sees
Not only snow, but driven snow, nor driven snow
But on the sacred summit of an Alp
Immaculate, and on the whitest peak,
Whiter than white; the flower not only fair,

But fragrant, and the light not only warm,
The fire not only bright ; the summer fruit
Sweet to the taste but sweeter to the eye,
And over all its tangible a bloom
That never can be touched.   She, only she,
In her least work, as in her greatest, shows
To his confessing eyes the unattained
And unattainable, and tho' his pride,
Stung to its strength, outstrain the furthest stretch
Of man, and bring the trophies of the world,
She, still unsatisfied, by Day and Night
Points upward, saying,—'Be ye perfect as
Your Father in the Heavens!'   Thou hearest me not ;
Thy cheek is wet with tears ; thou art pale and red ;
Amy, my little child !

  Amy.   Oh, Love, I live !
I am ! I feel !   The Earth is not a dream !
The Prison doors are broken ! I am free !
I stand forth in the sun ! I know the wind !
The utter world doth touch me !   I can grasp
The hands that stretch forth from the mystery
That passeth ! I am crowded with my life !
It is too much ! the vital march doth stop
To press about me !   Air, give air—too much,
Too much—forgive, forgive, forgive——

  Balder.   My Loved !
My Lost ! my Wept ! my early-risen ! I clasp thee
Fresh from the dead !   'Tis past ; new-waked from sleep

Sudden amid the concourse of sweet sounds,
The rush, the pageant tumult, and this tramp
Of Being, the weak sense bewildered laughs
And weeps by turns.

   Amy.   Husband, till now, thy speech
Was my sole music, whereunto I kept
The maimed attendance of these feeble feet ;
To-day 'tis but a note—the first, the best—
In somewhat that fills all this sunshine space
With sound——since 'tis for sound to stir the heart
Unseen.

   Balder. Here let us rest. Thou hast said well
'Tis Resurrection-day. For I remember
Once in a sleep of childhood I looked forth
Thro' a wide summer window, on a still
And Garden-world. Eden, as at the first
I saw, and all the summers since the first,
Above it like a golden silent sea,
Lay warm and sweet and slumb'rous, soaking deep
All things in honeyed light—flowers, fruits, and trees,
Which breathed their gums and amber, and let down
From their festooned fair tops that no wind stirred
Visible odours—and the tepid Lakes
And the dissolving Hills. And far below,
Down thro' green warmth of the relaxed sod
To hidden secrets of the inner Earth
Slow sank incumbent, sinking, sinking Light.
'Twas Resurrection-morn. Where I beheld

City had never stood, nor ways of men,
Nor place of funeral.   But the Dead came up
Like spring-Flowers, white and golden, thro' the ground,
Lifting a little earth, as snowdrops lift,
On their strange heads.   This morning, as I stood
Beside my open window, ere thou camest,
And looked upon the day, methought I saw
My childhood's dream.   Is it a dream?   For thou
Art such a thing as one might think to see
Upon a footstone, sitting in the sun,
Beside a broken Grave !   ' [*They sit musing.*

    Amy.   Thou hast been silent
So long, that the slow shade of the tree-top
Moved like a dark hand o'er the grass, and took ·
Another daisy.

    Balder.   I do know this moment !
This is the very wind that long ago
In the first morning of sweet life we breathed
By the open gate of Love, when thou and I
Went happy in together, knowing not
The place, nor heeding if 'twere Earth or no.
We were so young, thou wert so pure, the woes
And weary ills that keep the gate of Love
Looked on us as on shapes concerning whom
They had no charge ; the guardians of the trees
Slept all, and with us the sublimer Fates
Dealt softly as with children.   Did we dream
A dream of years upon some flowery knoll,

And do we wake where we lay down? Is this
The outer world? Is this the common day
Of all the living? Oh Amy! my own child,
I could believe this fancy; never since
I felt this wind upon me in my youth
Have I beheld thee as now. Dost thou remember
The old days when at trysting-time thou camest
Forth down the winding valley to the stile
To meet me, and beside me all the sweet
Meandering way trode back in silent joy,
With downcast eyes that ever sought the ground,
But tell-tale smiles that could not choose but come
Me-ward; quick smiles that every word of mine
Stirred up anew so often that they met
Like sudden roses caught in a warm wind,
And did provoke each other, ruffling sweets
In dear confusion, and in all the change
Of my swift fancy changing till they lay
Upon thee like the thousand lines of light
Upon the shimmering water that the west
Moves with a sigh? So we past slowly on,
And so, fond gazing on thy silent face,
I poured the glorious wine of love into
A vase of crystal, where it blushed and shone
More fair. Sometimes I marvel when I think
Of those first days of love; love that unknown
Knew not himself, and still went in and out
Among the happy inmates of the heart

As an unconscious prophet walks amid
His brethren ere his equal lips be touched
With the live coals of fire. I that so long
Spake, and we knew not that I spake of love
Because it filled my speech, and being all
Seemed nothing, I who that I saw it not
Never believed it present, nor remembered
That the sole face on which I cannot look
Is this men know for mine—how did I win thee?
Canst tell me?

    Amy.   I can sing a little song.   [*She sings.*
The sun he riseth up on new year's day,
And looketh on the earth and goeth down;
The earth she stirreth to be looked upon.
The faithful sun he riseth day by day,
And looketh on the earth and goeth down;
The earth she trembleth to be looked upon.
The faithful sun he riseth day by day,
And looketh on the earth and goeth down;
The earth she blusheth to be looked upon.
The faithful sun he riseth day by day,
And looketh on the earth and goeth down;
The earth she smileth to be looked upon.
The faithful sun he riseth day by day,
And looketh on the earth and goeth down;
The earth she sigheth to him from the south;
The earth she stands before him all in flowers;
The many-voiced earth, she calleth him;

She singeth at his chamber that he rise,
And long time holdeth him lest he go down.

Balder. Thou wert as silent as a bird that sits
On her dear treasure, and while steps pass nigh
Is hushed and hid, but, when the plunderer nears
And only silence could have saved her, cries.
I ne'er forget my little Amy's face
Upon the blessed chance that owned us one ;
The happy chance that struck me by her side,
And all heard that which else had died unheard !

Amy. How did she look ?

Balder. She looked in her surprise
As when the Evening-Star ta'en unaware,
While fearless she pursues across the Heaven
Her Lover Sun,—and on a sudden stands
Confest in the pursuit before a world
Upgazing—in her maiden innocence
Disarms us, and so looks that she becomes
A worship evermore.
The bare hill-top
Shines near above us ; I feel like a child
Nursed on his grandsire's knee that longs to stroke
The bald bright forehead ; shall we climb ?

[They ascend the hill.
The fort
Is won, and here I plant the stalwart sign
Of sovereignty. A little while this staff
Shall be the solar centre of creation.

All that thou seest is thine !   [*He lies down.*

                        How passing sweet
To rest the weight of this mortality
Upon such friendly turf, while the free soul
Released from earthly shackles shines a star,
Above the great horizon of this world,
Giving and taking Light.

                        Lo, the wide sea
Of air from the high shore whereon we lie,
To the far mountains.   Thou couldst lay thy fair
And buoyant breast upon it, and go down
Into the limpid ocean as the swan
Goes down into the lake.

                        How strange to know
Yon dim old British camp across a plain
Of fifty waving miles.   Dost thou remember,
Dear love, when we two in the central green
Of that mauled mountain which our giant sires
Had clipped and cropped as 'twere a Dutch-land tree,
Sat a long summer day, and far and near
Saw the great martial circles widening out
Ring after ring, as tho' the snake that dwells
In the world's core had wound him forth and lay
Motionless in the sunshine, coil in coil,
His great head in the midst, and the green grass
Sprang up and knew him not, his one hour's sleep
A thousand years.

                    Hark, hark, the gathering herds

Round the low valley pool.   What ! tears again !
Bright summer showers !

   Amy.   ,   Oh love, the song of life !
Oh love, the music of the world ! my ears
Are open ! since the years I was a child
I have not heard it !   Tho' mine eyes have seen
The ordered pomp and sacred dance of things,
And marvelled at the measure, it passed on
In silence, but to-day, to-day, I hear
The voice to which it moves !   Too sweet, too sweet.
                                [*They pause.*

   Balder. And now my years come on me, and the life
That shall be !   I am faint with too much light,
But as a death-bed soul exults in death,
My spirit soars triumphant as I sink.
The day is full of suns ; I lie a-dream,
And o'er me the colossus of my fate
Stands to the white heavens from the shadeless earth,
And casts no shadow !   This is that same hour
That I have seen before me as a star
Seen from a rushing comet thro' the black
And forward night, which orbs, and orbs, and orbs,
Till that which was a shining spot in space
Flames out between us and the universe,
And burns the heavens with glory.   [*Pauses.*
                    Now I live !
The weakness has gone by.   This seasoned body
O'ermasters the strong element, and turns

The potent draught to balm ; the Olympian wine
That made me reel throbs thro' these larger veins
A nobler blood.   Come such a day as melts
The hard earth back to her primeval drop,
And I could look it in the face ! my chains
Break from my ampler limbs.   If thou didst start
I could believe that I sprang up a god,
And am a god for ever.   Do not kiss me,
Lest the remembered touch of those dear lips
Bring back a mortal pleasure.

       Amy, Amy,
Will we not save the world ?
  Amy.   'Tis a fair world !
  Balder. Look down upon it in the sunny haze
Of silent noon, sole in the void of heaven
Asleep, divine with the unconscious smile
Of everlasting beauty.   A well-spread
And ordered world ; not the bright elements
Innumerous of unrespective change,
The broken argosy of the universe
On spangled waters ; but a multiform
Supreme event, the single continent
Of all ; like immaterial deity,
Full of the coloured thought of an unmade
Creation.
  Amy. 'Tis thy kingdom, 'tis thy kingdom,
My king, my king !
  Balder.   I will arise and reign :

As God contains the world I will contain
Mankind, and in the solvent of my soul
The peopled and unpeopled ages. They,
Born and unborn, are one in me, and freed
From the disturbing thrall of space and time
Take each and all, in one eternal whole,
Ordained places, like a heaven of stars.
Thou hast said well 'tis a fair world, but what
Do the trees hide ? and yon far cloud of smoke
Over the sulphurous city?   Amy, Amy,
I yearn towards my race !

       I have been like
A prophet fallen on his prostrate face
Upon the hill of fire.   Mine hour is come,
The earthquake has yawned by me, I have seen
The seething core of nature, both these ears
Are deaf with voices, I am blind with light,
My heart is full of thunder !   In the form
Of manhood I will get me down to man !
As one goes down from Alpine tops with snows
Upon his head, I, who have stood so long
On other Alps, will go down to my race,
Snowed on with somewhat out of Divine air,
And merely walking thro' them with a step
God-like to music like the golden sound
Of Phœbus' shouldered arrows, I will shake
The laden manna round me as I shake
Dews from this morning tree.   And they shall see

And eat, and eating live, and living know,
And knowing worship. We will lead the flocks
Of the whole earth, walking before with staves
Of light——

 Amy. I—I, too, even I? ah, husband, .
To feel beside thee !

 Balder.   But I see them, Amy,
Whitening the world like harvest.   Wheresoe'er
We stay they pasture ; in the temperate sun
Disport on hills for ever green and fair,
Or at our word with universal feet
Pass to new fields, their great sound overhead
Borne like a banner : under favouring skies
Drink of salubrious streams, in innocent lands
Lie down to harmless sleep, and rise with us
To follow day and summer round the globe !

 Amy. My husband !

 Balder.   Sing a song of love to me,
This glory burns me up ; fetch me some tears.

 Amy (sings). There grew a lowly flower by Eden-gate
Among the thorns and thistles.   High the palm
Branched o'er her, and imperial by her side
Upstood the sunburnt Lily of the east.

The goodly gate swung oft with many gods
Going and coming, and the spice-winds blew
Music and murmurings, and paradise
Welled over and enriched the outer wild.

Then the palm trembled fast-bound by the feet,
And the imperial Lily bowed her down
With yearning, but they could not enter in.

The lowly flower she looked up to the palm
And lily, and at eve was full of dews,
And hung her head and wept and said, 'Ah these
Are tall and fair, and shall I enter in ?'

There came an angel to the gate at even,
A weary angel, with dishevelled hair;
For he had wandered far, and as he went,
The blossoms of his crown fell one by one
Thro' many nights, and seemed a falling star.

He saw the lovely flower by Eden-gate,
And cried, 'ah, pure and beautiful !' and turned
And stooped to her and wound her in his hair,
And in his golden hair she entered in.

Husband ! I was the weed at Eden-gate,
I looked up to the lily and the palm
Above me, and I wept and said, 'ah these
Are tall and fair, and shall I enter in ?'
And one came by me to the gate at even,
And stooped to me and wound me in his hair
And in his golden hair I entered in

Balder. Nay the poor wanderer, fallen from
    heaven, drew near
The guarded gate; but with his forfeit skies
Had lost his privilege and master-sign,
And turned aside and plucked an asphodel,
And, wearing, passed unchallenged.

Amy.   Hist! who comes?
Ah husband, we must be alone to-day!
I feel new-married and do blush to speak.
Let us go hence.

Balder.   An artist by his satchel.
Lie silent he will pass us. (*Starts up.*) What! my
    comrade!

Artist.   My old friend!

Balder.   Welcome! but how many days
Before your assignation?

Artist.   Fairly asked.
Sooth is, I was a wooer of Dame Nature
Down in your sylvan valley there. My goddess
Left me love-tokens, but denied herself;
I wearied, you may guess; and every night
Looked upward to these western tops and saw
Her footsteps, and the cloudy draperies
She put aside in passing, closing red
Behind her, dyed with honour. So I came
To sit here and waylay her.

Balder.   Amy, this
Is that good Gerald whom thou knowest well

By many a song and fireside history.
Dear old companion, we must meet again ;
This is a sweet and solemn festival
Which we two keep together, she and I.
But ere you leave us for my sake remember
One of the songs we used to sing of old;
We sang it three at once, and it was called
' The Song o' the Sun.'   The glowing orb of joy
Within my head must shine, or 'twill consume me.
You, each of you, chime in the needful chorus.
I am the sun !

    Artist.   With all my heart.   Begin.

    Balder.   Thou knowest it, little Amy ?

    Amy.   Did I e'er

Forget a word of thine ?   [BALDER *rises to his feet.*

    Artist.   Phœbus-Apollo !

    Balder.   Earliest bird
               Thou hearest me,
               Me afar off
               Thro' the dark.

Roll O days into the years, and O years into the ages,
    and O ages into the mystery of God !
Oh Love, oh Life, and all ye jocund train
Virtues and Joys, my lusty Company,
Be loud around me !   Sing because I sing !
Call each to each as I call unto you !
Love calling unto Life
' Oh Life ! Oh Life ! '

Life calling unto Love
' Oh Love ! Oh Love ! '
' How beautiful oh Life ! '
' How beautiful oh Love ! '
I am the sun singing behind the mountains !
Thou heaven, that didst watch for me on the hills,
Sitting upon the hill-tops above the valley of beauty,
Thou hearest me afar off singing behind the mountains,
And hast let fall thy mourning, and thy bosom is pale.
Also blushes are on thy cheeks lest I see thee, oh
    thou most beautiful.
But I will see thee, O thou most beautiful !
Robe thee in purple, take thy clouds about thee,
Rise up, O queen, with gold upon thy brows,
Behold I reach thee forth my golden sceptre,
Behold I give thee morning as a garment,
Sit on thy hill, and I will touch thy hill.
And thou shalt sit upon a diamond throne,
And shalt be glorified before my world !
For I see thee, O thou most beautiful !

Quiet valley, valley deep and still,
Dost thou hear my voice behind the mountains ?
I will come gently as a father peepeth
Over the cot, over the cot of beauty,
So will I lift my face up over thee.

Love, love, love, how beautiful oh love !

Art thou well-awakened, little flower?
Are thine eyelids open, little flower?
Are they cool with dew, O little flower?
Hath the south touched thee? Hath the fairy kissed thee?
Wilt thou come forth, come forth, into my day?

Ringdove, ringdove,
This is my golden finger
Between the upper branches of the pine!
Come forth, come forth, and sing into my day!

Butterfly, butterfly,
This is my golden finger,
I will feel for thee down among the roses,
Sweet in the roses, in the climbing roses,
And put thee from thy bed into my day!

Love, love, love, how beautiful, O love!

I will arise, I will awake the world!
They shall be glad because of me, I feel
The joy-light shining thro' their lids of sleep,
Like music from the hollow of the earth!   [*They sing.*

It is time,	It is time,	It is time,
O ye leaves,	O ye streams,	O ye bells,
On the tree-tops	On the hill-tops	In the grey spire
Of morning;	Of morning;	Of morning;
Laugh down	Run down	Ring down
The trees,	The hills,	The spire,

That the pastures	That the valleys	That the hamlet
May wake !	May wake !	May wake !

Awake !

I am the sun, I am above the mountains,
My joy is on me, I will give you day !
I will spend day among you like a king !
Your water shall be wine because I reign !
I stave my golden vintage on the mountains,
And all your rushing rivers run with day !
I am the sun, I am above the mountains !
Arise, my hand is open, it is day !
Rise ! as men strike a bell and make it music,
So have I struck the earth and made it day !
Move, move, O world, on all your brazen hinges,
Send round the thunder of your golden wheels ;
Throng out, O millions, out, O shouting millions ;
Throng out, O millions, shouting, shouting day !
For as one blows a trumpet through the valleys,
So from my golden trumpet I blow day !

O earth, O flowers, O birds, O   , O men,
Day is proclaimed !   I called until I heard
The caverns echo !   Day is everywhere !
White-favoured day is sailing on the sea,
And, like a sudden harvest in the land,
The windy land is waving gold with day !
As for you whom I have awakened, do
As shall seem good in all your shining eyes,

Your eyes still wet with morning.   They shall dry,
And day shall fade.   But I have done my task :
Do yours !   And what is this that I have given,
And wherefore ? look ye to it !   As ye can,
Be wise and foolish to the end.   For me,
I, under all heavens, go forth praising God !

 Artist. I also.   And I also singing lauds
To see you both so happy.   [*Exit.*

 Balder.   Brave old friend !

 Amy. Shall we walk, husband, to yon shady tree
Above the little stream ?   [*They walk.*

 Balder.   Alas ! that one
Should use the days of summer but to live,
And breathe but as the needful element
The strange superfluous glory of the air !
Nor rather stand apart in awe beside
The untouched Time, and saying o'er and o'er
In love and wonder, ' these are summer days.'

 Amy. Let us sit here.   [*They sit.*

 Balder.   Under this ash, last spring,
I saw a sight more sweet than ever clown
Came on a-sudden in a fairy-ring
By summer moon.   A growth of primroses,
Thick as the stars by night, and like the stars
In constellations and in orbits due,
Shone round the central tree.   I could believe
Queen Flora, on a royal progress tired,
Halted beneath it, and her flowery court

Pitched their fair tents about her, or, well-pleased,
Sole or by twins, in fragrant converse, lay
Upon the enchanted ground.   Thou hadst a song,
A country song, a chanted calendar,
Fit to be timbrelled to the tambourine —

[AMY *interrupts him.*

Amy (sings).

First came the primrose,
On the bank high,
Like a maiden looking forth
From the window of a tower
When the battle rolls below,
So looked she,
And saw the storms go by.

Then came the wind-flower
In the valley left behind,
As a wounded maiden pale
With purple streaks of woe
When the battle has rolled by
Wanders to and fro,
So tottered she,
Dishevelled in the wind.

Then came the daisies,
On the first of May,
Like a bannered show's advance
While the crowd runs by the way,
With ten thousand flowers about them they came trooping
through the fields.

As a happy people come,
So came they,
As a happy people come,
When the war has rolled away,
With dance and tabor, pipe and drum,
And all make holiday.

Then came the cowslip,
Like a dancer in the fair,
She spread her little mat of green,
And on it danced she.
With a fillet bound about her brow,
A fillet round her happy brow,
A golden fillet round her brow,
And rubies in her hair.
No more, no more, for I am tired of singing,
I'll make a garland, as in olden days,
And crown thee as of old.

[*She runs off to neighbouring flowers.*

Balder.   Thou most pure essence,
Wilt thou exhale i' the sun? Being from me
Tho' but a little way mine eyes do fear
To leave thee, as they fear to leave the light
In a dew-drop. Happy perchance for thee,
If the spell brake and light returned to light!
Yet the strong Fate that mixed us hath wrought well.
I am for thee; thou mightest have crossed this world
Among our grosser motions as a spirit

Unseen, nor having organs to discourse
The rare ethereal of its too divine
And necessary beauty ; but O soul,
O woman mere and absolute, O Amy !
Upon a sacred moment thou didst come
Into the body of my Love and Power,
And henceforth art a worship, being seen
And known unto the eyes and hearts of men
For ever ; to whom temples shall be built,
And nations offer gifts of sighs and tears.
Thou, little one, who sittest twining flowers,
White flowers that lie like dew upon thy breast
Thou fairer blossom, and salutest each
With such new joy and fond discovery
As if thou least of living things couldst spare
A loveliness, and to thee most of all `
'Twere wondrous to be fair,—Thou who, too rich
And poor, when thy dear arms are round my neck
Hast no belief in human lot more proud,
Nor knowledge of a place in the wide world
So regal—little knowing what thou art,—
If I could tell thee all, wouldst thou grow pale
And tremble? I know not.   Nay if this hour
The green hill and the world below the hill
Fell from thee, and thou shining like a saint
Ineffable in mid heaven wert left bare
To the assembled and upturned gaze
Of this great Universe, I could believe

Thou wouldst no more than lift up thy pure eyes
Unconscious, and walk forth among the stars,
As in a planted garden.   Well for thee,
Dear child, in thine eternal childhood more
Than I who wrestling would join arms with gods !
Do these things haunt thee ? Dost thou ever dream
That thro' all human precincts evermore,
Wherever Love hath honour and Beauty fame
Thou shalt be welcome ? Dost thou think at all
Of those who in the centuries to come
Shall seek thee ? Men who in a golden time,
Noblest, shall rule a nobler race than ours.
These shall have read the shining scroll on high
And known what thoughts they be that God writes down
Upon his starry tablets, and for these,
Full-grown, this Mother Earth round whom to-day
Men stand as children spelling Truths unknown,
Shall close the open book upon her knee,
And tell out of her deep invisible heart
The secrets of her youth ! But these shall pause
To hear thee, Amy ; bending from their thrones,
Among which thou with simple step and sweet,
Dressed in thy country life, goest in and out
By right, for thou art mine !
                              In penury,
In cold oblivion, in a tortured life,
Have strange looks lightened from thee ? Hast thou seen
How proud they are who in the years to be

Would give their queenly crowns to change one day
With thee, or have it for a moment said
Of them as it shall be for ever said
Of Amy? Has it been that thou hast lain
Grandly upon the racking hours, aye curved
The paly channels of thy tears with pride?
Smile on, for well thou may'st! If haughty eyes
Refuse thee, and the front of jewelled state
Thine unadorned poor presence, if false tongue
Blaspheme thee, or cold heart look lightly on
Thy woe, doth ever music in the air
Perplex thee? Doth the mist of morning shape
Altar and arch and all the fretted pile
Pompous and grey, where men one day shall sit
Upon the graves of them who passed thee by,
And use their sculptured pride to rest the weight
Of the forgotten flesh that the wrapt soul
May hear me well because I speak of Thee,
In terror or in beauty?   And my love
A rushing mighty wind goes thro' the place
In thunders whereat underfoot the dead
Move the cold stones, and the great roofs and aisles
Are shaken as with passion!   And thou, Amy,
As a white bird across a sunset sky
In likeness of an angel to and fro
High wingest thro' the tumult of the dome,
In the red windy music.
                         Or, the storm

Being spent, and stillness like the sudden dark
Fallen on the listening senses, in the pause
I breathe upon the dumbness of the air
And heal it, and my breath sweet thro' the hush
Floodeth the fragrant silence which unstirred
Fills full of me, as an unclouded noon
Of balmy light ; and thro' that golden noon
Thou sinkest slow while reverent heads are bowed,
And bosoms heave, and the cold thrill of awe
Pales the proud face and bends the feeble knees
As if a God came down.   For thou art mine,
And I will have it so.

    Amy (returning).   A crown ! a crown !

    Balder. My beautiful !

    Amy.   Am I ?   Then give me now
The long long promised lesson ; teach me what
Is beauty.   I am very well to-day,
My brain is like that sea of glass and fire
Whereof we read together, whereupon
The angels walked.   Let them walk thro' my soul.
Dost thou remember idle days when we
Lay here, and thou didst roll the broken rocks
That spun into the valley round as stars ?
So take the worlds and bowl them round about me,
For well I think thou canst ; and I'll not flinch ;
Nay try me !

    Balder.   And thou liest among the bells
And blossoms, and lookest up to any star,

And thinkest in some Angel's face to read
The mystery of beauty ?   Loveliness
Is precious for its essence ; time and space
Make it nor near nor far nor old nor new,
Celestial nor terrestrial.   Seven snowdrops
Sister the pleiads, the primrose is kin
To Hesper, Hesper to the world to come !
For sovereign Beauty as divine is free ;
Herself perfection, in herself complete,
Or in the flowers of earth or stars of heaven.
Merely contained in the seven-coloured bow
Arching the globe, and still contained in each
Of all its raindrops.   This, my thought, I give
To thee, and am no poorer ; no, nor thou
Still giving, nor a singular of all
Who ever shall possess it, tho' my thought
Become the equal birthright of unborn
Nations of men, in every heart a whole.
There cannot be a dimple on the cheek
But all an everlasting soul hath smiled ;
Day is but day to all the eyes on earth,
No less than day to mine.   Love strong as death
Measures eternity and fills a tear ;
And beauty universal may be touched
As at the lips in any single rose.
See how I turn toward the turf, as he
Who after a long pilgrimage once more
Beholds the face that was his desert dream,

Turning from heaven and earth bends over it,
And parts the happy tresses from her brow,
Counting her ringlets, and discoursing bliss
On every hint of beauty in the dear
Regained possession, oft and oft retraced,
So could I lie down in the summer grass
Content, and in the round of my fond arm
Enclose enough dominion, and all day
Do tender descant, owning one by one
Floweret and flower, and telling o'er and o'er
The changing sum of beauty, still repaid
In the unending task for ever new,
And in a love which first sees but the whole,
But when the whole is partially beloved
Doth feast the multitude upon the bread
Of one, endow the units with no less
Than all, and make each meanest integer
The total of my joy.   Yet I have stood
And clasped the earth as if she were a maid ;
And held her, bearing all her sparkling stars
Upon her like a vase of Castalie
Upon a Greek girl's head, and made my boast
Of her, and as a lover let her fill
My feeding eyes !   Or I have hovered far
Upon the verge of all things, and beheld
The round globe as a fruit upon a tree,
The spangled tree that night by starry night
Stands o'er us, and have seen an angel pass,

Pluck it and cool his lips, and drop the hull
To chaos, and this earth, that I have loved
And worshipped, fall out of the universe
As unrespected as a dead leaf falls
From summer aspen, while the innumerous stars
Twinkled and quivered in the wind of God
Walking between the shade of fruited heavens
Untold as once between the river-trees
Of Eden.   But wherever I beheld
Or one or every one, the whole or part,
Some better thing that is not either or all
For ever putteth forth from all and each
A hand, and toucheth me, as he of old
Was touched in sleep; and I as one in sleep
Know not or how or where, but, having felt,
Believe, and serve the Invisible Unknown,
Calling it Beauty.   Therefore in sweet awe
Tread the bright mystery of the sod beneath
Thy feet, thou priest of Beauty! who dost stand
Bareheaded neath the stars, nor dare to slight
Her presence in the floweret of the field!
Beware, for beauty, as a maid, delights
In summer ambush.   Often the mere hem
And flutter of her garment doth betray
Her covert; or low murmurings of the leaves
O'er-fond about her naked loveliness,
Or jealous whisperings of envious winds,
Or voice of birds when her unwonted smile

Makes sudden sunshine in the dusky dell,
Or stir of showers that fall like kisses on her,
Or song of streams made happy by her limbs,
Is all her bruit.   And oft she buried is
—Rapt from her upper realm by gnomes and ghouls,
A moment powerful in the pause of Fate.
And her immortal body thrust in haste
Below the earth some lingering tress reveals
That floateth like a floweret in the wind.
There shalt thou stand, and say thy counter-spell,
Bard of the future ! Master-Prophet ! Man
Of men, at whose strong girdle hang the keys
Of all things !   Lo, the gaping earth and all
The breathing presence of the Goddess risen,
At thy shrunk side full statured from the grave.

> *Amy.* Art thou not he ?
> *Balder.*   The day shall answer.
> *Amy.*   I

Will answer for the day.   And being He
Thou must be born to feel as no man felt
Before thee.   Husband, to be born to feel
As no man felt before thee !   I do yearn
To know !   Not yonder panting lamb that kneels
To drink is more athirst—

> *Balder.*   My beaming Amy !

I stroke the tresses from thine eager brow,
And looking on thee deem the prodigy
Already wrought.

Amy.   Thou wilt not mock me, husband;
Thou must have somewhat in thee hid and deep,
Which, when the future Truth shall be revealed,
Will rise to meet it. Try thy soul for me
With many thoughts as fishers try a lake
With flies; it may be thou shalt find a shape
Whereunto something in thy soul shall rise
That never yet hath risen. Hast thou no guess
Like the dim pictures of a blind man's brain,
Or as altho' thou touch me in the dark
I know the hand is thine.

Balder.   The man born blind,
Having felt fire and handled a round ball,
Hath better image of the luminous sun,
Nay is more able to conceive the truth
Of some ethereal colour indescript
By gross experiment and thick contact
Of palpable occasion, than my soul
To know the Absolute. Nevertheless,
I have my blind man's dream, and tell it thee
As Blind to Blind. In Deity, my child,
There is which no man hath seen, nor can see,
Nor in the eternity to come will see.
To know it undestroyed were to be God
Indeed. That Work of God's which is concrete
Of this tremendous attribute we name
Sublime; and in the corporal Idol own
What angels and archangels in their hour

Of ecstasy when they look up to God
Undazzled, and outpierce the watching eyes
Ineffable before the throne that from
Eternity and to Eternity
Ever awake and waking ever new
From a past lesser sense as from a sleep
In the unchanging Glory more and more
And more for ever and for ever know—
Day without dark—a still increasing light,
Cannot behold. We feel annihilation
As 'twere afar off, and mortality
Is moved with muffled pangs. For so God wills
His worship, and the strange perfunctory flesh
Hath charge concerning us and bids the soul
To rites unknown, as a dumb servitor
His Lord to prayer.
               Also there is in God
Which being seen would end us with a shock
Of pleasure. It may be that we should die
As men have died of joy, all mortal powers
Summed up and finished in a single taste
Of superhuman bliss : or it may be
That our great latent love, leaping at once
A thousand years in stature—like a stone
Dropped to the central fires, and at a touch
Loosed into vapour—should break up the terms
Of separate Being, and as a swift rack
Dissolving into heaven, we should go back

To God.   What incarnation doth obscure
This attribute to safety and the health
Of mortal apprehension, I accept
As beautiful.   Thus in all forms I see
A mediator between God and man
After the order of Melchisedek,
A priest and king.   Ruling them as a king
Who have no God ; but in the sacred sight
Of a diviner faith as sovereign priest
Being God with us.   And thus the shows of earth
Must needs survive this world.   And thus produced
From their adverse far points in time and space
All extant opposites of love and fear
Meet somewhere in the heavens.   How of this truth
The inward voice not knowing what it saith,
Like a daft maid that hath a tale by rote,
Age after age to immemorial man
Unwearied nor to weary taketh up
The world-old parable !   In every tongue
Speaking of the Sublime and Beautiful
As of eternal twins, one dark, one fair,
She leaning on her grand heroic brother
As in a picture of some old Romaunt.

  Amy. Now I will crown thee.

  Balder.   Wherefore ? for we rule
By right which any diadem on earth
Nor gives nor takes.   Here on this summer bank
With neither gold nor tinsel, cap nor crown,

Hocus nor title, puck nor premier, gown
Nor robe of state, nor conjuring rod nor sceptre,
Nor high nor low grimace of sovereignty,
To lie here thus and find the earth and air
Conscious; or mid their fealty and unclaimed
Allegiance, free as the wild phantasy
I follow, and as far from common men,
Sole wandering like an unasserted god
Displendoured undeclared but not unknown
Thro' the sequestered places of my reign,
Lone glens and glades, dells and enchanted streams,
Silent hill sides, and holy mountain tops
Untenanted, without the care of kings,
Counsel or forethought or the toil of change,
But pausing in mere power where'er I love,
As the heart beats to people them at will
From heaven !—my Amy, my throned queen, is this
Royal?

    Amy. My dread lord, my dear husband, oh
My teacher, friend, and father, all in one,
My poet !

    Balder. Shall I do a miracle
To please thee? This green realm of thine, this fair
Sweet hill is lonely. Yon much-whispering stream
Interprets no fond lovers; the old thorn
Flowers for no village maid; the aged oak
Shades not the hoary council of the dale;
Yet ne'er was silent wilderness more apt

For vocal habitation. Say wilt thou
Be monarch of a Pastoral? Shall I
Endow thy reign with subjects?

 Amy.   Whence and how?

 Balder. This empty space above the turf is full
Of living shapes, that shapes as yet are not,
But possible to my strong-gazing eye
Charming the air. Shall they come down to thee?
There are necessities they must obey,
Laws which these undimensioned wanderers
Cry out to think of; thou hast heard them cry
When we have sat together on the hill
Upon a night of wind, for well they know
That whoso of their viewless race shall pass
Hapless across the field of poet's gaze
Is bound.

 Amy.   Thou seest him?

 Balder.   I but feel the place
Informed with presence, which my fixèd eye
Constrains, till having broken the first law
The essential motion self-perpetuate
Of spirits, and unhesitating change,
Time holds and all the straits of lower life
Compel.

 Amy.   Alas! Alas!

 Balder.   I see them yield
Ponderable, visible, subdued
To mortal separation and the lot

Of self and substance ; flushed with earth, and sad
With human beauty.

    Amy.   Pity !

    Balder.   My own Amy !

    Amy.   Heed it not, Love. A shower out of yon
      Heaven
Depeopled. Tell me.

    Balder.   These existences,
Won from the elements, and of a life
Unknown, nor bounded by the days of ours,
Cannot regain estate and order in
The evermoving orbit and weird dance
Of spirits whence they fell ; which, while mine eye
Detains them, desperate, is beyond the verge
Ethereal and inexorable revolves
Careering thro' the spheres. They, lost, return
No more to airy being, but, having touched
This globe, are thenceforth a terrestrial part ;
Assume our fate, and clothed· upon as we
Take human functions, but, by gross decess
Of organs and the lower use of speech
Cannot convey out of their charged souls
The secrets of the past ; and looking wrongs
Untold, and incommunicable woes,
And strange imprisoned joys for ever dumb,
Go forth disguised in manhood to enrich
A thankless world.

          Thou art wistful, my fair face.

To thee I dream.

 Amy.   Dream on !

 Balder. .   Nay, not for thee

The populous fever of a poet's brain.

 Amy. To-day ! To-day ! To-day thou saidst to me

I should be with thee in thy Paradise.

 Balder. Ay, but the three days in the heart of the

   earth ?

Dear happy child of sunshine, bless thy lot !

The grave for me ! For thee, who watchest in love,

The garden of the sepulchre !

 Amy.   I ask not

To see thine awful visions, but the Prophet,

Having come down the hill, interpreteth

To feeble ears. And all the shaking signs

And thunders of the mountain may be read

In whispers. Therefore put me like a sense

Behind thine eyes, and let me know the unknown

Thicken to apprehension.

 Balder.   Come and see.

At sultry noon, when earth and heaven are still,

And everywhere the full and helpless air

O'er-fed with summer weighs upon the lids,

Hast thou, long looking thro' the trance o' the time

To the far misty distance, pale with heat,

Beheld what more beheld became a cloud,

Mountainous. But, at first, being less than seen,

Did stir thee with no more than an unwilled

Attention, subtle consciousness of great
Approach, as yet beyond the shadowy verge
Of knowledge; which, being grown, became a sense
Of form behind the veil, and quickened still
Through the swift dawn of vision to the day
Of perfect sight.

              Ask me no more.   Alas !
Thine eyes are dim, my child, as if their rays
Shone inward; look forth on me ! This is thine,
This sun-light world ! Sport thee, Proserpina,
In upper air, with native things that are !
Enough for thee, O fairest, that the flowers
Are fair; enough for them that, being born,
Thou takest them to a breast more fair than they.
Not thine to seek them in the earth, not thine
The gendering caves and secrets where the spring
Is gestate, and the summer yet to be
Seethes dark. That underflow and subterrene
Wherein the future heaves, and time to come,
Like an embowelled earthquake yet unbelched,
Disturbs our world, is mine.

    Amy.   I cannot play;
My heart is heavy with thy strange sad thoughts;
The daisies look too happy; tell me, love,
Some sorrowy history.

    Balder.   I had a dream
Last night; and it was sad enough to tell
In a wan autumn night of falling stars.

Thou wert most beautiful, but some dread fate
Had touched thee, and dried up the hidden springs
Of mortal being; like a famished plant
Which fills its outer blossom from the core
Of vital substance, the material life
Within thee fed a phantom, and did pass
Transmuted into beauty.   I beheld.
I clasped thee as the circling shore doth clasp
The ebbing sea, or one that loves a ghost
Straineth the vain air in his void embrace;
As who should take the snow into his breast,
I took thee pale and cold, and bared my sword,
And glaring upon heaven and hell defied
The hosts to touch thee; and above, below,
There was such silence that the bitter laugh
Within my empty heart rose out of me
To the four corners of the world, and came
Back like the mockery of exulting fiends!
Thou wert exhaling, as a flower that spends
Its soul in fragrance, and I seized the flower,
And in the hollow of these passionate hands
Strove in my mortal agony to shut
The breath of life; oh how I cherished thee!
I took thy trembling lamp, and in my robe
Of love enwinding wrapt it from the wind,
And made a tabernacle next my heart,
And drew my soul out of the universe
To watch it there, and see with deadlier truth

The soft unflickering flame burn low and low.
If Death had come to snatch thee from my arms,
We had fought sore, and my wild grasp had proved
Too strong even for him ; but thy life died ;
And while I held thee, faded from my sight
Like autumn in November.   And I hugged
—A desperate infidel—the limbs wherefrom
The sap did sink, and even while I gazed
The beauty fell.   Calling on summer time,
And giving names of gladness to the sparse
Sick leaves that waited thin and flushed with death
The last dread gust, but inly cursing God,
And groaning in my soul for whomso lay
In straits like mine.   Then, in the wont of dreams,
We were apart.   As when some pair in lands
Of buried thunder, walk forth side by side,—
The unknown line of fate between—and earth
Yawns, and each, moonstruck, on a separate shore
Receding diverse, swift thro' sounding glooms,
Knows but a lengthening distance and a black
Abyss.   Anon, I must return ; what sprite
Of eager evil rode upon the wind
I wist not, and I knew not in my dream
What dreadful need compelled me, nor what hands
Innumerable, wheresoe'er I turned,
Thrust me to thee ; nor how thro' ill on ill,
Battling and bruised, with the blind might of love
I sought thee, nor why drawing near I saw

One as expectant on the threshold stand,
And one that kept the stair, and ready doors
Oped as I came, and no man asked me whence,
Till at the highest of the creaking house
Lo the strewn rushes, and a hush of awe !
And some who in the way would check my speed
With words unheard ; and, through the whispered press,
Fevered and loud the dread and hissing breath
Of mortal throes.   Then cried I once as he
Who takes his death, and sprang in, and fell down
Wild on my knees beside thee, thee upon
A low poor pallet by the hasty hand
Of pity rudely curtained, and above
The bed, thro' a mean lattice wide for air,
The still and starry heaven that I saw not
Shone.   I rent back what hid thee, and beheld
The tortured witness of thy dying face,
Thy face,
Which thou didst lift a little way to me,
Silent, as conscious all the fearful tale
Was writ there, and didst creep upon the arms
That clasped thee, and being pillowed once again
On the sole breast where thou couldst sleep in peace,
The struggling life gave way before the wont
Of rest.   The painful limbs contract with pangs
Relented, and with sudden weight and strange
The fleshless form wan as a withered child
Sank low.   I felt ; and a great wind of fear

Struck down my heart, and deadly consciousness
Of present evil met an outer sea
Of flooding ill unknown, that surged me in
From all the black horizon of the night,
Drowning the world.   I clenched thee where my heart
Had broken, but thou stretched out madest no sign.
No, tho' I bent above thy face, and all
The throbbing functions of my desperate life
Forsworn that thou didst live, stood still to see.
Thy tongue is silent, and thy moveless breast—
Thou hast gone down out of thine eyes, 'tis dust
The tugging earth doth claim ; the strife is o'er,
And the stern universe too strong for me.
Then I looked up, and a great inward cry,
With the whole utterless strength of my mad soul,
Arose.   Whereat my inner frame convulsed
Quaked and rocked Reason from her seat.   No man
Heard it, no, not the listening mourners round .
The chamber door, no, not thyself, tho' late
Perception lingered in the ear of Death ;
But it filled Heaven, Amy, and the very stars
Shook.

       Wherefore art thou putting back the wind
As if it were an enemy ? Alas
Her flushed cheeks ! and her hands upon her brow !
My little Amy, I am near, fear not !
We are awake ! I touch thee with my hand !
Thou hast not stirred—this is the very place

Where we two sat, and knew that we were happy—
It must be well with thee—

    Amy.   My pain ! my pain !
Oh Husband, tell me it is evening ; say
The sun is set ; say it is dark to thee ;
No, no, it comes ! it comes ! Husband ! it comes !
Like a great Vampyre blackening all the air
Milking the day of light and sucking blood
Out of the cheeks o' the World.   My pain ! my pain !
                                      [*Pauses.*

Why dost look wretched, Husband ? we are fools.
No, there was nothing fair ! 'twas all a dream !
A flight of happy angels stopped to rest
And stood upon the earth and hid it out !
And now they rise again ; hark how they rise !
And all that seemed the surface of the world
Goes up, and the foul earth is like a skull
Scalped of its golden hair.   Do not go up !
Do not go up ! I catch your skirts ! my child,
My little child, my little child,—me also—
Me also—oh me also !

    Balder.   The sun shines,
This flower is the same colour ; the bird sings ;
The clouds, the plain, the mountains, are not changed.

SCENE XXV.

THE STUDY.

BALDER, *solus.*

Balder. Who is He
To whom this toilsome and producing earth
Is as a cunning workman? what are they
Whose lot is to enjoy as ours to lose?
To what fair soil do they transplant our bliss
And batten on the harvests that did sprout
In blood of ours?

                Where be those planted fields
Wherein the everlasting flowers are full
That budded here;—whose tender germs, forsooth,
In all the universe could find no place
Warm as this bosom, and that would not root
Save in a human heart?

                Where art thou, joy
Of yesterday? In whatsoever world
Whatever eyes inherit thee, what lips
Would taste, what hands majestical possess,
What breast contain, I interdict them all!
Thou art mine! Do thou but bless them with thy least
Enjoyment and I curse thee with my curse,
A Father's! What! am I but dung, you Heavens,
To grow your lush delights?

                                    Fool, fool, fool, fool !
What is the flower but that on which it fed ?
The same continued atoms now reset
In fashion to be glorious ! Are we not
As he who lay a hundred years ago
In yon cross road, an elm-stake thro' his midst
That burgeoned, and he went up thro' its veins
Out of his prison into the bright air
And laughed green leaves, and so his felon shame,
His rotting shame, dark in the wormy earth,
Sprang to a tree, that with ten thousand hands
Greets the familiar winds, and first and last
Salutes the sun ?
                        Ay, if I could go up !
If all these whirling passions lifted me
As whirlwinds lift the sea or the Simoom,
Dust such as I !
                        Oh Earth, that every year
Conceivest and hast no power to bring forth,
And year by year beginnest a psalm unsung,
So as with thee is it with all of thine ?   '
As one who in a crowd of recreant men
Begins a chant of freedom, and with brow
Lift to the glowing sun, sings the first stave
Triumphant, but no ring of bold refrain
Surrounds him pausing for the wonted shout,
And he looks down to pallid lips and eyes
And all the silent treason, and, undone,

Sinks on the sward, and hides his shamèd face ;
So ever looking to a golden time
At each new year, impatient, thou criest out
' There shall be ! '—and art silent, casting dust
Upon thine head.
                  Oh, season ever new,
Oh Spring that risest with us, sun by sun !
Whither thine hurrying stream, where thy full tide,
Thy neap excess, and overflow ? What vale
Far off in heaven, dost thou yearly flood
With rainbow waters worthy of thy well,
Ah fountain Arethuse ? For never here
Thy consummation ; but what time we hail
Thine outleap, and the pulsing channels sing,
Somewhat beyond the verdurous verge drinks down
The sudden waters, leaving yellow sands
That autumn gathers, till the rock beneath·
Shines in the frost of winter.
                  Where on earth
Is the unknown meridian of that day
Which to the Morn I met upon the east,
Should be as man to babe ? Doth the young moon
Complete her promised light or multiply
Her beauty by her days ?
                  Where is that rose
Which he who gave its bud as hieroglyph
Of budding love would own the equal sign
Of love's full-flowered perfection ?

                                        Of what blood
And changeling race are we who fill this earth,
Whereunto, hour by hour of every day
And night of all its fruitful centuries,
Children are born?

                        Oh little child, girl-child,
Last daughter of the old manorial house
In the green village, thou who when the sun
Is rising, and above, below, around,
The dew-drops shine, as every bough and spray,
Blade, leaf, small petal and least acrospire,
Yea, the unbodied joyance of the air
Had eyes, and smiled to see him, comest forth
Into the morning as an element
Of such etherial season duly sweet
And sweetly due, while singing birds and bees
Sound like the bubbling of that stream of day
Whereby thou, tripping, givest song for song !
Fair happy child, who goest at thy will
Into the sunny midst as a white bird
Into the crystal water that reflects
Spotless a spotless image, pure in pure,
And each unlessened still enhancing each,—
The image whitens the white wave, the wave
Adds the pure image to the floating snow ;—
Thou who art native to the good of all ;
For whom the unsullied fairness of the earth
Guards not herself, nor deprecating hands

Mystic arise out of the Beautiful
To put thee from the beauty ; who dost tread
The daisies like a morning-wind and spill
Dews from lithe buttercups that fill again
With drops of pleasure ; Oh thou unknown essence !
So near the eyes, so distant from the heart,
When dost thou take our nature, and become
No more than we ? Something within her looks
A strange light through her lashes, and a joy
Beyond our throb. It cannot be that this
Abideth with her, for such bliss fulfilled
Thro' all the coming seasons that must yet
Accomplish woman, and increasing still
Within the ampler temple, were a sight
To breed rebellion in the universe,
Burn every world with jealousy of her's,
Summer this earth, and make the schooldame Nature
Break thro' the ill-assumed severity
Of her enforcèd aspect, with a cry
Be all the mother, catch thee to her heart,
Begin the golden ages, and in thee
Restore mankind. Therefore, thou most fair child,
Here thou hast no completion. In what hour
Of what set night wilt thou give up this ghost,
Exhaled as the last fragrance from a flower
Unchanged in hue ? Upon what destined morn
Shall she come down a stranger to the board
Where the same face and form shall take a place

Not hers, and answer to familiar names
That have no owner upon earth?   Of them
Who loved her is there one who shall be grave
With an unconscious sorrow, knowing nought,
But saying in himself, since such a day
My heart is poorer? Is there one of all,
Who thinking of a blissful time gone by
That floats in on his day-dream, like sweet air
From heaven, sun-bright and full of golden sounds
Going and coming, at one happy voice
Among the choir, starting, shall cry 'Ah whose?'
And muse, and pass his hand across his brow
Perplexed?   Will they be sodden with a spell,
Nor lift astonished eyes and hands to see
Her shining crescent fill no fuller moon
Than others?   Nor so much as droop a lid
Sighing, as when the pulsing heart of youth
In mere abundance of young life's excess
Beats an unknown approach that never comes,
And we look up expecting, and look down
With melancholy wisdom mildly sad,
Smiling moralities?

                They will behold,
And she shall grow and marry, breed and die,
Even as her mother, and of many none
Shall question her.   Nevertheless at last
Truth shall be justified.   Of them who deck
Her bier, or chant her thro' the pompous aisle,

Or load the blazoned marble with her broad
And gravid virtues, or in sable grief
Swell the dark progress winding long and slow,
Stately to honourable tombs, no hand
Will write upon her coffin, ' This is she
Who played among the roses.'

        Bitter heart,
That art so sternly just, is she as far
From the dear promise of her youth as thou
From yesterday?

      Thou little phantom child,
That merely passing thro' my trancèd soul,
Hast left thy bright path, like the quivering track
Of any fleeting star, what is that scheme
Of life where this divine emotion finds
Its equal place, and in the balanced whole
Of still renewed proportion gives and takes
Worthy consent? Where doth the Man complete
The Poet? My chief impulse, and king-thought,
Capital virtue, and consummate act,
To what consorted system, yet unknown,
Do these belong? Of what colossal frame
Do I, like some rude hewer of the rock,
Dishume the giant limb from my rent heart,
And cannot guess its fellows?

        Mystery
Of mysteries, like some great vapouring cloud
Topping a cumulous Heaven of mysteries !

         [*A long pause.*

Have we been all at fault?   Are we the sons
Of pilgrim sires who left their lovelier land,
And do we call inhospitable climes
By names they brought from home?

       Who shall declare?
Which of us hath beheld what first was called
'Order'?   Since bad hath worse, who testifies
That our serenest spectacle is not
The prime Confusion?   Where the human sight
That ever looked on what they name in Heaven
Beauty and Good?

      That which we fondly deem
A happy universe of part with part
Well-placed, and call it the full countenance
And noblest front of things, I could believe
To be upon the very skirts of God,
Ay where they roll in tumult, and do flap
In the wind of his going.

     This is Chaos,
The Chaos whereof Poets sang, and sing
Unconscious, never having seen or heard
The harmony of Nature.   This broad light
Is darkness.   I who speak of me and mine,
Am but a living hand rent from its trunk
In the black vortex, and amid the waste
Of loaded disproportion and the foul
Incongruous ferment of these elements
Which might be worlds and men, touching at once

The grains of all unlikeness, to and fro
And up and down among the seething mass
For ever lifted, grasping dust or flame,
Each while I hold it Me, and each alike
Put out for any other. Nought between
A god's heart and the abominable extremes
Of the worst brood of sin's most loathsome world
Impossible ; nought certain but the pain
Of finding all unsure.

SCENE XXVI.

THE STUDY.

BALDER, *solus.* *Through the door the voice of* AMY.

Amy. Surely the Lord is cruel but to me,
And over bounteous to the race of men
With mercy taken from my single lot.

I am the dwarf of this great family,
The favoured lips do drink the wine of life,
And all the mingled lees fill up my fate.

I am a place where music music meets,
Putting it out ; by how much joy is loud,
I am the darker silence : all the lines
Of sorrow cross above my wretched head.

They are grown sour with sweetness, they are proud
With pleasure, they care not to keep awake
Even to be happy.   Like a slave they bid
Their bliss abide their time, and, like a slave,
It fans their happy faces while they sleep.

Ah Heaven ! they sleep upon the flowery banks,
And daylight flowers fill them with honey dreams,
And pleasured smiles do light their languid lips.

Ah Heaven ! they stand amid the fruited trees,
The golden-fruited trees, and every wind
Daubs the ripe fruit upon their sated lips.

Ah Heaven! they lie beside the living stream,
And the superfluous stream o'er-wells his banks,
And laps sweet waters to their happy lips.

Where they do most enjoy my need is worst ;
The living cup they spill would save my life ;
The joy that wearies them would give me rest.

I lie down in the night but cannot sleep;
I keep vain vigil for my plighted bliss;
l strain after the fruit I may not touch,
And cannot reach the river tho' I die !

SCENE XXVII.

THE STUDY.

BALDER, *solus.*

Balder.   And is this your device, you Heavens,
When ye would have the music of our groans?
The feeble lamentations of such pale
Hereditary anguish as is born
To pangs, and with the dread entail receives
Inheritance of patience, the dull howl
With which accustomed guilt receives his stripe
In skin that thickens to the lash, each ill
That carries with the wrong the slow redress
Cries not for you; the lax and languid strings,
Which Nature, careful of herself, doth loose
To save her heart, cannot ring out such sounds
As startle pleasure in your sated ears.
They should be giants who make sport for gods!
As we enjoy we suffer; legends tell
That Eden is the utter wilderness,
And the archangel's stature did become
The measure of the fiend.   Therefore, ye eld
And sager gods, whose reeking Vulture once
Did gorge your youthful vengeance on the rock
In Crete, ye have grown wise, and no more

Subtract the needful vitals that may throb
A lustier pang, nor bleed the bull ye bait.
Prometheus, keep thine heart !   There is no trick
Of Hell's contrivance that can plague thee so,
Nor with as subtle mastery dispense
Such dire infliction !   Even the rude skill
Of mortal cruelty hath learned to breed
The gladiator to die hard ; and they
Who roast the human feast upon the shore
Do supple him with kindness.   What nice nerve
Thrills the best pleasure twangs the sorest pain ;
The sense that faints with bliss will faint with woe :
And he who dieth of a rose is damned
Upon the thorn.   Therefore, ye jubilant gods,
Pamper the victim, fill his veins with joy,
Build him of soft endurance, tender and strong
As a flayed lion ; finish each stern power
To such an exquisite final that it ends
A plumèd feeling ; let delicatesse
Weave his thin cuticle, and mesh him in ;
Be his most sensitive structure the extreme
That meets and makes a whole with matchless strength—
Even as the dread Apocalyptic beasts
Were full of eyes.   Thews of asbestos, ribs
Of adamant, wound in so fine a thread
Of life produced and ambient that he stands
The heroic total of great opposites ;
Firm as a tower in any wind that blows,

And trembling to a fragrance in the wind !
Then on some human pyre whose dainty frame,
As 'twere of frankincense and gums of Ind,
His vital heat might warm into decay,
Stretch him out, like the prophet on the dead,
Limb upon fateful limb, and bind him down
With the strong bonds of love, and rivet fast
What everlasting anguish could not break !
And fire the pile! and let your ready flames
Wrap the incumbent health and scorch the strength
They not consume! unguarded, unsuspect,
Naked, and toiled, not as a hero falls,
Nor in the wont of battle to receive
His fate, and, by contending, half subdue ;
But bound and prone, expatiate with nice art
To the invenient horror, oped and spread
To the elective lust of keener flame,
Lifting with incommunicable throes
The inevitable torment, leaping high
In vain and higher, every desperate strain
Stirring new fires that burn a loftier bound
That fans worse anguish and more wild despair
For ever self-renewed, let him plunge, gods,
And cheer Olympus!

SCENE XXVIII.

The Study.

BALDER.   *Enter* DR. PAUL.

Balder.   Come ?   Thanks !

Doctor.   How ? is she worse ?

Balder.   I know not that.
I sent for thee to hear yet once again
The story of her sorrows.

Doctor.   The old errand !

Balder.   Not so.   Thou hast been here in vain to seek
A hope, but I send for thee now to find.
Cure her !

Doctor.   Four solemn times within this month
Have I told thee——

Balder.   Paul, Paul, if I can bear
My portion in this venture dost thou blench
At thine ?   Is it so very much that thou
Who canst sit careless of the stars, whose hand
Shakes not already with adverse aspècts,
Shouldst draw the horoscope once more for me
And cast the fates anew ?   'Tis the last time.
I swear that what conjuncts for bliss or bale
This sovereign hour determines I accept
As doom.   Therefore be patient.   Strain thy skill !

Draw it so well that were the burning sun
Nought but an eyeball, and his sight to thine
As he to thee, he could not magnify
Thy deviation ! Thine art is not mine,
I am no Esculapian, but I know
Less alteration than our sense can mete
Would make the inexorable asymptote
Close like fond lips. Get thee new instruments ;
No pinhole points and measure of mortal hairs,
But compass that shall set his foot between
. Two feathers of a butterfly ; a scale
Scored with——

    Doctor.   Well, well, I'll see her, and do my best.
But hope for nought ; if even thine anxious gaze—
And love is more than science,—can discern
No better sign.

    Balder.   Full many a time and oft
I have sat still thro' all a summer day,
And listened to its change as to a book
Read by untiring lips. Thou wouldst have sworn
The day was like a field of buttercups,
Where every shining moment stood and smiled
Beside his golden likeness ; but not I !
I know the hours, and call them by their names,
As a shepherd his sheep. So in thy world
The microcosm——

    Doctor.   Ah that word microcosm !
A true word, my dear poet, a true word,

For in six days God makes us, and, alas,
If the seventh day wherein He rests be not
The sabbath of the grave——

Balder.   .   In that world, Paul,
Which is thy study, as this other mine,
I would look with thine eyes.

Doctor.   As you will, friend.
Shall I go in?

Balder.   Ay, no, I had forgotten;
She sleeps; I'll waken her.

Doctor.   Not hastily.

Balder.   With saddest music.

          [Goes to his harp by the open window.

                Do ye well to smile
Superior, ye wise Heavens, because ye see
I am a coward and fool 'Time to keep
Fate at the door?   All this and more I know
No less than you.   I am as wise as you
If this be wisdom!   I pray you cloud over.

          *[*BALDER *sings.*

In the hall the coffin waits, and the idle armourer
    stands,
At his belt the coffin nails, and the hammer in his
    hands.
The bed of state is hung with crape—the grand old bed
    where she was wed—
And like an upright corpse she sitteth gazing dumbly at
    the bed.

Hour by hour her serving men enter by the curtained door,

And with steps of muffled woe pass breathless o'er the silent floor,

And marshal mutely round, and look from each to each with eye-lids red,

'Touch him not,' she shrieked and cried, 'he is but newly dead!'

'Oh, my own dear mistress,' her ancient Nurse did say,

'Seven long days and seven long nights you have watched him where he lay.'

'Seven long days and seven long nights,' the hoary Steward said,

'Seven long days and seven long nights,' groaned the Warrener grey,

'Seven,' said the old Henchman, and bowed his aged head;

'On your lives!' she shrieked and cried, 'he is but newly dead!'

  Then a father Priest they sought,
  The priest that taught her all she knew,
  And they told him of her loss.
 'For she is mild and sweet of will,
  She loved him, and his words are peace,
  And he shall heal her ill.'
  But her watch she did not cease.
  He blest her where she sat distraught,
  And showed her holy cross,—
  The cross she kissed from year to year—

But she neither saw nor heard ;
And said he in her deaf ear
All he had been wont to teach,
All she had been fond to hear,
Missalled prayer, and solemn speech,
But she answered not a word.

Only when he turned to speak with those who wept about
  the bed,

'On your lives !' she shrieked and cried, 'he is but
  newly dead !'

Then how sadly he turned from her it were wonderful to
  tell,

And he stood beside the death-bed as by one who
  slumbers well,

And he leaned o'er him who lay there, and in cautious
  whisper low,

'He is not dead, but sleepeth,' said the Priest, and
  smoothed his brow.

'Sleepeth ?' said she, looking up, and the sun rose in
  her face !

'He must be better than I thought, for the sleep is very
  sound.'

'He is better,' said the Priest, and called her maidens
  round.

With them came that ancient dame who nursed her when
  a child ;

'Oh Nurse,' she sighed, 'oh Nurse,' she cried, 'oh
  Nurse !' and then she smiled,

And then she wept; with that they drew
About her, as of old ;
Her dying eyes were sweet and blue,
Her trembling touch was cold ;
But she said, 'my maidens true
No more weeping and well-away ;
Let them kill the feast.
I would be happy in my soul.
"He is better," saith the Priest ;
He did but sleep the weary day,
And will waken whole.
Carry me to his dear side,
And let the halls be trim ;
Whistly, whistly,' said she,
'I am wan with watching and wail,
He must not wake to see me pale,
Let me sleep with him.
See you keep the tryst for me,
I would rest till he awake
And rise up like a bride.
But whistly, whistly!' said she.
'Yet rejoice your Lord doth live ;
And for his dear sake
Say Laus Domine.'
Silent they cast down their eyes,
And every breast a sob did rive,
She lifted her in wild surprise
And they dared not disobey.

'Laus Deo,' said the Steward, hoary when her days were
   new,

'Laus Deo,' said the Warrener, whiter than the warren
   snows ;

'Laus Deo,' the bald Henchman, who had nursed her on
   his knee.

     The old Nurse moved her lips in vain
     And she stood among the train
     Like a dead tree shaking dew.
     Then the Priest he softly stept
     Midway in the little band
     And he took the Lady's hand
     'Laus Deo !' he said, aloud,
     'Laus Deo,' they said again,
     Yet again, and yet again,
     Humbly crossed and lowly bowed,
     Till in wont and fear it rose
     To the Sabbath strain.
     But she neither turned her head
     Nor 'whistly, whistly,' said she.
     Her hands were folded as in grace,
     We laid her with her ancient race
     And all the village wept.

Balder.   I think she stirs.   Go in !

     [*The* DOCTOR *enters, remains, and reappears.*

Balder.   Is there no change ?

Doctor.   None that brings hope.

Balder.   That day seems scarcely past—

That day of——

    Doctor.   My poor friend, when a ship strikes
Long time on the mad surge she heaves and falls,
And dips in winds and waves her leaning spars :
Till, like a dying horse, with a last plunge
She rises, reels, and over from the reef
Goes mast-down in the deep.   To see her rise
Rises the landsman's cheer along the shore,
And sinks with her.

    Balder.   Enough.

                      Paul, long ago
I said a time would come to raise the veil
On yonder scroll.   Lift it to-day.   I owe
No less excuse for my relentless gripe,
And thy still barren labour.   Read out, Paul,
For I would hear what I have lost ; albeit
To me those words are but a rosary,
As unlike what they count as beads and prayers.
Read slowly, and with a minute respect,
As thou wouldst touch the enchanted elements
On a magician's table—poor to look on,
But things that, being moved, perplex the stars,
And knot the threads of Nature.   Do but fail
Or falter, and by Heaven ! I strike thee dead !
Aye, marvel at me, for thou knowest not
What I shall see.   For thee, as men infer
From maps and charts the living earth and heavens,
Learn there what once was she—what is she now

Thou knowest.

    Doctor (aside). He is pale,—pale to his lips,
His eye is set. I'll humour him.

      [DOCTOR *lifts the veil, and reads the scroll beneath.*
(*Reads.*)   'In HER,
Nature's first thought was beauty; she conceived
Her image sitting in her robe of white
Thinking of spring, and, at the fancy moved,
Smiling breathed softly, and did turn to make
The firstling snowdrop of the stainless year.
And, as the year arose, her fairer thought
Took substance, and, consummate in her care,
Grew with the growing year; for at her will
Day after day past by, and passing dropt
Its own memorial flower, the better sign
Of all; and night by night, when shades are deep,
And that mysterious sorrow is transact
Unseen, and there is weeping in the air,
She, understanding all, midst common dews,
Caught the accepted tear that makes the hour
So holy. Nor herself in greater deeds
Forgot the less, thro' each surpassing mood
In which with higher ecstasy she wrought
Abundant summer, whatsoe'er confessed
Her happier hand—elect and dedicate
Encreased the secret store; and over all
Frequent and fond with dainty change and wise—
As meet perfection of each part admits

Phœbus or Dian,—various balm of life
She poured from golden and from silver vase
Of sun and moon.   But when the year was grown,
(And sweet by warmer sweet to nuptial June
The flowery adolescence slowly filled,
Till in a passion of Roses all the time
Flushed, and around the glowing Heavens made suit)
And onward through the rank and buxom days,
Tho' she ceased not to work and help the year
Great with the burden of the honeyed past,
And gave her good deliverance and great pomp
Of harvest, and in royal glory robed
Matron and mother, to her dearer hoard
She added nought, nor what her love had hid
Unclosed before the broad unclouded face
And heated welfare of the lusty world.
But when the destiny that haunts the proud
Did tardy judgment, and the prosperous year,
Struck in her young maternity, beheld
First born and last lie low, and wrapping wild
The early mists about her, on the ground
Amid her prostrate hopes disconsolate
Sat veiled : or standing forth with upstretched hands
And strange appealing eyes, and wildered face
Hectic with fate, looked like her spring-time self
Transfigured on some martyr pile of woe
Seen through the flame ; then Nature knew her hour
And at conjunction of the setting signs

Opened her sacred Casket and took forth
Well-pleased : and of the lone and latter rose,
Pale autumn violets, and all hapless blooms
Did make in mournful fragrance sadly sweet
The mortal breath of beauty.'

   Balder.   Do not smile !
This is no dream, for she came in September,
And if she were o'erlaid with lily-leaves,
And substantived by mere content of dews,
Or limbed of flower-stalks and sweet pedicels,
Or made of golden dust from thigh of bees,
Or caught of morning mist, or the unseen
Material of an odour, her pure text
Could seem no more remote from the corrupt
And seething compound of our common flesh !
Nay, as I oft have told thee—a whole year
Ere she was born, her mother fed on fruits.
Read on, Sir Science, for thou readest truth !
Truth is a Janus, Paul, but either face
Herself, therefore be reverent.

   Doctor reads.   ' I have seen
The poet in his pride, who of his urns
And lachrymals and crystal chalices
Hath one, most treasured of his treasure-house,
To which he goeth only with full heart
And leaves the fulness there ; ambrosial blood
As of that cluster, weeping wine, wherein
The blessing is, its vintage all unpressed

Save by the purple and spontaneous touch
Of too abundant being.   Nature thus,
The Poet Nature, singing to herself—
Did make Her in sheer love, having delight
Of all her work, and doing all for joy.
And built her like a Temple wherein cost
Is absolute, dark beam and hidden raft
Shittim, each secret work and covert use
Fragrant and golden, all the virgin walls
Pure, and within without, prive and apert,
From buried plinth to viewless pinnacle
Enriched to God.

      ' Ah, was the very air
Etherial round her, so that whoso breathed
Revived to his best nature and grew bright
For her sake, as a mote from dim to dim
Sails the sunbeam ?—What deity indwelt
Her still small voice, which was her perfect self
Audible—that most happy voice, which when
It rose to gladness made men rich and glad
Unminished, and receiving but to spend
Sweeter abundance with a lovelier will.
Gayer for gaiety, but of the gay
Still gayest, as bright sun o'er brightened fields
Seems brighter, gaining from the light he gives.
That voice which was to sorrow as its sigh,
And by the side of wonted circumstance
Went as the tinkle of Titania's feet,

Ringing the hour of day on fairy bells
Marriage or funeral.   Nor less blessed when
It fell into the bosom of the poor
Like gold and silver.   That dear voice which when
She sang her life, the charmed listener hearing,
Accepted for consummate loveliness
Till she was mute, and, his divided soul
Returning to the eyes, her silent beauty
By the higher sense perceived, seemed insomuch
Diviner music.
               ' Oft have I admired
When the poor wayfarer on whom she looked
Clothed in his tattered fortune did take rank
A moment in her smile, and could not ask
The alms his famine craved ; the passing thief
Had virtue in her service, and the clown
Grace to be hers.   The maimed who chanced to meet
Her far-off beauty on the way, aside
Drew into shadow till she passed, nor begged
Aught that might turn the light of her fair face
On the too conscious fault ; and Lazarus
Covered his sores with deeper sense of ill.
Rude country-wives to whom in lane or mead
Happened her sweet regards. with honoured face
And thankful did obeisance going by
As owning bounty and a duty known
Unschooled ; the village children at the door—
Little two-year children—having gazed,

Ran to her as she passed and caught her skirt
And looking up laughed strange intelligence,
Abashed and pleased, in the mere act repaid,
And wiser than the three-score-years-and-ten
That chid the holy freedom, being purblind.
For they who saw her were as one who knows
A mystic sign and smiles with consciousness.
There is a soul unto the grosser sense
Of spoken language, an unuttered thought
Virgin and peerless, which no man hath said
Nor hath the hope to hear upon the earth,
Tho' it be dear as the unbodied dream
Of early love, familiar as the wife
Upon his breast, albeit untouched as maids
In Paradise. In every human speech
No speaker but hath with him, undeclared,
This angel; and doth bear about a thing
Too lovely for his lips, beloved unnamed.
As every heart upon its secret, so
The world did look on her ! Where'er she went
Nature, in dale or hill, in cot or grove,
Owned her, and in the shepherd or the lamb
Confest no less. The Lamb which to her knee
Came fearless, unsuspicious of the gray
Grim guardian of the fold who harmed her not
Nor challenged her just right what-time she took
The lambkin willing, to her purer breast.
Thus or in haunts beloved or foreign fields

Her equal way was all among her own,
Unquestioned still, nor anywhere or new
Or strange.   We had a wonted bower, secluse,
Of honeysuckle wild in mossy dell
Facing the noon, and sheltered from the north
By denser shade ; flowery it was and deep,
And caught the flowing light as chaliced leaves
The sunset.   In the inner sanctities
Shy birds did nest, and all the summer through,
Entering, with tumult of distress I shook
The troubled verdure, but she came at will
And sat there ; and the birds went in and out
As tho' she were so merely beautiful
That nought betrayed her limits and she mixed
She, undistinguished—with the love-lit air
The fragrance and the summer joy that lived
In that green bower,

      ' So lovely in her rest
More lovely her awakened beauty played
The smiling pastime of her innocent life
Gracious and holy, wherein fairest thought
And fond performance thro' melodious hours
Rhymed like a gentle ballad.   All she did
Expressed her.   The mild lore and simple arts
She knew and loved might exercise unblamed
Chaste Flora's self or what pure essence warms
The happy difference of a morn of May.
Song and answering lute, and mute delight

Of pencilled touch, and nice dexterity
Of bending Eve in gardened Paradise
Were hers ; she had a faërie forestrie
Of birds, and bees, and summer flies ; she knew
Sweet mysteries of sunrise and sunset,
Of seasons, moons, and clouds.   But chief in joy
Her skill was among flowers, which in her hand
Took·better hues, and fell under her looks
Into an ordered beauty as before
Their queen ; and when they crowned her, unaware
The butterfly did court the rose as still
Upon the blushing tree.   Yet more I loved
An art which of all others seemed the voice
And argument ; rare art, at better close
Of chosen day, worn like a jewel rare
To beautify the beauteous, and make bright
The twilight of some sacred festival
Of love and peace.   Her happy memory
Was many poesies, and when serene
Beneath the favouring shades and the first star,
She audibly remembered, they who heard
Believed the Muse no fable.   As that star
Unsullied from the skies, out of the shrine
Of her dear beauty beautifully came
The beautiful, untinged by any taint
Of mortal dwelling, neither flushed nor pale,
Pure in the naked loveliness of Heaven.
Such and so graced was she. ·

' But not alone,
Ah purest ! not alone in thy first reign
Of placid pastures and beseeming woods
Palatial, where the conscious waterfalls
That leaped in bliss beside thee did no more
Than all that gave thee thro' the loyal year
Duteous attendance, not alone by glen
Or mountain wert thou absolute ! nor he
Who passed thee, tutelar, amid the wilds.
Of thine accustomed sanctuary alone
Thy worshipper !   Hers was no vulgar glare
Startling the dazzled crowd to blink and gaze,
Nor came she glorious as a summer noon,
Melting all looks to pleasure and all limbs
Relaxing as with heat, and thro' the sense
Sending soft breath of love and southern joy.
The happy paths she blessed led not to courts
Or cities.   Loved and loving she would live
No more accompanied than by what train
Is love's, and in the love-feast of her days
Served while she sat or sat whileas she served !
To know where winding from the ancient tree
By the gray style thro' copse and daisied dell,
In every mood of immemorial mind
The simple village went a thousand years ;
Or o'er the brook upon the stepping-stones
To follow unperplexed thro' bosky maze,
The feet of sorrow to her shyest lair ;

Or at the ruined cot, and down the dim
Deserted path, to watch under the dust
The unwonted grass rise slowly up and lift
The memory of the dead from off the earth ;
Or round the wildered garden to convince
The graceless moss of greed ; Or from lone lane
At summer eve to trace some ancient track
A-field and learn what need or joy of life
Saw viewless landmarks in the devious way,
Her daily pleasaunce. But where men are met,
If unpropitious hap or lot unsought
Awhile constrained her, fate that did the wrong,
Jealous, allowed no other ; as a King
Seizing his bride, rapt from her native bowers
Circassian, in the amorous crime completes
His cruelty and makes the captive queen.
Not otherwise, and looking like a flower
Dropt in the city street—some blossom fair
That grew dew-nursed and lone green miles away—
Into the heedless crowd that knew her not
She came uncrowned, and they wist not she came ;
Till simply sitting in the parlous midst
Her presence like a silent virtue spread
About her. For a little while she sat
Unhonoured, but a consciousness disturbed
The spot, and as a holy influence
Did touch the unwilling people into awe,
Whom gentle observance and sweet respect

Disposed, till who partook her magic ring
Still or discursive, sole or sociable,
Each in his several function did denote
Her place.   Nor customary in mere use
Perfunctory, and rite of cap or knee,
The general homage ; but of some inborn
Content and central sanction in the soul,
Inmost and earlier than where creeds begin
Or doubts divide.   Men turned and asked not why,
Nor, seeing, marvelled that they turned ; but apt
Took reverent distance : nor, decorous, ceased
The fealty of regard.   With decent eyes
And with no louder sign nor needless bruit
Of the unuttered reason than what-time
On wintry day they face by mute consent
The seldom sun.   Thus she who came unknown
Into the stranger crowd with modest step
And eyes that rather would be ruled than rule,
Having no need of praise, nor hope of fame,
Nor conscience of dominion, did subdue
Its chaos to her nature, being divine.
And merely present could no less than stir
The dull and grosser essence to revolve
About her, as by instinct and hid force
Of that well-ordered universe whereof
Its matter was a part.   Herself informed
The jarring elements, till, as her sway
No utter sign enforced, nor shows of power,

Nor but a golden sweet necessity
Sovereign, unseen, the subject heart gave like
Confession.   Not as they confess a queen
With sudden shout, but as two friends regard
A rising star, and speak not of it while
It fills their gaze.   The loud debate grew low,
What was unseemly chastened, and the fear
Of Beauty waking her moralities
Sent thro' adjusted limbs the long-forgot
Ambition to be fair.   Nor sex, nor rank,
Nor age, nor changed condition, did absolve
Her rule, which whatsoever was remote
From sin the more saluted.   Everywhere
Babes smiled on her, and women on her face
Did look as women look in happy love.

So the world blessed her ; and another world
Like spheres of cloud that interpenetrate
Till each is either, met and mixed with this.
And as the angel Earth that bears her Heaven
About her so that whereso'er in space
Her footstep stayeth we look up and say
That Heaven is there—SHE moved and made all times
And seasons equal ; trode the mortal life
Immortally, and with her human tears
Bedewed the everlasting, till the Past
And Future lapsed into a golden Now
For ever best.   She was much like the moon

Seen in the day time, that by day receives
Like joy with us, but when our night is dark,
Lit by the changeless sun we cannot see,
Shineth no less.   And she was like the moon,
Because the beams that brightened her passed o'er
Our dark heads, and we knew them not for light
Till they came back from hers; and she was like
The moon, that whatsoe'er appeared her wane
Or crescent was no loss or gain in her
But in the changed beholder.   I, who saw
Her constant countenance, and had its orb
Still full on me with whom she rose and set,
Knew she had no lunation.   In herself
The elements of holiness were merged
In white completion, and all graces did
The part of each.   To man or Deity
Her sinless life had nought whereof to give
Of worse or better, for she was to God
As a smile to a face.   Ah God of Beauty !
Where in this lifeless picture my poor hand
Hath done her wrong, forgive; she was Thy smile,
How could I paint her?   That I dared essay
Her image and am innocent, I plead
Resistless intuition, which believes
Where knowledge fails and, powerless to define
Or to confound, still calls the face and smile
Not one, but twain, and contradicts the sense
Material, which, beholding her, beholds

Essence not Effluence, nor Thine but Thee.'

Doctor. Aye—veil it over !

Balder.   Once again I say
Cure her !

Doctor. And, good friend, hear me once for all.
I have brought to your wife's lamented case
What skill I own,—and twenty years of cure
Have taught me something—but for much esteem
Of her and you, I made her malady
The subject of my college.   I stand here
A simple country surgeon, but where'er
Men worship Science, some one of her Priests
Calls me his friend ; whatever oracles,
As yet unbruited, murmur from the cell,
I learn from these.   Therefore in my poor words
You hear a verdict sworn to by the prime
Of Europe.

Balder.   There is no most rare device
Occult, or cunning of the eye or hand,
Or mastery of subtle elements,
Beyond thee ?

Doctor.   No.

Balder.   Whatever lesson new
These latter days have spelled in the unread
And polyglot palimpsest of this body
Is thine already ? Thou hast it within
By rote ?

Doctor.   Yes.

Balder.   Let us speak of other things.
The sun must be near setting—shall we watch him
From the old rampart of my Ruin?   Follow.

    Doctor.   With all my heart !

                     [*They ascend to the ramparts.*

    Doctor (emerging).   Truly the light is sweet !
That winding stair—two hundred steps and more——
My head swims.

    Balder.   'Tis a fearful height.   My Dog,
Whose stature thou didst praise, seen hence appears
Notably less.   His kennel which thou knowest
Befits a mastiff of the English breed,
Might house a cur.   We have a legend here.
A maniac dwelt in this old tower and hence
Throwing his keeper, hid the battered corse
In yonder tarn.   His ghost preserves my fish.
A dalesman would as soon drop line in hell
As in the murder-pool.

    Doctor.   I shudder.

    Balder.   Sounds
The old tale credible? How say thy craft?
Is the leap death?

    Doctor.   Death to a hundred lives !
His mother would not know the face that reached
Yon stones from these.

    Balder.   Thou art a feeble man,
I am no giant, but am thrice thy match ;
Cure her !

Doctor. Thou hast mine answer.

Balder. And thou mine.
Cure her.

Doctor. I cannot.

Balder. In mine art I know
Passion and terrible occasion make
Men poets, poets gods. Thine may have like
Apotheosis. Cure her!

Doctor. Hands off! see
The precipice we stand on——

Balder. Ah! ah! ah!
Cure her!

Doctor. Thou jestest with me!

Balder. By the Heavens
No!

Doctor. Stand back!

Balder. Cure her!

Doctor. Free me! Mercy! Help!
We have been friends, thou wilt not murder me?

Balder. We have been lovers, but I sent a shaft
Into her heart. If thou canst draw it forth
Well; but if not——

Doctor. Nay, I can fight for life!
Madman! Hold! Murderer! Mercy! Mercy!

Balder. Cure her!

Doctor. Spare me! my wife! my children!

Balder. Cure her!

Doctor. Christ!

God! oh God!
 Balder.   Cure her!
 Doctor.   I will!
 Balder (*releasing him*).   Thou wilt NOT!
Liar! Begone! Haste! Lest in my despair
Thou 'scape not twice.

SCENE XXIX.

THE STUDY.

BALDER, *solus.*

Balder. I will sit down
And let the stars roll on. Such pitiless signs
Cannot for universal health maintain
An hour's ascendant. If the heavens could halt
I might despair, but the worst orb that moves
Betters my fate.

SCENE XXX.

THE STUDY.

BALDER *sits by the open window.*

Balder. Thou dull tree,
What and hast thou gained nothing? Not a twig,
A leaf, a flower, a colour? By my count

Thou shouldst have leafed and summered, seared and
    died
Since I sat down beside thee. Nay, if I
Had lifted up this head that thou dost shade,
To see thee branchless, thy dismantled trunk
Worm-wemmed in hollow age—I could have said
'Why this is well, yes, thou and I, old friend,
Have filled our days.'   [*Turns to papers on the table.*
                How goes the human year?
The first of a new month! I take my times
And seasons as a traveller in the night
Kneels by the stone beside the unknown way,
And gropes with patient finger the moss-grown
And mouldering miles; while at his trembling touch
Out of the ignorant strange dark comes forth
The old remembered name, and or the light
Of home, or the intolerable flash
That sends him scorched and moaning.
                    I remember
A year ago to-day I left my fields
To dwell in cities. How that black sad time
Frowns back to this. The first dark day it rained,
An inky rain blackening the civic shrubs
And birds apostate whom my heart knew not.
Between the door-sills flowed the narrow street,
Betwixt the house-tops crept as foul a mirk,
Soaking and cheerless, as if overhead
Another street, inverted in the air,

Let down an answering ooze; and I beheld
Nor felt it was not well; till suddenly
Upon the morrow eve the sun shone in,
The country sun—and I rose up in haste
And clasped my hands and cried 'not here, not here
For pity!' as she cries whom secret shame
Hath soiled, and puts away with passionate tears
The old familiar kisses.   The third day
I went; but in those three days saw strange sights
And many, which men told me that the eyes
Which dwell there daily saw and did not weep.
I saw the palaces of thronèd Law
Where Law supreme in red and ermine sits,
And, like the fool's cap on the telescope
With his pert sheepskin shuts out sun and stars.
I saw the man-fruit on the gallows-tree,
It hung up like a fruit and like a fruit
Shook in the wind, like a fruit was plucked down
And the dark wintry branch stood bare.   That day
I saw a withered woman in her rags
Watch by a door and snatch what lay within
And feed her young.   I saw a stout arm seize
And hale her to a dungeon.   The same hour
I saw a young man in the flush of youth
Broad in the sunshine of the city street,
Meet a poor soul that once had been a maid;
She knew that she was desolate, and he
Spat in her ruined face because he might.

I did not hear that he was hanged or chained.
And so the world went on.   But was it thus
That in the Eye of Him who made the world
While it was yet unmade the thing to be
Did golden revolution, and appeared
So lovely that He made it?   If this earth
Be but a Lazary, a madman's cell,
A gaol, a charnel, wherefore was it reared
So like a temple?   Hath a den of thieves
The gates called 'Beautiful?'   Or are these hills,
Whereon the consecrated Noon doth set
The golden candlestick, and robèd Eve
Shall light her late burnt-offering in the west,
The changers' tables?   Yet ah, who shall say
' My Father's House,' and by that right divine
Dispose unblamed within? Whose sinless cords
Shall cleanse it?   What sufficient touch of faith
Removing the great mountain that on high
Holds back the imminent Hyaline, unsluice
The second deluge?   Where is he on earth,
At whose great word I, who sit here to-day
In her fair porch and royal gate of all
One sore from head to heel, should rise and walk?
And at what word that did not make me whole,
Would I, for all the beauty of my place,
Lift from the chaste chryselephantine floors
One leprous limb?   Yet who shall dare to cast
A stone upon my sin, or with white hands

Hale me beyond the portals?   Drugs there be
For every ill, and in their books the wise
Apportion each to each; but who shall bring
The living instance to the written saw?
For every sickness of a human soul
There may be balm in Gilead, but what eye
Infallible shall find, what lip shall name
My hid disease?   To hell, ye empirics !
And burn your statutes.

                Who shall legislate
For the unseen performance of the heart?
Or in the balance of his justice weigh
The imponderable soul ?   By what gross word
Of this her rude interpreter assess
Her necessary silence?   By what work
Of menial senses judge her viewless hand,
Her secret enterprise, her unobeyed
Commandment; good in service turned to ill,
Or ill so carried that it looked like good ?
What profiteth to draw your lines about
A haunted house, or hem a ghost with trench
And scarped epaulment?   Canst thou chain the wind,
Or put material fetters upon thought
That bloweth where it listeth ?   Or debar
The Soul from her delight ?   Who shall keep watch
O'er the forbidden treasure, and attach
Her going out and coming in ?   Show me
The etherial captive naked in the sun,

Bound at thy chariot wheels ; bend at thy will
Her free immortal limbs ; pass, under seal,
The charter of her rights, repeal this sin,
Enact yon virtue, with a single groat
Endow a starved remembrance, confiscate
That in the past that I could tell thee of,
And I will hear ! Aye, send thy Sheriff, King,
Into this bosom ; apprehend this pang ;
Touch Me or these ; arrest that bloody knife
Wherewith I quiver ; standing by my side
Thrust in thine arm if thou art man, oh King !
And stay these burning hands that 'day and night
Are felon here !

             ' King !' Aye, that word crowns all !
Where is our King ? If there be some man built
For each due office, and no man alive
But in his place is matchless, where is he
The head and master workman to dispose
Tasks fit for all, and each to his fit task ?
For we are the disordered elements
Of that tremendous engine which, compact,
Should put a soul into this floating earth
And drive her thro' the stars ; make headlong way
Dead in the wind of chance and all the tides
Of fortune, laugh to scorn the storms of fate,
Make white the deeps of chaos, and, at last,
Cast her eternal anchor on the shore
Of far applauding Heaven.

                                    But now unplaced,
Constrict in bonds inordinate, or ties
With hopeless lesion lax, in unexplained
Society consorted to no end,
Or from connexion apt or impotent
Absolved and separate, dissolute, poured down
In orderly disorder, quick or dead,
Inert or vital, as the several part
Motive or to be moved fulfills in vain
Its own peculiar, fruitful now no more
In general welfare and the good of all—
We lie on heap, and each constituent finds
Disastrous sloth or detrimental use ;
Dead in himself, or motionless as dead
Oppressed beneath his fellows, or, uplift
By wilful hand of hapless circumstance
And so applied, in sad unequal case
With unadapted organs ill performs
Unsuited functions, fine with gross, and gross
With fine.   If One Infallible might speak
And make these dry bones live !   If any sign
Could daily end this dire perplexity !
We are the sons of anguish ; we are born
In labour and to labour ; toil and pain
Begin us, and shall end us.   It is well.
We are your slaves, work your high pleasure on us !
Aye, load us till we crack, and our great wills
Shall not be less than yours !   None of these things

Move us, for none of these things our proud hearts
Arraign or shall arraign you, O ye gods!
We are no rebels; this our loud demand
Is not the ill blooded and morose complaint
Of secret hate, or the promulgèd war
Of overt treason, but a claim of right
Preferred by lips still loyal in the phrase
Of sweet subjection, the ensheathed appeal
Of armed allegiance, the obtesting cry
Of a forgotten people.   Ye are gods,
And we are men; so let it be.   But ye
Speak not our language nor we yours.   If one
Might rede aright to us your dark decrees,
Whereof we pay infraction with the blood
Of ignorance!   If any daily voice,
Were it no larger than this grasshopper's,
In our own tongue could only say to us
' Well done, well done, thy feet are in the way,
This path beyond the darkness is the same;
Thou hast not walked in dreams, nor in thy sleep
Hath any passing mischief carried thee
Far from the roads of morning!   Nought is lost.
That which thou sawest thou sawest, what thine ear
Heard hath been spoken; thou art not yet false;
This that thou callest good is good : go on,
It shall be well with thee in all the worlds!'
But now am I as one blindfold and bound,
Who, 'mid a sounding pageant, pressed and thronged

With tramp of steeds and shout of changed event,
Roar of innumerable multitude,
And banners' proud advance and clang of horns
Dying the gaudy air with hot acclaim,
And flux and reflux of resistless tide,
Doth take from side to side with helpless face
Blind buffet of the surging turbulence
And strong bewilderment, and feels his blood
Down-dropping, and his wounds ; but heedeth more
The wonder of his heart, and moans and moans,
' Alas that I could see ! '

                 ' I ? ' who am I ?
Whence ? How ? Why ? Whither ?

                      This old world that stands
Before me day and night, what ? wherefore ?

                           Down
Thou pompous and intolerable ruin !
I weary of thee !   Thou art out of knowledge ;
Thy centuries untold ; thy Builders where ?
Thy fashion lost ; thy substance without name ;
The very need that thou didst satisfy
Forgot.   Why cumberest thou the fields of air,
Incantada ?

           The cardinal intent,
The regnant virtue, final element,
And master good, the better truth of all,
Which on its ordered arms upbears these shows
As leaves upon a tree ; that which beheld

Infers the necessary universe
As substance shadow ; and, being known indeed,
Is the old fruit which, eaten, maketh gods,
Who shall discover and therein first find
Himself and all his race? There is some truth
Unknown, whose very footsteps are more bright
Than any visible face, and on whose track
Unlooked for the glad heart in loud surprise
Doth open like a hound. Sometimes I pass
Plain after plain of many-trodden life,
And never cross it ; and anon when Hope
Grown careless hath unleashed his pursuivants
And all the long invariable way
Stretches in lifeless waste—my dazzled eyes
And the long trail of light ! This panting heart
Racing pursuit where as she runs the run
Gives strength to run and warm and warmer air
Leads on the nose of capture, mad to win
O'ertakes the brightening leagues ; then all at fault
Stands fixed and bays the sky. As one should trace
An angel to the hill wherefrom he rose
To Heaven, and on whose top the vacant steps
In march progressive with no backward print
A-sudden cease. Sometimes, being swift, I meet
His falling mantle torn off in the wind
Of great ascent, whereof the attalic pomp
Between mine eyes and him perchance conceals
The bare celestial. Whose still happier speed

Shall look up to him while the blinding toy
In far perspective is but as a plume
Dropped from the eagle? Whose talarian feet
Shall stand unshod before him while he spreads
His pinions? Who shall take him by the hand?
I have tried all Philosophies; I know
The height and depth of science; I have dug
The embalmèd Truth of Karnak and have sailèd
Tigris and Ganges to the sacred source
Of eastern wisdom; I have lived a life
Of noble means to noble ends; and here
I turn to the four winds, and say ' In vain,
In vain, in vain, in vain ! '

                The end is come.
I stand upon the Babel I have built,
I have surpassed the mountains, the great globe
Lies inexhaustible below, my days
Are still before me; these unconquered limbs
Invulnerable hang by my strong side
Brawny with toil; but I have worked my last.
I cannot lift these arms. I have attained
The furthest realm aërial where the air
Is gross enough to breathe, and Nature's self
Refuses to o'erbuild the vital bound
And lift me into death. I lay me down
Upon my life-long work the wretchedest man
That ever fought and lost. What I have done,
No more being done, is vain, and more being done

Unsouls the bulk that went before, and rears
A pyramid to hold into the sun
The offence of my mortality.   My pride
Hath climbed till I can hardly see the earth
Beneath me, and from that last possible height
Looks up with fainting eyeballs to behold
A heaven no whit more near.   Is there no help?

[*A pause.*

O Thou Invisible, whoe'er thou art,
Who with sufficient presence and plenary touch
Extensive, whether in the unfathomed east
And west or in the terrible extremes
Beyond the Pole Star and the Southern Cross
They mark the immeasurable round of heaven,
At once distendest with co-equal life
The order'd spheres ; either withdraw thyself
From the serene and golden harmony
Of that inspirèd matter overhead
Which circleth irrespective day and night
In heedless welfare ; either give up realms
That once were Chaos to the mortal shock
Of the last anarchy ; let maddened day
Scorch hope to ashes, and the flaming night
Affright us till the yell of our despair
Rise in the howling regions ; be exhaled
O Power, let me behold the sudden stars
Meet in omnipotent havoc that results
To utter space and ebbs and flows and ebbs

In vast conflux and infinite recoil
Systole and diastole, till lo !
A universe that like our mortal lot
Panteth to death, and in the hopeless sight
We leap to final flames ; or now at last
Unveil Thyself and save us !   Come forth strong
To judgment !   Justify the shows of things,
And heal HER and this world !

SCENE XXXI.

THE STUDY.

BALDER *at his table in act to write.   Through the door the
voice of* AMY.   *As she sings he rises and rushes from
the room.*

   Amy. That I might die and be at rest, O God !
That I might die and sleep the sleep of peace !
That I might die and know the balm of death
Cool thro' my limbs and all my silenced heart !
O God, that I might die ! that I might die !

Death, Death, thou wilt not take me ? should I bring
Disquiet to thy kingdom ?   Yesterday
Was pain, and had a yesterday of pain
Whereto it was to-morrow ; and pain, pain
This dark to-day, to-morrow's yesterday

And yesterday's to-morrow ; then why not
To-morrow ? and why less because with thee ?

I know the wanderer in the desert heat
When the well faileth and the cruise is spent
Sees with his eyes his great necessity
And hears the murmur of his strong desire
And speeds—to drearer wastes and deadlier sand.
If I am he, O Death, and thou my Thought
Hast lain so long before me cool and sweet
And art the mirage of a wretched heart !

In what fair shape hast thou beguiled me not ?
O Death in all this vision of the world
What have I seen, Betrayer, if not thee ?

Sometimes I climb, and thou upon the height
My mother waiting for her weary child
With outstretched circling arms and bosom bare !
Or I am falling in a draw-well deep
Red round with infinite depth of hateful eyes
And night-mare mocking faces, and below
Thou liest like a smile of love and peace.

Sometimes I am a maimèd captive, bound
To the swift chariot of the pitiless sun,
And thou art night that dost unloose my chain !

Or I a pilgrim at the gate of heaven,
Torn with the thorniest way, and thou O Death
A virgin angel met upon the verge,
And pitiful thou dost divesture me
And there of all my tattered earthly weeds
Spreadest a bed where I may sleep my last
Nor enter weary on the happy land.

Or I a floating vapour, white and wan,
Casting a shade and shedding doleful dews,
And thou a sunshine from a sun unseen
Dost touch me, passing, to a rarer change.
I float and sadden not the summer air
Nor shed a doleful dew nor cast a shade.

Or I am sailing on an ocean wild
And o'er the bark I bend me, fain to die,
And hopeless look into the sea ; and eyes
Shine up like drownèd jewels from the depths,
And somewhat riseth in the deep to me,
And in the waters a familiar face
And a hand waving to the mermaid-cells.

Touch me, O Death !　This moment let me sleep !
I can do all, O Death, but doubt in thee.
Touch me, O Death, least I be wild with fear !
Aye, now thou art again as thou hast been.
Stay with me ; lay thine hand upon my brow,

Cool, cool ; bend o'er me ; let thy shadowy hair
Shut out the distance from my aching eyes.
Stand between me and the unsetting sun ;
Console the frailty of my feeble limbs
And task me with a burden I can bear !
I fling me on the shore ; I cannot try
The ocean of interminable life.
Hush me, and sing me to a better mind.
A little rest, a little rest, O Death,
Ere the great labour of the world to come !

SCENE XXXII.

THE STUDY.

BALDER *sits at the table, turning the leaves of a MS.*

    Page after page ! from earliest light of dawn
To the first evening star, and still in vain !
The eye indeed perceives, but the shut soul
Hath no reception. As in a great house
Upon a day of mourning when the lord
Pines in his closet, and the eager crowds
Fill the contentious vestibule and keep
Jostling attendance, what the sense admits
Stands in the outer precincts of my head
But gains not me. Nay, thro' dull walls I hear
The intolerable murmur, and go back

To darker depths.   If these ears would forget !
These eyes contain their uses in the straits
Of function, and the strong impediment
Of wood and stone !   A little rest !   An hour's
Oblivion !   Six days have I sat as now,
In the same chamber, at the well-known place,
In the same chair, before the wonted table,
With the same pen dipped in the self-same horn,
The altar laid as when the god came down,
And every duteous rite of sacrifice
But not the fire from heaven !   You pitying gods,
I am content to suffer; as ye will
Work all your pleasure on me ; but I pray,
Having so far advanced my monument,
Let me not die unhonoured.   I ask not
Space for the dearest business of life ;
But if we are to die unloose these limbs
A little season, grant but what reprieve
May place the final stone which shall surmount
Our ashes, and these votive hands shall shed
The blood ye long to taste ! these mindful arms
Embrace your vengeance !   [*Pauses.*
                              If ye ever heard,
Save what is left of me !   Ye will lose nought ;
I shall die nobler game.   Hack me to earth
By this slow baiting and the inglorious wounds
Will mortify, and I that might have roared
At bay upon your foremost, and, upreared

Like a wild desperate Lion, have made sport
For your divinest prowess, may turn tail
And trail my hinder death along the ground
Of craven faint retreat.   Now ! now ! ye swift
And interposing powers ! the cry I the cry !

             [AMY *is heard thro' the door.*

    Amy. Blind, blind I stand and dare not stir for fear.
Blind, blind I turn my face up to the sky.
I have no hope to hide my bruisèd face
Which evermore a strong hand in the air
Smites with a burning rod and will not rest.

SCENE XXXIII.

THE STUDY.

BALDER, *solus.*

Through the half-open door is heard the voice of AMY.
            [*He rises and shuts the door*

    Balder. In vain ! There is but one wall upon earth
Thou canst not pass : One door that being closed
Is closed on thee ; one refuge where even thou
Art silent.   If I hide myself in deeps
Of lonely woods the murmuring trees take up
Thine argument ; if in the further wilds
Of the waste hills, my heart is full of tongues
And each to either in untiring round

They tell thy story.   She of old who fled
Before the humming fly, and coursed the world
Uncomforted, wild with the ceaseless sound
Susurrent, was in better case than I
Who have no hope of change, and with swift flight
Should bear as swift a woe.   I am impaled
Here where I stand ; my hurt, alas, not mortal,
But touching at the very hinge and crank
The springs of action and the palsied limbs
Of staring struck desire.   'Tis hard, 'tis hard,
To lie upon this earthly battle-field
Among the sick and helpless in the rear
And see the strife and the eternal prize
Borne off by other hands, and hear the trump
And all the victory which thou canst not share.
But nature smooths the pillow that she spreads,
The fevered hand is weary of the sword,
The fallen warrior's eye hath lost its fire,
His voice its thunder ; his unstanchèd wound
Hath bled ambition, and the sick man's pap
Is not the bait of war.

                     Ask what he feels
Who with the pulse of promise and the limbs
Of young performance and the lusts of youth
Swelling and flushing on unconquered brows
And favouring heavens above him and great signs
In the consenting earth, mounts to his dear
And proud intent, and hears already rise

The shout of conquest, and, in grasp of all,
Yea in the triumph of his measured strength—
That leans over accomplishment to close
With forward acquisition,—stops stone still,
Spell-bound.   And spell-bound, locked and motionless,
With unseen prowess of inglorious war
Hid in his silent body, strives with fate
And spends his might within.   (As one doth grind
The set teeth down, and in his clenchèd palm
Break his own bones, and cram his chargèd veins
To bursting, string each muscle till it crack,
Hold but a little breath with will enough
To bind the winds of Heaven, and stay a hand
With force that could arrest the headlong world
And no man knows it.)   He thro' starting eyes
Sees all that should be his, and, like a fierce
And hungry mastiff held back by a chain
In the full scent and sight of his near prey,
And strong to seize, that gasps and claws the ground
And wears his bloody talons to the bone
With unrelaxed endeavour, he beholds
While the auspicious light goes down the sky
And high in Heaven the awful omens change,
And 'mid the murmurs of impatient earth
He stands for ever straining to the breach
Of still denied occasion.
     My keen ears
Heard each careering star that rounds the sky,

And knew them by their sounds.   But now to list
In vain, nor know if the great march of worlds
Stand still !   When life was sweet I would have died
That men might happier live ; when hard existence
Toiled thro' its sweats of blood, I would have lived
That men might nobler die; but now alike
To live unfruitful and to die unblest !
Heavens ! that the creak of passing wain should hide
The voice that drowns the rolling universe !
That thou, despite of me, canst fill the world,
And no more pressure of this hand than holds
A bundle of unbruised buttercups
Could still thee !   That the bannered host of man
Under my leading starts on its white way
Down the rejoicing ages, and thou, Amy,
Canst take the car of glory by the wheel
And stop it ; with a single touch arrest
That wondrous wingèd horse whereon I rode,
And throw mankind in me.

SCENE · XXXIV.

A FIELD NEAR THE TOWER.

BALDER, *solus*.

Oh God ! to how great office was I born,
To how proud exaltation came I in

Unquestioned as one comes unto his own.
For nor was it forbidden me to hold
The pen of sovereign Nature when she bent
To send her message to the sons of men,
Nor,—being her Scribe, and finding in her eyes
Maternal favour—undismissed to sit
At her dread feet, while her much-musing Voice
Like muffled thunders of a storm unburst
Did murmur to her heart.   Nor she disdained
In royal leisure to remember me ;
Keeping her eyes upon the wilderness
In mercy, and dividing to my sense
The o'er-great burden of her gaze and speech.
And I being asked made answer, having grace
To speak.   Nor unto me was it denied
To hear responsive secrets from her lips.
Nor to behold her undestroyed what time
She held her court and all the subject Powers
Of the obedient Universe appeared
To hear her bidding, and to each her hand
Dispensed his several task.   Nor unto me
Wholly inhibited, nor by these orbs
In this dark day forgot, the blinding sight
Of that all incommunicable hour
And ecstasy when she who wears the stars
Sitting alone amid Infinitude
Nor seeing from her all-surveying throne
Sovereign or peer, doth veil her awful head

And own a Master.
                         Naked from the womb
She took me, and she clothed me round about,
Nor have I other garment than the robe
She gave; wherefore I, driven forth and disowned,
Displaced, dishonoured, cut off once for all,
Outcast and unauthentic, by my weeds
Still seem her servant. .All that seek her grace
Salute me, and my hands are full of bribes.
They whom she loves are free to me in speech
No longer mine, and uncommanded slaves
Contend to do me service.   Hereabout
I am confessor to a thousand flowers
And wheresoe'er I stand some one begins
Her unsought confidence : each several Oak
Standing above me, hoarse with waving arms,
Makes me companion of his difficult strength
As Cromwell spake to Milton.
                              From what state
Am I cast down !   Where shall I rest who lay
In the hid core of silence and did sleep
Cradled in central calm ?   In what world find
A dwelling ?   Under what less potentate
A new allegiance?   Beneath what dark Heavens
A worship ?   From what spot of lower spheres
A Universe ?   In Heaven, Hell, Earth, or Air,
Aught that can satisfy a heart which once
Beat in the very breast and vital seat

Of all things, and being forced to the extremes,
Resents the unblest deformity and hath
No function of a heart?

              Oh Queen, oh Mother,
Take, take me back !

                   I that ne'er wept before !
Thou seest !

           Silent ?   Silent and these tears !
Nay this is to outrun the Destinies.
True I am fallen indeed, but not yet dead !
Dead ?   How if dead not fallen ?   And perhaps
From the high place I filled no more removed
Than that her mournful and imperial hands
Might urn me in a star?   And as one bears
A heavy sleeper with fast closèd lids
Whose dreams like shadows of the truth repeat
The outer perils darkly, in this sleep
I have had visions?   Hence wild phantasy !
I live!

          Hast thou forgotten me ?   This brow
These limbs that at thy feet thou hast so oft
Looked down upon in love that I have seen
The spheres grow pale missing their wonted light,
How are they less than then ?   A friend—a foe—
The beneficial difference of the sword
Is in the using !   Something I have done,
Something may do.   Chaos hath still his standard.
Speak, or I join it ! lead the dark attack

By the most secret way ; betray thy counsels ;
Make thy hid thoughts the common sport o' the air,
Map thy designed war, and thine arch-foe
Forearm with master-spells.

                      Aye silence, silence.
Why not ?　How should I move thee, O sublime
Invulnerable ?　Though I not behold
Thy countenance, I know that if the smile
Dimmed on thy lips, or round thy brow serene
Tempered the gracious summer, these whose sight
Attains thy face had drooped their sudden heads
With hopeless frost.

                 But is it wise in thee
With this imperial scorn to rouse an arm
Which once was worth thine honour ?　To send forth
Wrath which was once thine angel ?　And unloose
A tongue which learned its language .on thy breast
Amid the nursling thunders ?　Thou art there
And shalt be ; nor can I aspire to shake
Thy throne.　But this terrestrial sovereignty,
This sublunary verge and late domain
Of empire, who shall save it ?　Speak to me !
Or by a conscript hell——　　　　　　　[*Pauses.*

                  In vain, in vain !
Smile on ! I see it all.　Thou hast ta'en thought
Of this defection.　What I lift is not
The hand that moved the heavens.　Thy pride hath
      snapped

The weapon it disused.   The self-same touch
Put me at once from duty and disservice,
And dwarfed me from my native healthful height
Below obnoxious stature.

                Shall I look
Into the wayside pool to see my face,
And shall a water-beetle blot it out?
I could believe no less.   Poor mannikin,
Prate as thou list—pray, sing, preach, rave, despair,
Square to the sun, defy the stars!   Thou art free!
Royally done!   I am too mean a thing
To have mine anger reckoned.   This weak arm
Is warrant for desertion; this cold heart
May throb for whom it list; this scrannel voice
Pipe here or there unchallenged.   Everywhere
Misfortune hath the privilege of treason
And impotence prescription to rebel!
Once it had not been thus; no, nor couldst thou,
Oh Unapproachable Serenity,
Have heard me all unmoved.

                       But now sit calm.
Wert thou the merest maid that ever lay
Well-portioned and well-pleased before her glass
Braiding her locks and shining thro' her curls
Upon the kneeling lover at her feet
Enough refusal, insolent and vain,
Round her most dainty finger slow and cold
With equal touch and languid cruelty

Twining his heart-strings and her golden hair,
I could not harm thee.

                    I, who from thine height
Beheld, and,—since we claim for corporal self
Whatever bears the living head wherefrom
The soul looks out—I that saw down from thence
To the far footing of the solid dark
My starry stature; I who with stern eye
Did gaze into the opening infinite,
And on the scale of that perspective scan
This measured earth; I who would equal space,
And as a thing apart in outer courts
Contain creation; I am even contract
To the dimensions of some elfin world.
This checquered field shall be my vast expanse;
Yon tree Igdrasil; any passing cloud
In golden distance o'er my sinking head
Shall arch sufficient Heaven; the nightly Moon
Toil the horizon of a fairy ring
As once I led her the majestic march
Of this great globe, and in impatient power
Danced round her steps as David round the Ark,
And wheeling into utter depths returned
About her languid motion. Day by day
Shall bring my grain of wheat and drop of dew
Content; and I shall see the rising Sun
Above the Mole-heaps as I saw him once
Above the hills of God !

SCENE XXXV.

THE STUDY.

BALDER, *solus.*

Balder.   I could believe I heard myself grow thin,
The slack and empty sail cling close and dry
Upon the cordage masts and stays of life,
My bare unmuffled bones collapse and clank
And what was round and cheerful in this body
Fall out of observation.

                Let it fall,
It has survived my use—this goodly space
And palace of· the flesh which hall by hall
I have given up, retreating from a voice
Without, till, more than housed in the strait bounds
Of its most secret cell, I find at last
How little it bested me.

                I that laid
My hand upon this breast and deemed I throbbed
Beneath ; who held my unity of powers
In such most sweet conversion that it seemed
Love was essential in the tranquil soul
And wisdom cordial in the beating heart,
Where am I?   Did the echoes of the house
Deceive me, and the murmur of the shell?

My soul hath gone back like a sea on heaps
Before a Prophet's rod ; leaving that bare
Which never saw the light—the gulphs and deeps
And all the infand unknown which since the first
It covered but was not.   And I sit here
Within my passions ; and that writhing round
Of rooted serpents rises like a ring
Of licking flames about me.   Some are dead
And others gnaw them.   Of the living, some
Lie lank as worms ; some roar as dragons ; all
Enjoy or suffer ; and I see unmoved
How each fulfils his office ; coils and glides,
Plays as when Eve stood smiling, warms, desires,
Swells, springs, falls, maddens, struggles, twists and dies,
Strangled in its own knots.   I see them,—mine
Not me ; myself in the hot midst, a cold
Calm lidless eye that neither hopes nor fears
Nor loves nor hates nor smiles nor weeps nor prays.
It cannot last.   I am a living man
Not an anatomy for time and change
To scalpel when they teach the younger gods
And show them subject man.   You heavens, what right
Makes me the bleeding instance ?   Why am I
The Paragon of woes ?   How dare they seize
These organs to discuss the novel signs
Of unaccustomed torture ?   Must I bear
That they may be instructed ; with keen edge
Distinguish what is mortal from the threads

Of inconclusive anguish, and in slow
Discovery one by one dissect away
The stamens of endurance, with fine point
Experimental and touch exquisite
Detect of each rare core the central sense,
Open the vesture of the secret nerve,
Make bare the naked torment and lay out
The warm and quivering Nature styled and strung
For vital exposition ?   Malefactors,
Who in the last resource of desperate hope
Yield up their breathing bodies to the schools,
Die under such division.   Human hate
On choicest victim of her direst hour
Hath not accomplished it ; the subtlest pains
Of her most fell invention cannot pass
That Lethe through which pitying Powers convey
The wretch for whose worst crime in their just eyes
'Tis more than expiation to be aim
Of such unheard-of purpose.   Hell itself
Hath no such agony ; the very Damned
Are plunged in whole.

SCENE XXXVI.

A Hill near the Tower

BALDER, *solus.*

Balder.   Like a sailing eagle old
Which with unwavering wings outspread and wide
Makes calm horizons in the slumbrous air
Of cloudless noon and fills the silent heaven
With the slow circulation of a course
More placid than repose, this shining still
And universal day revolves serene
Around me, hasting not and uncompelled.
But the tumultuous thought within my head
Is a poor captive beast, that to and fro,
Wild in the trepidation of mad pain
Beats its red bars in blood.   Gods ! how it climbs
This throbbing dungeon, leaps and falls and leaps
In strong attempt, and strains a battered face
Against the narrow outlets, gnaws the holds
Of iron and shakes loud with desperate will
The adamantine doors.   What ! have I caged
A leopard in my pleasure-house ?   Am I
A doomed city ? are these halls a roost
For owls and dragons ?   Shall the bittern cry
Out of the stagnant courses of my heart
And the fox litter in her palaces ?

My seat wherein I sat is overturned,
My images are broken and cast down,
My set and sacred places are defiled,
My fair adornèd walls dismantled all
And all the tattered tapestries of life
Rent on the floors of Ruin !
                I do not rage
Nor rave ; but I ask you O ye blue heavens,
What have I done ?
                I do remember me
That on a cottage threshold once I saw
An idiot child.   His blue orbs in his brow
Were as when some round rosy cloud of morn
Opens deep azure eyes and we see thro'
To heaven.   On his calm countenance there lay
A lazy day of self-sufficing hours,
And all the changes in his face were made
By the soft feet of pleasure slow and fair.
Is there a soul behind you ?   There was none
In him !   He was born deaf and dumb and blind
And foolish.   But he was as bright as you.

SCENE XXXVII.

A Glen among the Hills near the Tower.

Balder, *solus.*

Balder. I will return.
Sitting down here this morn I turned my back
Upon the sun, and now he sees my face.
Waste hours—where all are waste ! A round of sand
Built in the endless sands with walls of sand.
That the red Tartarean world I feel
Within me hath reality without
Amid the discord of my soul I yet
Can make denial heard. And as a man
With whose disloyal organs ruthless Fever
Hath tampered till some play him false and all
Are treasonable, touching one by one
His harlequin environment constrains
Protean shapes to stand and give response,
And of attested qualities constructs
A synthesis more sure than the sick eye,
I, whom nor morning gladdens nor meek eve
Consoles, do know my desperate malady
And testify that fruitless eve and morn
Have both done well. I will not be deceived,
And so my day becomes a manifold
And drear induction that sets Truth from Truth,

As the blind hesitating sire of old
Jacob from Esau ; and with tender strength
Of one who going must divide fond arms
Enfolding, and unravel with stern love
Soft intertwining fingers of dear hands
That clasp him, doth unlock the enfoundered hulls
And spars of the strange worlds I see and feel,
And bid them pass as twain.   Here where I sit
The sun must needs be sweet,—the bees sing in it,
And yon large fly—a hawk among his kind—
Still in the very level of mine eye
Keeps on the wing, with shining long delay
Or sudden flash of capture.

       On the bank
The nodding moor-hen lands to preen her quills.
The trout hath left the alders of the pool
And basks.   Her beak the brooding king-fisher
Shows, breathless, at her callow hole above
The brook ; within the eddies of the brook
The water-mouse dissolves and reappears ;
Therefore 'tis halcyon weather.

     [He rises and walks homeward.
       The small flock
That lay but now, fleece upon panting fleece,
About the knees of yonder aged oak—
Their lusty lord upon a gnarled root
High in the cooler midst—descend and fill
The lengthening shade.   The weed that shuts at noon

Is closer than a sleeping infant's lid ;
And the pale evening rose hath not yet set
Her chalice for the dews ; therefore it is
That heavy hour of silent afternoon
When even grief can slumber and forget.
For me I know no seasons, nor will trust
The tale of the extravagant heart that tells
Between the orient and the setting sun
A year of days, and calls the outer world
Chaos let loose.   [*Enters the Garden.*
          This green turf nicely fine
A fairy host marshals its serried spears
Innumerable, and of all not one
Hath turned an edge ; a human conflict here
Had trodden it as o'er our helmèd heads
The wrestling gods contending trample down
A field of legions.   Up the new spread walk
Well-trimmed, my morning footsteps where I came,—
Eight hours since by the dial,—still remain ;
None other near them : therefore I have been
Alone, and as I walk I print a like
And solitary record, therefore now
I am alone.
          If I went forth at morn
Thro' a well-tilled soft garden, and came back
This very hour to find it trodden hard,
Stamped to a summer floor, and all my home
Threshed out upon it, flying here and there,

Chaff on the wind, 'twere less incredible
Than this approven solitude.

                           Across
My doorway I perceive the gossamer
Drew silver bars behind me.   They have lost
The immaterial beauty of the morn,
When passing on the gleaming wind they seem
Rather effect than cause, the cutting sheen
Of somewhat on the eye too swift for sight,
Or hung across the early way appear
A shining prohibition in the air
No more.   But these are stiff as rods of glass,
And flat with drought.   Therefore since I went forth
None hath gone in or out.

                    This looks like peace,
And I must needs believe it.   *[Enters a room.*
                    How the motes
In idle sunshine slowly circulate,
A little heaven of worlds as calm and sweet
As any stars above us.   Eh ! my breath
Sucks gulphs beneath the golden equipoise
And sets a viewless tide that bears away
Systems and suns.   Thou great astronomer,
Perplexed by some new motion, WHO on high
Beyond thy telescopic organ stands
Breathing ?

           A wood wren ! and the open lattice
He passes deftly with familiar wing.

No chance intruder, or the crystal panes
Had toiled him, and my first step at the door
Had been his fearful signal !   Is the day
Such and so comparably native here
That even the tenants of the silent wood
Deem it their own possession ?   Peace—

               [*Enters an inner room.*

                   Asleep !

Her pallid head upon her hand, and all
The blighted harvest of her locks unsheaved
Upon her pillow ; whence a single hair
Hangs its sweet tendril and by duest time
Still kept to the fair rise and shadowy fall
Of her white breast denotes how undisturbed
The obedient air about her !   To my cheek
'Tis hot and angered as with glare of fire !
But the Mimosa by her doth not fade ;
Some dew is on the blossoms that she wears,
Plucked, doubtless, in the shadow of the dell ;—
And I observe yon frail-winged butterfly
Which fluttered through the eastern casement cool
With freshest odours—and whose fairy fans
Had shrivelled in a heat which cherishes
This human flesh—doth palpitate unharmed
Mid through the glow that scorched me.

                 Inch by inch

Adjusting every witness of the soul
By such external warrants, I do reach

Herself, the centre and untaken core
Of this enchanted Castle whose far lines
And strong circumvallations in and in
Concentring I have carried, but found not
The foe that makes them deadly; and I stand
Before these most fair walls and know he lies
Contained, and in the wont of savage war
Prowl round my scatheless enemy and plot
Where, at what time, with what consummate blow
To storm his last retreat and sack the sense
That dens her fierce malease.

      I am as one
Who hearing music thro' the dark doth press
Straight towards the sound and comes upon a tower,
And feels along the impediment whereby
To pass it; and the walls still put him back
And the contained voice still calls and he
Still pressing to the sound still journeyeth round
His hid desire; and now by ear led on
Draws nigh,—and now, when close pursuit should break
The skin of fleshed enjoyment, hears the voice
Fainter and fainter from the further cell.
And so unconscious treads a beaten ring
Following that moony voice that wanes and fills
And wanes, and at the worst again is new.
Till at the last, instructed by defeat,
Step by slow step he measures round the wall
The crescent sound, and at one loudest spot

Of proximate possession lays his siege,
And with his straining strength and bruised hands
Would force the unyielding Stone !
                          Thus have I tracked
That still unseen disturber of my days
Who in this holy sanctuary hath made
His sacrilegious dwelling; yea could lay
A finger on the small fair space that hides
Within such alabaster and most pure
Sarcophagus the cancerous atomy
Which with its black disease, as with a stench,
Infects this gracious world.   From the wide air
Thro' the freed earth and up the very stairs
Of home, entrenched against me, hold by hold,
Implacable with steady overthrow
Of hounding hate incessant I dislodge him,
And here before a scale of living bone
Come to my final stop ! and though my arms
Can hem him in, and his unforced place
To these avenging and swift hands be near
As their own marrow, know him here at last
Impregnable.   Heavens ! that the very knife
Which doth uproot a weed would cut more deep
Than should eradicate from the restored
Sweet universe that thread of bitterness
Which feeds the mighty shade that poisons all !
That with one little stroke I could cut out
This œcumenical and central wrong,

And dare not do it ! With no stronger use
Of no more muscles than would rend this hair,
This little hair—I could end once for all
That sole accursed evil which hath been
My Master ! That the mortal chase hath brought
Mine enemy to ground, and he lies here
As far off from my just revenge as in
The farthest of the stars !

SCENE XXXVIII.

THE HILL-SIDE.

Enter BALDER.

Balder. Was this world built for happiness, that man
In all his agonies since pain began
Hath, as of intuition, changed its use
And customary order ; made the Night
A banquet-hall for his cold feast of Death,
And Day his weary chamber ? Or was't wrought
In equal seasons, that the separate walls
Of twain but neighbouring mansions might contain
The happy and the wretched ?

                            I. that walked
All this long night upon the bare hill-top
Grow heavy in the sunshine and would sleep.

      [*He lies down and sleeps—after a while starts up.*

This dream! why I came leaping out of it
Half-witted and half-dead as one escapes
From dungeons into air. I must have wept, too,
The grass below my face is all bedewed,—
Away!   [*Turns and sleeps.*

                            [*Leaps up with disordered looks.*
No, no, it cannot be, it must not be,
It shall not be!—Amy!   .

                    [*Looking up, his eye catches the clouds.*
                        You white full heavens!
You crowded heavens that mine eyes left but now
Shining and void and azure!—

                            Ah! ah! ah!
Ah! ah! ah! ah! ah! ah! ah! ah! ah! ah!
By Satan! this is well.   What! am I judged?
You ponderous and slow-moving ministers,
Are you already met?   Are crimes begot
Above?   And do we sin to give the train   '
And hungry following of the stately gods
An office?   Doth their pastime tarry there
Because I lag?   Is it to be endured
That while I sleep the ready forum forms
About me, and the conscript fathers wait
The unaccomplished wrong?   Hence! clear the heavens!
Break up!   What! can I not so much as dream
But your substantial thunders must surround
The ghostly fault, and with material towers
And bodily environment hem in

The thin unflesh'd commission?   Do you close
Upon me like a weary prey run down,
Stalked to the final onset?   But I live!
Will you sit at the board while the meal walks?
How if you are too soon?   Who sees the game?
Look down upon us here—which is your man?
What have I done?   My hands are white—behold!
You solemn imperturbable o'er-high
All-seeing and prededicate avengers,
For once ye sit in vain!   My will is not
Yours; nor shall any terrors of your loud
Discomfiture, nor any warning sign—
No, tho' the rocked right half of heaven rolled o'er
And stood at heaps on the sinister side—
Unplant my fixed resolve.   Mine eyes do pierce
The lower ostentations of your brief
And temporary royalty to reach
A Paramount Supreme.

SCENE XXXIX.

The Study.

A Writing-table, with Paper and Pens.

Balder.   Yes, I will bear, forbear, hope, labour, wait,
Yet once again.   He who from love of day
Doth end his life in the obscurest hour

Of long-lived night flies not from aged Nox
But from unborn Aurora.   'Tis the part
Of wisdom to endure.   Whatever clime
Surround, more fair, this sublunary scene,
Howe'er we name those undiscovered Powers
That rule us and do place our weal and woe,
The problem of the wretched is to pass
Not the set circumscription of his known
And ordered ill, but the unsearched confines
Of their supreme disposals.   Failing that
All fails; and the poor slave for whom extends
No safe inviolable shore, no last
Red Stygian frontier where the angry hordes
Of hurrying hell must needs stand balked and droop
The unavailing scorpions,—had best bend
To his worst task, nor heat the blood of swift
Inevitable vengeance.   Once again—

    [*Through the open door,* AMY *is heard.*
 Amy.   If thou art not, O death, if thou art not,
I am immortal and not born to die,
And time hath no dominion over me.
Is this the secret of my wretched lot,
Is this the secret of a happy world
And all the joy of life that glads not me?

I think I am immortal; I do think
My unrespective being takes to-day
The further woes of an eternal fate.

In vain the earth is happy, and in vain,
In vain, a little space above my head
The dread and over-arching destiny
Is calm and fair ; I feel from pole to pole,
Nor know the year that doth devour mine heart !
Oh, God !   Thou hast not made me for my lot,
I faint in prospect of the shoreless sea !
I cannot stand under the universe !
That it would sink and crush me once for all !

That I were broken as a thing defect,
Wholly rubbed out as of no right to be,
And as a heedless error of the hand
Cancelled for ever from the book of life !

                 [*After a long silence she is heard again.*
That I might die and be no more at all,
That I might cease out of the scheme of things,
And all my place be filled up evermore !

I am galled with my destiny ; that one
Would take my lot out of my scorched hands,
And all my heritage in heaven and earth.
Oh, God, forget me from thy universe,
Oh, God, I have retired out of my life,
The functions of my soul are dead, and I
Am but a burning hope of not to be !
Oh, God fulfil me ; I am but this thirst,
This all-consuming thirst, quench it and me !

                 [*After a long silence she is heard again.*

My punishment is more than I can bear,
Oh, men, oh, living men, oh, passers by,
No, this was not my sentence, no man yet
For such a fault hath heard so hard a doom!
For a small matter did they shut me in
Upon the eve of war, and on the morn
The tower was taken and the gaoler fled!

My cell is in the dank and hollow ground,
The ruins fell above it ; no man knows
Its place ; I am forgotten in my land.

I lay my hand upon the creeping thing,
The worm crawls o'er me ; the snail harbours up
My limbs.   I am as dark and all-forgot
As any stone that never saw the sun
And is and was and will be in the earth.

I hear the sound of life above my head,
The toads leap with it, and the very rock
Shakes with the overgoing ; but I know
The fallen ruins lie on heap ; my cry
Can never struggle to the day ; no man
Will ever seek me.

                    Hist! they move the stones!
Fast, faster! or I famish! This was not
My sentence! I was not shut in for this!
No man could treat me so! oh, men, oh, men,

The tower was taken and the gaoler fled,—
Let me out, let me out! I starve! I starve!

[*Listening to this he rises.*

    Balder.   You great Gods,
Here like a night-mare do I shake you off!

[*After a pause.*

Poor child,
Come hither, perchance I can help thee.   Hear me.

[*She comes.*

By all her wrongs,
Her unrespited Patience, unreleased
Endeavour, unremembered sighs and tears;
By her unheard poor prayers, her unfulfilled
Long hope, her uncrowned faith, her love unblest,
Her unallayed incomparable sorrow;
By all that hath no worthy place on earth,
All that hath won no summons from the skies,
I swear to set her free!

    Amy (kneeling before him).   To set me free?
Am I to be free? oh to set me free?
It cannot be so.   Sir, thou knowest not;
They have forgotten me where I do lie;
The tower was taken and the gaoler fled;
The ruins fell on heap; the many stones
Are o'er me; no man can come near nor tell
The under earth is hollow. ‵ Oh to help me,
Oh to come near me, oh to set me free!

[*She sinks on the floor weeping.*

Balder (*musing*).   This leprosy
Of murder being fairly out on me
Hath lost its worst disease.   The dark excess
That for so many days o'er-loaded all
My swollen veins, strangled each vital service,
And pressing hard the incommoded soul
In its unyielding tenement convulsed
The wholesome work of nature, is expelled.
The crisis of my malady is past
And leaves me sane but hideous.   I do stand
Blood-hot from head to heel but cool within.
Blood-wet and steaming blood from every pore
Incarnadine, but retching at those mouths
The red surcharge that killed me.   I am calm
And being calm shall better aim the bolt
Forged and flung down amid the thunder-rain
Of Passion.   That great rain that did so drown
The present where it fell that all beyond
Looked back upon already seems a world
Before the flood.

            I will even let her forth
As a poor bird out of a burning cage.
Nought in the direst caverns of the dark
Untried unknown can be less kind to her
Than I have been.   Somewhere, perhaps, in space
There may be better places than this world;
No worse.   Yes, I will let thee forth, poor child,
Aye tho' the seven times sacred bars be built

Of the twelve holy jewels, and I break
The door that will not open ! Amy ! Amy !
She sleeps !   What ! hath the very breath of murder
Such odour of its substance that the air
About me brings her to a doze like Death ?
'Tis well ! so can I test the untried strength
That seems invincible.   How now—how then ?

[*He bends over her.*

Now,—These dark tresses that I lift aside
To see the brow they shade, and, in my hand,
Having no sensible motion yet do lie
With something of agreement ; nor as things
Wholly inert, but lighter than their weight
With strange and inner help :—*then*—Nay for if
The hair grow after death ?   I have read so.
Now a most pallid cheek and leaden lids
Closed lids still livid with her latest pain ;
And on the cheek and on the lid two tears.
Then—but they'll scatter morning flowers upon her,
And if some dew-drops fall upon her face
They must needs be as these—no lovelier
No purer, nor less meet to call to mind
The briny taste of human sorrow.   *Now*
A little stirring of the breast—*then* none.
Now not so much as drives away the fly
Upon her bosom—*then*——

You Gods, I curse ye !
[*After a pause.*

I did not tremble, therefore I can do't.
      [A very long silence, during which she still sleeps
                        at his feet.   Clock strikes.

Another hour, and thou that sleepest there
Hast like a rosy Angel that o'erstands
The pale flat corse that is and is not she,
Stood in my eyes and tried me.   Am I bent
Grey, weathered, travel-stained?   The hidden truth
And secret of that strange geography
We traverse in the journey we call life
I know not; but I know that in this hour
I have inhabited each backward spot
Left long ago, long past and, by my count,
Almost as far behind as Heaven before.
Whenever I did take thee by the hand
With fatal purpose, thou sweet looking up
Didst lead my ignorant steps and charmed eyes
To some dear olden scene and moment where
I could not kill thee.   None seemed far and none
More near than any other.   But I turned
Upon the bruisèd body at my feet
And would not see the phantom.   Then it sang.
And then I heard thee like a bell i' the air,
Stirring the silver silence circulate
About thee into music; while around
Dreamy upon the wind the floating past
Circled thee shining, as stained clouds about
The watery moon, and all the ancient joy

Came forth revolving in the coloured void,
Well-wonted, nor life-weary, but with looks
Terribly sweet, as waiting on thy voice
And only lacking thee to be again.
And I am shaken with grief and my black fate
Shrieks as a night of tempest at my head
And the dream passes like far village chimes
Blown on a rushing twilight full of rain.
I did not tremble; therefore I can do't.
Who if not I?   Poor Dove, Poor Dove, I caught thee
In the eagle's talons and did carry thee
Up to the heights I dared nearest the sun
And scorched thee blind!   And shall my pinions fail
To hurry thee beyond the temperate bound
Of mortal anguish, or refuse that great
And consummating mercy-stroke that cleaves
The last of vital ether and doth end
Captive and captor in the final blaze
Of solar conflagration !   I can do it.
Whether these mortal Dædalean wings
Will bear me living to the central pyre,
The dire event must try.   Enough to know
I shall not die till I have seen thee first
In safe destruction; this most exquisite flesh
These tender filaments will have transpired
Invisible in incense filling Heaven
Ere I am ashes.
                    Oh my Beautiful

My Beautiful why wert thou ever mine?
Why didst thou love me?   What had I to do
With thee?   Oh Eve, oh happy happy Eve,
Why didst thou hear my voice?   Was Paradise
Too narrow to content thee?   Paradise
That if thou wert immortal would have brought
Some better flower for every sweeter day
Of thy still blest for-ever; nor had asked
More answering care than this—that for the fame
Of her dear handiwork thou shouldst not bend
Thy cheek above her blushing rose nor wear
Her lily in thy breast!   What dost thou here?
Have I the hand that pencils the white page
Of snowdrops, or doth hang on the fine ear
Of each unhurt fair blossom morn by morn
Its pendulous jewel; is my manly texture
Soft as the silken slopes of Venus' thigh,
That I should touch thee?   Can 1 give thee food
Celestial? or what vital element
Dissolve in a sweet draught of delicate air
And serve thee?   Is my home an amber tent
Of April cloud?   Are my black oaken floors
Light-paven levels such as spirits walk
At moon-rise?   Can I take an evening mist
And dip it in the west and clothe thy limbs
With gold and purple?   Have I zephyr-winds
To wait upon thee, and to snood thine hair
With gossamer?   Then wherefore art thou mine?

That any immortality of pangs
The damned know not might buy this boon for me,
This only boon—to set thee back again
In thy first best estate! to wrench mine heart-strings
From thy life's web and burn them in deep hell!
What weary Angel exiled from the skies,
Her baby at her breast, with failing strength
Paused at this earth and left thee? Thou wert not
Of us and being grown up shouldst have gone
Back to thine heaven; or having business here
It should have been in some excepted task
Set out and sacred from the common lot.
If there be any still and vesper hour
More pure than all the day, thou shouldst have been
Its tutelar, to lead it in and out,
Versed in the duteous season and each rite
Of welcome and farewell. This changeful earth
Should be to thee a garden where we take
Rare pleasaunce and in happy weather walk
But do not dwell. Thou shouldst have dwelt afar
With everlasting Morning, going forth
With her and from her chaste urn unrebuked
—Dipping thy sinless hand—shouldst sprinkle dews
Or at the side of Spring, her handmaiden
Bearing her violets, what time she comes
Over the hills descending shouldst have passed
Into this valley blessing it and me.
And shouldst have loved me only while the fields

Were sown, nor pitied me forlorn, nor heard
My vows, nor faithless to thy Goddess-queen
Forgot thy better duty, but have gone
When she went, singing o'er the southern slopes
Joyous beside her; turning on the height
For my sake and in richer violet-beds
Betraying that thine hand relaxed with thought.
So thou shouldst still have left me and returned
With the pervading year, for ever young,
Till that sad season when thy tearful care
Found not the old man on the wonted hill
Nor by the thorn nor the memorial tree;
And made a time of strange forget-me-nots
And melancholy flowers that love the rain
Setting the fairest banks with saddest blooms
And by a grassy mound in one deep dell
Beating thy breast let fall the store of spring,
So that to other vales the spring came late
Tarrying for thee.   And whenceforth thou being given
To sudden sighs and musings didst not keep
Thine old unblamed attendance, and no more
Didst sow thy flowers with free impartial hand,
But, sick with fitful fancies, oft delayed
Oft hasted, till for many hapless years
Spring lost her fame on earth; nay had a weird
And crazy name, because that fall by fall
Thou still remindful didst steal back alone
To trim my grave, and ever and anon

After the snows were white didst visit me
Being ill at rest; and lo! in that strange dell
Unseasonable thaws and timeless flowers
And none knew why.

              But I have taken thee
And in my coarse and savage ignorance
Put thee to mortal uses.   Bent these hands
Which from some flowery chalice should have fed
The early bee, to grind the daily bread
Of household travail, set to vulgar toil
These tender fingers which were made to unfold
The plaited wings of butterfly or know
One violet from another, and this frame
For which if she had found it anywhere
Forsaken Nature of herself had wrought
Peculiar season, left a prey to harsh
Inclement fortunes, torn by winds of woe,
Bit by the frosts of poverty and struck
To the scorched marrow by the burning stroke
I did not feel. 'Thou art avenged! avenged!
Oh Amy! wilt thou go back to thy fields
Of childhood, and the walls of the old home
That loved thee? Wilt thou wander late at eve,
When all the west is still and black, and pass
Among the dim trunks of remembered trees
Like a returning sunset? Will the flowers
Be fairer there to-morrow, and grey men
Look on the year and praise it with the years

Of youth, and all the village that so long
Had drooped for thee, like a revivèd plant
That drinks by dark a subtle sustenance
Which no man seeth, lift the sudden head
That yesterday was low?   There wilt thou be
Oread and Naiad, or from many oaks
Whisper thy secret, wander like a sigh
Thro' green woods where we wandered, or persuade
Misfortune from the happy cots we loved,
Or spread by tranquil Night or genial Day
Felt but unseen a necessary health
Within, without, thro' all the charmèd place,
The hearth serener and the happier bed,
The ways auspicious and the waters safe?
No go not there !   The very paths are yet
Bare with my footsteps.   I shall haunt thee still.
I have distraught thy world, and thy poor skill
Can never recompose it.   Night by night
Thou shouldst behold me in the western sky
Dyed with thy blood. Spring, Summer, Autumn, Winter,
Should be the racking seasons of the day
I killed thee ; every custom of mankind
A various form of murder ; aye the knife
Upon the unoffending cottage board
Round which the children sit, should rise unheld
And stab thee to the heart.
                              Rather return
Into this general nature, whereof thou

Art not so much a part or element
As the consummate whole in a given space
More visible,—a ripple of the sea.
The whole is happy; sink into the whole.
I think there is no separate tenement
—No, though thou wert an angel far in heaven—
Where thy meek subject soul would. dare refuse
Ingress to mine.   Better be re-dissolved,
Nor have one atom of thine unconstrained
Free essence so defined as to receive
The local weight of sorrow, nor a sense
So fashioned to contain a human thought
As to remember me !

SCENE XL.

The Study.

BALDER, *solus, at the open window.*

Balder. Oh you o'er-arching and high heavens on
  whom
I call, because that as remote from me
. Ye must be good ; that as diverse from me
Ye must be strong; that as serene above
The comprehension of my human sense,
Ye may be happy ; is it well, you heavens,
That ye look down on such a thing as I ?

If your innumerous hosts be seraphs crowned,
Thronèd, with radiant limbs and upturned eyes
Reflecting God,—and such, methinks, but now
I saw at eve ere the great choir was filled
Taking their thrones expectant of the hour,
And for the general anthem one by one
Tuning their harps and shedding dewy tears
Ecstatic,—if they sit there to adore,
And have perpetual function of mere praise,
Were it not wise, ye heavens, to draw your clouds
Between us?   I was faithful once as they,
And mighty as the mightiest who doth sweep
His golden starry strings, and with the sound
Lighten these tuneless deeps.   If I were God
They should not see this heart.

SCENE XLI.

The Study.

Balder, *solus, by the window.*

Balder. And once since then it hath been night and
      day.
Before my open eyes the useless sun
Perfunctory again hath been drawn up
Over yon east.   Why I know not, nor care,
For in my soul the season hath not changed.   [*Pauses.*

It must be done.   *How* I have learned so well
That the dread lesson going to and fro
On the bare surface of my beaten brain
Hath trod out its own footsteps.   Yet once more
Let me dispose it in the attitude
Of due performance.   This most sovereign gift
Of long-sought death should be the last and best
Of all our sweet love-tokens, and bestowed
In the ripe moment and receptive throb
Of her consent, my hint and cue to be
Her own entreaty.   Good.   ·   [*Pauses.*
     ' That I might die,'
And then I strike.   [*Pauses.*
   —Who struck?   Liar, not I !
For in this forehead came the mortal dint
And stunned me ! Down from my flayed shoulders thou
Intolerable weight that like a beast
Hast dropt on me out of the mystery
And blackest umbrage.   I have enough to bear,
I hurl thee off—aye, tho' thou clawest my life
And rollest into Hell.   I have not sinned !
It is no sin !   Did she not beg for death ?
Is it not blessed to give ?   And if the gift
Bankrupt the giver—how?   You heavens, if I
Am merely poor that she who gave her mite
Was Crœsus' widow !
     Did she not pray too ?
Have I not heard her at midnight and noon ?

And she was righteous, and her righteous prayer
Must needs avail : what is to come must come.
Whether by thunder-bolt, or secret touch
Of plague, or undetermining event
Of irrespective hap, or by the hand
Of love, how guiltier?   Beast, I have not sinned !
Off !—Why 'tis well.   Thus as with sudden shout
I scare it from me, and these worse within
That like a pack of hungry wolves disperse
A moment into darkness and return
Ravening the more.   Vain labour to vain end.
Even let them gorge their full.   My pride is carrion
And stinks to be devoured.   Hie in you hell-dogs
And split your hides !   There is no good in me ;
Why cavil in what fashion I shall wear
The necessary evil of an essence
Inexorably bad?   If that which lives
In this detested arm had warmed the sap
And swelled the branches of some innocent tree,
A murderer would have plucked it.

      Do you weep
Ye heavens?   Let fall your balmy tears in vain.
Aye, make the grass green that she may not tread ;
Let brooks prate idly, fill the empty earth
With wasted flowers.   What matter?   Have your will
Niggard or good.   None evermore shall see
Or hear.   My Beautiful, my Beautiful,
Thou art slain ! Thou art slain !

God, that I had not been ;
That I had perished in my father's veins !
That some fore-blasting flash had dried me up,
And nature had not known an hour or womb
So cursed as to conceive me !

[*He sits silent for two hours by the window.*

Forty times and five,
And every time to each twin beak a meal ;
Two meals and but a single fly to each
Fourscore and ten ; but I perceive the bird
Feedeth by favour, and the further beak
That hath a forward air and overhangs
The pendant threshold at each dole enjoys
A double bounty.   Do both parent birds
Concern in this fond labour ?   I think both.
They seem alike ; but measuring with mine eye
By the small boles and bosses of the nest
I mark that the alternate visitant
Plants its right tiny foot where the left claw
Of the last comer rested, and this so
Not once or twice within the laws of chance,
But in such due succession as bespeaks
Or choice or habit personal.   If choice
Then both by differentia, since in birds
The sense of numbers, if such sense exist,
Solely perceptive must of need omit
Numerical relation, and if habit
Both by the hypothesis.

                                    Oh thou great grief,
That like a lion at the foot of a tree
Dost wait for me—gape thy red jaws ! I come !
It must be done.   The very day is doomed.
A shut and funeral city hung with black
Is not more different from the daily streets
Than this day from another.   As on morn
Of foul and horrid execution
The sullen Tyrant orders from the North
His hideous hordes upon the glowing land
That loved the captive, Winter ere his time
Upon the genial season hath advanced
Sudden with all his Power.   Down the moist walls
The long snail slimes ; cold things of fen and pool
Come within doors and as a native stone
Do crawl the grisly hearth ; and in my soul
This palpable obscurity repeats
The outer darkness, and within, without,
Cosmic and microcosmic, as yon twain
Round answering hemispheres, world answers world.
I cannot see the hills or the mild sky,
Or aught of gentler aspect that beheld   .
Might yet dissuade me.   To mine inward eyes
That might have met unmanned such sweet array
Of sacred opposition, there is now
Nought but the inner mist and through the mist
A path stark clear.   Therefore it must be done.
As one who having stared upon the sun,

Turning his eyeballs downward doth bedaub
The blotted world with black, to my hot sight
A moving pall is in the air and when
I think of her it falls upon the face
I could not slay.   Therefore it must be done.
Nature herself consenting to the deed
Lets her veil round it, and to me shut in
Of all her universe doth leave alone
The victim and the knife.   Therefore, oh God,
It must be done.   [*He attempts to rise.*
                    I will arise.   Rare moment!
The slow will hath not reached the idle thews,
Yet, being dispatched, the irrevocable deed
Is now in act, and I that have not moved
Already am felonious.   What! is this
A dream, that the strong cause o'ershoots the effect
And passes with its message the untouched
Dull functions it should stir?   At length I stand.
What! am I chained?   Have I trunk-hose of lead?
The door—the door—my limbs do help the ground
Sucking me in.   The threshold is not yet.
I labour against the stedfastness o' the air,
Which bars my breast, and, as two walls of ice
Falling together with mine head between,
Enlocks me.   Hands, hands, nothing but hands—Ah !
Is it so horrible that very nothing
Conceives to stay it?   Off! I will be free.
Darkness at noon !   Aye,. aye, the flood swells fast.

This lightning——   [*Sinks in a swoon.*
                    [*After lying long he recovers and sits up.*
A swoon? So best. Zero once past is past,
And the uncounted scale beneath hath not
A credible extreme. I am a man
Who with the very gate of death shuts out
Each earthly work behind him, and, with all
His human powers in one, comes back to do
A single office. By this strait I leave
The womb of failing nature, and am born
Invincible ; safer perhaps to know
The range of chance, and stronger to have felt
The worst of mortal weakness. Weakness? Bah !
I turned the sword of manhood in my hand
And with mine eye I tried it, and on edge
The broad attempered steel went out of sight.
A true Damascus blade !   [*Clock strikes.*
                    One, two, three, four,
Five, six, seven. Never trembling wretch that hears
The form of Justice, strained at the approach
Of that one final word that holds his fate,
As I for that last stroke.
I well remember that at eight o'clock
We, far asunder, kept a tryst in Heaven
Night after night for years. At that sweet hour,
She had a prayer she used to say for me,
And ever since I think the very time
Repeats it. I have need of prayers to-night,

And I do think the evening air so oft
Ensweetened with her deprecating breath
Will then be gracious for her.

                        I'll not haste
Nor to the moment of the deed abate
One jot that smooths the doing. [*Going to the window.*

                          Brittle world !
Thou hast another hour ere I do break thee.
For she shall live until the clock strikes eight.
Oh heavy, heavy curfew !

SCENE XLII.

THE VACANT STUDY.

*Busts, books, a harp, &c.   A locked writing-case on the
table.*

Enter AMY (*her face very pale,—her hair dishevelled,—
her dress disordered*).

   Amy.   Aye—this is the place,
This is the chamber of his nights and days.
Let me lie close.   Where be these mistresses
For which his lawful wife must sit in the shade?

              [*Taking up the writing-case.*
What are you in here?   [*Shaking the case.*

            Do you know me, girls?
This makes the treason full ; I have endured

Too long.   Have I not loved him like a god ?
Am I not beautiful?   Is it no shame
That he should leave these limbs for harridans
That I can shake together in a box?
It must be ended—I will wait him here
And he shall do me right. [*Crouches down in a corner.*

Enter BALDER.—*He stands a long time silent.* ·

Balder.   Ye pale companions, marble counsellors,
Who for so many years have been content
To ratify my will; or in the shine
Of whose mysterious influence I have been
The unwitting creature of a power unknown
Wrought by the pitiless necessity
Of your supreme ascendant; Deities
Or Slaves,—I know not whether—but not stones !
Ye who have darkened with me as white brows
Of the invulnerable rocks with thunder,
And in my triumphs have been moved as gods
Changing unchangeable with such a truth
Of inner motion that the deferent eye
Obeyed the conscious soul and saw a change
Sweeter than mortal beauty, like the smiles
That flit and flicker in dim light about
The lips of death !   Oh thou dear sanctuary,
Wherein as in a body I have dwelt
The informing spirit, finding more and more

My wish forelaid, my wants fulfilled in thee,
Till going forth from thee the plastic sense
Subserves thee, absent, and I stretch the hand
To the familiar distance, and raise vain eyes,—
As an unbodied ghost new given to air
Enfolds the immaterial arms, and strains
To lift the wonted limbs ! my stringless harp,
—Poor empty skull that hadst so sweet a tongue—
Ye broken tablets ;—

[Opening the case and taking forth a scroll.
Thou material soul,

Thou uncontained dimension, thou dead self,
Which art not I, and shalt perhaps revive
When this I am is nought ; thou wondrous voice
That canst be seen and touched ; thou strange parhelion
That wilt not set with me ; thou Ariel
Fast in the rifted pine ; thou Afreet dread
And fierce, whom, sealed by a strong sign of power,
As in a charmèd vial thus I hold
Inert and silent, so that a child's hand
May bear thee harmless, place thee here and here,
Take thee and leave thee,—thou that being loosed
Mayst leap forth like a blast of the simoom
And tear a host to tatters ; thou entombed
And mummied past ; thou colourless substantial
Which in a light unrisen shalt be called
A microcosm of beauty ; thou dull moonstone
Dark as cold lava now—that rushing o'er

The upturned heads of nations might'st have shone
A blazing portent, troubling thrones of kings;
Thou black uncomely root; thou trifling seed;
Thou grain of poison or of antidote
So little and so much; thou extillation
And sacred concrete of the golden cloud
That filled the azure of my years, and like
The legendary water-drop that falls
On Abyssinian summit and becomes
Egyptian harvests—wert to flood the earth;
Oh thou that I have made in fear and awe
And ignorance, knowing only thou canst smite
Angels and fiends, and shake the shrines of Gods;
Thou hidden secret, master Alchemy
And cunningest composition of mine art,
Which as a fireball with this unknown hand
Approaching through the dark I thought to throw
Into the smouldering ashes of mankind
And see, with thunder like the clap of doom,
From earth to heaven—as if a pillared light
Shot up from the rent centre of the world—
The midnight of my wretched race made day
With my unthought-of glory—

[AMY, *rising suddenly, approaching wildly, snatches the
    scroll and throws it through the open window into
    the moat.*

    Amy.   Glory? see!

Can it light up that pit down where I dwell

Out of the light of day and of the stars?
Out of the light o' the grave;—Aye, the dull earth
Below the dead is not so black with night
But the great day shall stir it!   Is it well
That the dull earth below the dead hath light
And I am dark for ever?   Is that well?
Is that well, husband?   Husband, is it well?
Oh yes, thy glory!   Yes—he must have glory,
Yes, he must have his glory; he can stand
All day in the sun, but he must have his glory!
He has walked here up in the sunshine world,
He has been in the wind and the sweet rain,
And none cried ' Upset the cup o' the honey-time,
Upset the cup o' the honey-time,'
And I am empty and dry.

> [*Looks vacantly on the ground.*

Thy glory?
I pray thee, husband, tell me what it is.
Is it a god that it can set me free?
Hath it limbs to burrow?   Can it reach me?
Is it any thing that I have known?
There was Love—I knew it—thou taughtest me.
How many songs hast thou not sung of love?

> [*Sings.*

 ' When first I courted thee, Amy,
  The years we knew were fair and few,
 I was gay as break of day,
  And thou wert pure as dew.

I looked into thy face, Amy,
 No word I said, no tear I shed,
My love-light true fell in thy dew,
 And came back rosy-red.'

Or,

 'Love broke his golden bow, chasing thee long ago,
  Then the boy cried,
  Thou didst in pity turn '——

     Nay not that, but,

  'Come love, and bring
  Sweet hope and joy '——

    Words, words ! what are they, down
Where I am ?   Oh, my husband, would it reach me ?
Dost think that it would reach me for thy sake ?
Dost think it would ?   And will it fetch me back
Being thine ?   I do remember all things thine
Did love me.   There was never dog of thine
But if I looked would run before my eyes
And bay for pleasure ; if I dropped my glove
'Twould carry it, poor Pompey !   Bay ?   Who spoke
Of Bays ?   Is this a time to mock me, Husband ?
Yet some one hath said somewhat of the sea ;
I think I heard it ; Didst thou speak of the sea ?
Why do I see the sea ?   And was it kind
That thou shouldst maunder to me of the sea ?
To me ?   To me ?   Alas ! the moonlight water !
Dost thou mind when we sailed together, love,
We two alone, and thou didst say the moon

Was like a silver boat,—and so the silver
Slanted—I know not how,—and I fell in
Deep, deep.   But I am deeper, deeper now.
I think the sea-rocks gaped and I fell here
With all the sea between me and the wind,
And the sea-rock between me and the sea.
I strike it thus.—

           [*Striking her head against the stone wall.*

Balder.   My Amy !

Amy.   Why how now?

Do not move me, but rather move it for me ;
For why should I lie here out of the world?
Thou knowest not, husband, what it is to lie
With all the sea between thee and the wind,   ·
And the sea-rock between thee and the sea.
I say why should I lie here?   Out of all
The beauty of the earth, the blessed chime
Of things, the touch and furthest cast of good,
The common warmth of human kind, the voice
Of man or God?   Out of the very sea
That rolls and rolls above my aching head
And will not cool these lips?   Man, what have I
To do with thee?   How long is't since we two
Drew near?   If I am altered since we met,
What then?   Have we dwelt at the further poles
For nought?   Because my puppet warmed thy bed
And filled thy chair have we been side by side?
Ah, ah ! didst never look in at the eye

And miss me? What, didst never hear my heart
Like a clock ticking in an empty house?
Husband? Ah, ah, ah, ah, ah, ah, ah, ah,— [*Pauses.*
Do not disbelieve.
They will scoff at thee, they will shake thy dream
Out of thy soul, they will deny, deny
This where I am, but thou hast heard a voice
Out of its depths, thou hast heard it ! does it sound
Like a beloved familiar? Is there fire
Above-ground that could smelt what thou didst love
To this? Hast met it anywhere on earth
My husband? Aye, and have I frightened thee
Into my mate? Shoot out thine eyeballs more !
See ! see !   [*Dancing before him.*
              Thou canst not shut up ears and eyes.
List to my voice, my voice which I upheave
As I did force it through a dome of brass.
Mine hour is come. I will cry in thine ears
And burst in crying. Canst thou tell how deep
By the sound? Black—black—Hast a good ear for
     colour?
It bubbles thro' it all, up—up—I think
Thou dost not hear me, but thou shalt hear once,
Once, only once, and I will be so silent,
So silent—thou shalt not look pale at me,
Thou shalt not chatter thy long teeth at me,
Thou shalt not show out thy black beard at me.
What, does it grow so fast? What, have I scared thee?

What, does the white skin shrink back down the roots?
Art thou a porcupine? What! Shall I dance?
Aye, husband, dance and sing; aye, hear me sing.
Hear! thou *shalt* hear; my voice is coming up;
Hark, hark, it comes; dyed with the dark, it comes!
Now it comes into me, now I will cry;   [*She shrieks.*
I am his wife! This is my murderer!
Make way, make way, this is a murderer!
I am in hell, slain, lost, robbed, murdered, mad,
He did it, he!

    Balder.   He knows it.

    Amy.   Mad, mad, mad.

                 [*Sinking in his arms in a swoon.*

    Balder. Now, now, my soul! it must be ere she wake.
I will bear this alone; she shall not know
The hand that strikes—This hand! Nor man nor fiend
Would do thee harm but me! Now—now—yet oh!
That it must be now. That it had been while
The fire of madness burned her, and she swelled
And blackened like a burning house, once home,
Now but a house in flames. For home is not
The stone that holds it; and the elements
That once were Amy, and which marked thy place
And made thee visible, were neither thou
Nor all thou wert to me, nor all thou art,
Lying this moment here, here as of old,
And with no sign in heaven or earth to say
That thou canst never waken as of old.

Yet one more kiss which thou canst not return.
Return?   And hast thou given thy last?   Oh, Amy,
Wake, wake! My last?   And taken as the others?
                              [*Bows his head into his hand.*
Accursed coward, and is this thy love?
Poor slaughtered innocent, thou hadst good right
To scorn me!   Closer, closer to my heart,
There thou didst find the bane, and shouldst receive
The final counterpoison.   [*Begins to divest her.*
                              Heaving breast,
How oft have I undone thy weeds as now,
And very softly, very silently
As now—and not more tenderly, no not
More tenderly, no, on thy bridal night,
No, not more tenderly.   But oh, you heavens,
Wherefore and wherefore?
                         Here, under her bosom,
It cannot fail here.   Hide thee, hide thee, Heart;
Poor fluttering bird, why wilt thou stir the lilies?
Dost thou not know me who I am?   Soft, soft;
Thou hast so often struggled in mine arms
Asleep, and I have wakened thee with kisses,
I pray thee do not struggle now, my child,
I cannot rouse thee from this dream.
                              Oh God,
If she should clasp her hands upon her breast
And moan! If she should feel through this thin trance
The cold steel ere it pierce and call on me

For help!—but I will hold thee fast, my child,
Fast in these arms altho' thou start and cry,
And shield thee from myself! If I strike ill
The first stroke, and she wake and strive for life ;
If she should ope her eyes but once too late
And go forth to believe for evermore
I struck unkindly—   [*Throws a kerchief over her face.*
         No, she shall not see me.
And now thy living face is gone for ever,
And I have murdered thee before thy time.
Nor God nor Demon could have wrung from me
This moment, this last moment, only thou,
Oh, only thou.—   [*Frantically lifts the kerchief.*
       Amy!
         Thou, thou, all thou!
Help me, my child. Aye, look so beautiful.
'Tis well ; if there be heaven this is not
To kill thee.—Now.

THE END.

LATER

MISCELLANEOUS POEMS.

LATER MISCELLANEOUS POEMS.

THE MAGYAR'S NEW-YEAR-EVE.

(1859.)

By Temèsvar I hear the clarions call :
The year dies.   Let it die.   It lived in vain.
Gun booms to gun along the looming wall,
Another year advances o'er the plain.
The Despot hails it from his bannered keep :
Ah, Tyrant, is it well to break a bondsman's sleep?

He might have dreamed, and solved the conscious throes
Of Time and Fate in some soft vision blest :
Sighed his thick breath in childhood's happy woes,
Or spent the starry tumult of the breast
On some dear dreamland maid, nor known how high
The blind heart beats to hours like this.   'Tis nigh !

Lo in the air a trouble and a strife ;
I feel the future.   Mighty days to come
Strain the strong leash a moment into Life :
Shapes beckon : voices clamour and are dumb :

And viewless nations charge upon the blast
That blows the spectral host to silence, and is past.

Hark, hark! the great hour strikes! The stroke peals
    ' one ; '
Again! again! God! Have the earth and sky
Stopped breathing? Will it never end? 'Tis done.
The years are rent asunder with a cry,
The big world groans from all her gulphs and caves,
And sleeping Freedom stirs, and rocks the martyrs'
    graves.

Oh ye far Few, who, battle-worn and grey,
Watch from wild peaks the plains where once ye bled,
Oh ye who but in fortune less than they
Keep the lone vigil of the immortal Dead,
Behold! And, like a fire from steep to steep,
Draw, draw the dreadful swords whereon ye lean and
    weep!

And oh you great brave harvest, that, war-ploughed
And sown with men, a grateful country yields,
You bearded youth who, beardless, saw the proud
Ancestral glories of those smoking fields
That now beneath ten grassy years lie cold,
Rise! Shew your children how your fathers fought of old!

But we are fettered, and a bondsman's ire,
Howe'er it flash, can only end in show'rs.

Who shall unlade these limbs? Alas, the fire
Of passion will not melt such chains as ours;
We have but heated them in wrath of men
To harden them in women's tears.   What then?

Less than both hands at once what Freeman gives
To Freedom?   Stand up where the Tyrant stands,
Draw in one breath the strength of slavish lives,
Lift the twin justice of your loaded hands,
And with that double thunder in the veins
Launch on his fated head the vengeance of your chains!

They hear!   I see them thro' dissolving night!
Like sudden woods they rise upon the hills!
The mountains stream with a descending sight,
The hollow ear of vacant landscape fills,
From side to side the living landscape warms,
To arms!   Yon bleeding cloud is spread!   Day breaks!
      To arms!

Aye, Tyrant, the day breaks.   Look up and fear.
To arms!   A greater day than day is born!
To arms!   A larger light than light is near!
A blacker night than midnight foams with morn!
Arise, arise, my Country, from the flood!
Arise, thou god of day, and dye the east with blood!

THE YOUTH OF ENGLAND TO GARIBALDI'S LEGION.[1]

(1860.)

O YE who by the gaping earth
　Where, faint with resurrection, lay
An empire struggling into birth,
　Her storm-strown beauty cold with clay,
The free winds round her flowery head,
Her feet still rooted with the dead,

Leaned on the unconquered arms that clave
　Her tomb like Judgment, and foreknew
The life for which you rent the grave,
　Would rise to breathe, beam, beat for you,
In every pulse of passionate mood,
A people's glorious gratitude,—

But heard, far off, the mobled woe
　Of some new plaintiff for the light;
And leave your dear reward, and go
　In haste, yet once again to smite

[1] Those 1,067 Cacciatori, who, after conquering in the Lombard campaign, set out, unassisted, and 'looking upon themselves as already dead' (vide *Times*), to complete, in face of a fleet and three armies, the work of Italian emancipation.

The hills, and, like a flood, unlock
Another nation from the rock;

Oh ye who, sure of nought but God
   And death, go forth to turn the page
Of life, and in your heart's best blood
   Date anew the chaptered age;
Ye o'er whom, as the abyss
O'er Curtius, sundered worlds shall kiss,

Do ye dream what ye have done?
   What ye are and shall be?   Nay,
Comets rushing to the sun,
   And dyeing the tremendous way
With glory, look not back, nor know
How they blind the earth below.

From wave to wave our race rolls on,
   In seas that rise, and fall, and rise;
Our tide of Man beneath the moon
   Sets from the verge to yonder skies;
Throb after throb the ancient might
In such a thousand hills renews the earliest height.

'Tis something, o'er that moving vast,
   To look across the centuries
Which heave the purple of a past
   That was, and is not, and yet is,
And in that awful light to see
The crest of far Thermopylæ,

And, as a fisher draws his fly
   Ripple by ripple, from shore to shore,
To draw our floating gaze, and try
   The more by less, the less by more,
And find a peer to that sublime
Old height in the last surge of time.

'Tis something : yet great Clio's reed,
   Greek with the sap of Castaly,
   In her most glorious word midway
Begins to weep and bleed ;
And Clio, lest she burn the line
Hides her blushing face divine,

While that maternal muse, so white
   And lean with trying to forget,
Moves her mute lips, and, at the sight,
   As if all suns that ever set
Slanted on a mortal ear
What man can feel but cannot hear,

We know, and know not how we know,
   That when heroic Greece uprist,
Sicilia broke a daughter's vow,
   And failed the inexorable tryst,—
We know that when those Spartans drew
Their swords—too many and too few !—

A presage blanched the Olympian hill
　To moonlight : the old Thunderer nods ;
But all the sullen air is chill
　With rising Fates and younger gods.
Jove saw his peril and spake : one blind
Pale coward touched them with mankind.

What, then, on that Sicanian ground
　Which soured the blood of Greece to shame,
To make the voice of praise resound
　A triumph that, if Grecian fame
Blew it on her clarion old,
Had warmed the silver trump to gold !

What, then, brothers ! to brim o'er
　The measure Greece could scarcely brim,
　And, calling Victory from the dim
Of that remote Thessalian shore,
Make his naked limbs repeat
What in the harness of defeat

He did of old ; and, at the head
　Of modern men, renewing thus
Thermopylæ, with Xerxes fled
　And every Greek Leonidas,
Untitle the proud Past and crown
The heroic ages in our own !

Oh ye, whom they who cry 'how long'
  See, and—as nestlings in the nest
  Sink silent—sink into their rest;
Oh ye, in whom the Right and Wrong
That this old world of Day and Night
Crops upon its black and white,

Shall strike, and, in the last extremes
  Of final best and worst, complete
  The circuit of your light and heat;
Oh ye who walk upon our dreams,
And live, unknowing how or why
The vision and the prophecy,

In every tabernacled tent—
  Eat shew-bread from the altar, and wot
Not of it—drink a sacrament
  At every draught and know it not—
Breathe a nobler year whose least
Worst day is as the fast and feast

Of men—and, with such steps as chime
  To nothing lower than the ears
  Can hear to whom the marching spheres
Beat the universal time
Thro' our Life's perplexity,
March the land and sail the sea,

O'er those fields where Hate hath led
   So oft the hosts of Crime and Pain—
   March to break the captive's chain,
To heal the sick, to raise the dead,
And, where the last deadliest rout
Of furies cavern, to cast out

Those Dæmons,—ay, to meet the fell
   Foul belch of swarming Satan hot
   From Ætna, and down Ætna's throat
Drench that vomit back to hell—
In the east your star doth burn;
The tide of Fate is on the turn;

The thrown powers that mar or make
   Man's good lie shed upon the sands,
Or on the wave about to break
   Are flotsam that nor swims nor stands;
Earth is cold and pale, a-swoon
With fear; to the watch-tower of noon

The sun climbs sick and sorrowful,
   Or, like clouded Cæsar, doth fold
   His falling greatness to behold
Some crescent evil near the full.
Hell flickers; and the sudden reel
Of fortune, stopping in mid-wheel

Till the shifted current blows,
   Clacks the knocking balls of chance :
   And the metred world's advance
Pauses at the rhythmic close ;
One stave is ended, and the next
Chords its discords on the vext

And tuning Time : this is the hour
   When weak Nature's need should be
   The Hero's opportunity,
And heart and hand are Right and Power,
And he who will not serve may reign,
And who dares well dares nought in vain.

Behind you History stands a-gape ;
   On either side the incarnadine
   Hot nations in whom war's wild wine
Burns like vintage thro' the grape,
See you, ruddy with the morn
Of Freedom, see you, and for scorn

As on that old day of wrath
   The hosts drew off in hope and doubt,
   And the shepherd-boy stept out
To sling Judæa upon Gath,
Furl in two, and, still as stone,
Like a red sea let you on.

On ! ay tho' at war's alarms
   That sea should flood into a foe !
   On ! the horns of Jericho
Blow when Virtue blows to arms.
Numberless or numbered—on !
Men are millions, God is one.

On ! who waits for favouring gales ?
   What hap can ground your Argosy ?
A nation's blessings fill your sails,
   And tho' her wrongs scorched ocean dry,
Yet ah ! her blood and tears could roll
Another sea from pole to pole.

On ! day round ye, summer bloom
   Beneath, in your young veins the bliss
   Of youth ! Who asks more ? Ask but this,
—And ask as One will ask at Doom—
If lead be true, if steel be keen ?
If hearts be pure, if hands be clean ?

On ! night round ye, the worst roak
   Of Fortune poisoning all youth's bliss ;
Each grass a sword, each Delphic oak
   An omen ! Who dreads ? Dread but this,—
Blunted steel and lead unsure,
Hands unclean and hearts impure !

Full of love to God and man
  As girt Martha's wageless toil ;
  Gracious as the wine and oil
Of the good Samaritan ;
Healing to our wrongs and us
As Abraham's breast to Lazarus ;

Piteous as the cheek that gave
  Its patience to the smiter, still
  Rendering nought but good for ill,
Tho' the greatest good ye have
Be iron, and your love and ruth
Speak but from the cannon's mouth—

On ! you servants of the Lord,
  In the right of servitude
  Reap the life He sowed, and blood
His frenzied people with the sword,
And the blessing shall be yours,
That falls upon the peacemakers !

Ay, tho' trump and clarion blare,
  Tho' your charging legions rock
Earth's bulwarks, tho' the slaughtered air
  Be carrion, and the encountered shock
Of your clashing battles jar
The rung heav'ns, this is Peace, not War

With that two-edged sword that cleaves
   Crowned insolence to awe,
And whose backward lightning leaves
   Licence stricken into law,   ,
Fill, till slaves and tyrants cease,
The sacred panurgy of peace !

Peace, as outraged peace can rise
   When her eye that watched and prayed
Sees upon the favouring skies
   The great sign, so long delayed,
And from hoofed and trampled sod
She leaps transfigured to a god,

Meets amid her smoking land
   The chariot of careering War,
   Locks the whirlwind of his car,
Wrests the thunder from his hand,
And, with his own bolt down-hurl'd,
Brains the monster from the world !

Hark ! he comes ! His nostrils cast
   Like chaff before him flocks and men.
   Oh proud, proud day, in yonder glen
Look on your heroes ! Look your last,
Your last : and draw in with the passionate eye
Of love's last look the sights that paint eternity.

He comes—a tempest hides their place !
   'Tis morn.   The long day wanes.   The loud
   Storm lulls.   Some march out of the cloud,
The princes of their age and race ;
And some the mother earth that bore
Such sons hath loved too well to let them leave
      her more.

But oh, when joy-bells ring
   For the living that return,
   And the fires of victory burn,
And the dancing kingdoms sing,
And beauty takes the brave
To the breast he bled to save,

Will no faithful mourner weep
   Where the battle-grass is gory,
And deep the soldier's sleep
   In his martial cloak of glory,
Sleeps the dear dead buried low?
Shall they be forgotten?   Lo,

On beyond that vale of fire
   This babe must travel ere the child
Of yonder tall and bearded sire
   His father's image hath fulfilled,
He shall see in that far day
A race of maidens pale and grey.

Theirs shall be nor cross nor hood,
　　Common rite nor convent roof,
　　Bead nor bell shall put to proof
A sister of that sisterhood ;
But by noonday or by night
In her eyes there shall be light.

And as a temple organ, set
　　To its best stop by hands long gone,
　　Gives new ears the olden tone
And speaks the buried master yet,
Her lightest accents have the key
Of ancient love and victory.

And, as some hind, whom his o'erthrown
　　And dying king o'er hill and flood
Sends laden with the fallen crown,
　　Breathes the great trust into his blood
Till all his conscious forehead wears
The splendid secret that he bears,

For ever, everywhere the same,
　　Thro' every changing time and scene,
In widow's weeds and lowly name
　　She stands a bride, she moves a queen ;
The flowering land her footstep knows ;
The people bless her as she goes,

Whether upon your sacred days
   She peers the mightiest and the best,
Or whether, by the common ways,
   The babe leans from the peasant's breast,
While humble eyelids proudly fill,
And momentary Sabbaths still

The hand that spins, the foot that delves,
   And all our sorrow and delight
Behold the seraph of themselves
   In that pure face where woe grown bright
Seems rapture chastened to the mild
And equal light of smiles unsmiled.

And if perchance some wandering king,
   Enamoured of her virgin reign,
Should sue the hand whose only ring
   Is the last link of that first chain,
Forged by no departed hours, and seen
But in the daylight that hath been,

She pauses ere her heart can speak,
   And, from below the source of tears,
The girlhood to her faded cheek
   Goes slowly up thro' twenty years,
And, like the shadow in her eyes,
Slowly the living Past replies,

In tones of such serene eclipse
   As if the voices of Death and Life
Came married by her mortal lips
   To more than Life or Death—'A wife
Thou wooest; on yonder field he died
Who lives in all the world beside.'

Oh, ye who, in the favouring smile
   Of Heaven, at one great stroke shall win
The gleaming guerdons that beguile
   Glory's grey-haired Paladin
Thro' all his threescore jousts and ten,
—Love of women, and praise of men,

The spurs, the bays, the palm, the crown,—
   Who, from your mountain-peak among
Mountains, thenceforth may look along
   The shining tops of deeds undone,
And take them thro' the level air
As angels walk from star to star,

We from our isle—the ripest spot
   Of the round green globe—where all
   The rays of God most kindly fall,
And warm us to that temperate lot
Of seasoned change that slowly brings
Fruition to the orb of things,

We from this calm in chaos, where
   Matter running into plan
   And Reason solid in a man
Mediate the earth and air,
See ye winging yon far gloom,
Oh, ministering spirits ! as some

Blest soul above that, all too late,
   From his subaltern seat in heaven
Looks round and measures fate with fate,
   And thro' the clouds below him driven
Beholds from that calm world of bliss
The toil and agony of this,

And, warming with the scene rehearst,
   Bemoans the realms where all is won,
And sees the last that shall be first,
   And spurns his secondary throne,
And envies from his changeless sphere
The life that strives and conquers here.

     .

But ere toward fields so old and new
   We leap from joys that shine in vain,
And rain our passion down the blue
   Serene—once more—once more—to drain
Life's dreadful ecstasy, and sell
Our birthright for that oxymel

Whose stab and unction still keep quick
   The wound for ever lost and found,
Lo, o'erhead, a cherubic
   And legendary lyre, that round
The eddying spaces turns a dream
Of ancient war! And at the theme

Harps to answering harps, on high,
   Call, recall, that but a strait
   Of storm divides our happy state
From that pale sleepless Mystery
Who pines to sit upon the throne
He served ere falling to his own.

LOVE.

TO A LITTLE GIRL.

(1862.)

WHEN we all lie still
Where churchyard pines their funeral vigil keep,
Thou shalt rise up early
While the dews are deep;
Thee the earliest bird shall rouse
From thy maiden sleep,
Thy white bed in the old house
Where we all, in our day,
Lived and loved so cheerly.
And thou shalt take thy way
Where the nodding daffodil
Tells thee he is near;
Where the lark above the corn
Sings him to thine ear;
Where thine own oak, fondly grim,
Points to more than thou canst spy;
And the beckoning beechen spray
Beckons, beckons thee to him,
Thee to him and him to thee;

Him to thee, who, coy and slow,
Stealest through dim paths untrod
Step by step, with doubtful glance,
Taking witness quick and shy
Of each bud and herb and tree
If thou doest well or no.
Haste thee, haste thee, slow and coy!
What! art doubting still, though even
The white tree that shakes with fear
When no other dreams of ill,
The girl-tree whom best thou knowest,
Waves the garlands of her joy,
And, by something more than chance,
Of all paths in one path only
The primroses where thou goest
Thicken to thy feet, as though
Thou already wert in heaven
And walking in the galaxy.
Do those stars no longer glisten
To thy steps, ah! shivering maid,
That, where upper light doth fade
At yon gnarled and twisted gate,
Thou dost pause and tremble and so,
Listening stir, and stirring listen?
Not a blossom will illume
That chill grove of cambering yew
Wherein Night seems to vegetate,
And, through bats and owls, a dew

Of darkness fills the mortal gloom.

Haste thee, haste thee, gaze not back !

Of all hours since thou wert born,

Now thou may'st not look forlorn ;

Though the blackening grove is dread,

Shall he plead in vain who pled

'To-morrow?'   Through the tree-gloom lonely

One more shudder, and the track

Softens : this is upland sod,

Thou canst smell the mountain air,

What was heavy overhead

Lightens, the black whitens, the white brightens !

Ah, dear and fair,

Lo the dazzling east, and lo,

Someone tall against the sky

Coming, coming, like a god,

In the rising morn !

And when the lengthening days whose light we never saw

Have melted his sweet awe,

And thy fond fear is like a little hare,

Large-eyed and passionately afraid,

That peepeth from the covert of her rest

Into the narrow glade

Between two woods, and doth a moment dare

The sunshine, and leap back ; yet forth will fare

Again, and each time ventures further from the nest,

Till, having past the midst ere she be 'ware,

Bold with fear to be so much confest

She flees across the sun into the other shade;
Flees as thou that didst so coyly draw
Near him and nearer, and art trembling there
Midway 'twixt giving all and nought,
In a moment, at a thought,
Bashful to panic, hidest on his breast;
Once again beneath the hill
Where round our graves these funeral pines refuse
The clamorous morning, thou shalt rise up early
When we all lie still.
Thou shalt rise up early while
Down the chimney, ample and deep,
Dreaming swallows gurgle, and shrill
In window-nook the mossy wren
Chirps an answer cheerly,
Chirps and sinks to sleep.
In the crossed and corbelled bay
Of that ivied oriel, thou
Lovest at morn and eve to muse;
But this once thou shalt not stay
To mark the forming earth. and how
Far and near, in equal grey
Of growing dawn, thy well-known land
Now to the strained gaze appears
The nebulous umbrage of itself, and now,
Ere one can say this or this,
Divides upon the sense into the world that is,
As the slow suffusion that doth fill

Tender eyes with soft uncertainties,
Suddenly, we know not when,
Shapes to tears we understand;
Such tears as blind thy eyes with light,
When thou shalt rise up, white from white,
In thy virgin bed
On that morn, and, by and by,
In thy bloom of maidenhead
Beam softly o'er the shadowy floor,
And softly down the ancient stairs,
And softly through the ancestral door,
And o'er the meadow by the house
Where thy small feet shall not rouse
From the grass those unrisen pray'rs,
The skylarks, though thy passing smile
Shall touch away the dews.
And thou shalt take thy way,
Ah whither? Where is the dear tryst to-day?
Trembler, doth he wait for thee
By the ash or the beech-tree?
With the lightest earliest breeze
The dodder in the hedge is quaking,
But the mighty ash is still a-slumber;
All its tender multiplicity
Drooped with a common sleep, by twos and threes,
That triple into companies,
Which, in turn, do multiply
Each by each into an all

So various, so symmetrical,
That the membered trunk on high
Lifts a colour'd cloud that seems
The numberless result of number.
Now still as thy still sleep, soft as thy dreams,
They slumber; but when morning bids
The world awake, the giant sleeper, waking,
Shall lift at once his shapely myriads up,
As thou at once upliftest thy two lids.
Ah, guileless eyes, from whom those lids unclose;
Ah, happy, happy eyes! if morning's beams
Awake the trees, how can they sleep in yours?
Look up and see them start from their repose!
Yet nay, I think thou wouldst forbid them hear
What some one comes this morn to say;
Therefore, sweet eyes, shine only on the ground,
Nor venture to look round,
Lest thou behold how subtly the flow'rs sigh
Among the whispering grasses tall,
And see thy secret pale the lily's cheeks,
Or redden on the daisy's lips,
Or tremble in the tremulous tear
Wherewith the warmer light of day fulfils
That frigid beauty of the wort whose stars
Look, thro' the summer darkness, like the scars
Of those lunar arrows shot
From the white string of that silver bow
Wherewith, as we all wot,

Because it was a keepsake of her Greek,
Diana shooteth still on every moony night.
What is it, then, that this close buttercup
Is shutting down into a golden shrine?
What hath the wind betrayed to the wind-flow'r,
That, on either side, it so adjures
Thy passing beauty, by such votive hands
Point to point with praying finger-tips?
I know not how such secrets go astray,
Nor how so dear a mystery
Foreslipped the limits of its destined hour;
Perhaps, the mustered spring, in whatsoe'er
Deep cavern of the earth, ere it come here,
It takes the flowery order of the year,
Heard the soft powers speak of this loveliness
That in due season should be done and said,
As if it were a part o' the white and red
Of summer; or perchance some zephyr, willing
To sweeten the stol'n fragrance of a rose,
Caught one of thy breaths, and blew it
To the flow'rs that suck the evening air,
And in it some unspoken words of thine
Went thro' the floral beauty, and somewhere
Therein came to themselves, and made the fields aware.
Thus, or not thus, surely the cowslips knew it;
Else wherefore did they press
Their march to this sole day, and long ago
Set their annual dances to it?

This day of all the days that summer yields?
Didst thou not mark how sure and slow
They came upon thee with exact emprise?
First a golden stranger, meek and lone,
Then the vanward of a fairy host
Following the nightingales,
Bashful and bold, in sudden troops and bands,
Takes the willowy depths of all the dales,
And, on unsuspected nights,
Makes vantage-ground of mounts and heights
Till, ere one knew, a south wind blew,
And a fond invasion holds the fields!
Over the shadowy meadowy season, up and down from
    coast to coast,
A pigmy folk, a yellow-haired people stands,
Stands and hangs its head and smiles!
And art thou conscious that they smile, and why?
That with such palpitating flight
Thou fleest toward the linden-aisles?
Ah, yet a moment pause among
The lime-trees, where, from the rich arches o'er thee,
The nightingale still strews his falling song
As if the trees were shaken and dropt sweetness;
No heed? More speed? Ah, little feet,
Is the ground soaked with music that ye beat
Silver echoes thence, and keep
Such quick time and dainty unison
With the running cadence of the bird

That he hath not heard
A note to fright him or offend,
While down the tell-tale path from end to end
Such a ringing scale has run thro' his retreat?
The limes are past, and ye speed on;
Ah, little feet, so fond, so fleet,
Fleeter than ever—why this fleetness?
Who is this? a start, a cry!
A blind moment of alarms,
And the tryst is in his arms!
Fluttering, fluttering heart, confess
Truly, didst thou never guess
That he would be here before thee?
Didst thou never dream that ere
The last glow-worm 'gan to dim,
Or the dear day-star to burn,
Or the elm-top rooks to talk,
Or the hedge-row nests to threep,
He was waiting for thee here?
Ah! ne'er so fair, ah! ne'er so dear,
For his love's sake pardon him,
Smile on him again, and turn
With him thro' the sweetbrier glade,
With him thro' the woodbine shade;
In the sweetbrier wilderness,
To his side, ah! closer creep,
In the honeysuckle walk
Let him make thee blush and weep,

While the wooing doves, unseen,
Move the air with fond ado,
And, lest the long morning shine
Show you to some vulgar eye,
To ye, passing side by side,
With a grace that copies thine,
Favouring trees their boughs incline ;
While, where'er ye wander by,
Hawthorn and sweet eglantine
From among their laughing leaves
Stretch and pluck ye by the sleeves :
And all flow'rs the hedge doth hide
Sigh their fragrance after you ;
And sly airs, with soft caresses,
Letting down thy golden tresses,
Marry those dear locks with his ;
While from the rose-arch above thee,
Where the bowery gate uncloses,
Budded tendrils, lithe and green,
Loosen on the wind and lean
Each to each, and leaning kiss,
Kiss and redden into roses.
Oh, you Lovers, warm and living !
And ah, our graves, so deep and chill !
As ye stand in upper light
Murmuring love that never dies,
While your happy cheeks are burning,
Will ye feel a distant yearning ?

Will a sudden dim surprise
Lift up your happy eyes
From what you are taking and giving,
To where the pines their funeral vigil keep,
And we all lie still?
Love on, plight on, we cannot hear or see.
Oh beautiful and young and happy! ye
Have the rich earth's inheritance.
For you, for you, the music and the dance
That moves and plays for all who need it not,
That moved and played for us, who, thus forgot,
In the dark house where the heart cannot sing
Nor any pulse mete its own joyous measure,
See not the world, nor any pleasant thing;
And ye, in your good time, have come into our pleasure.
Ah, while the time is good, love on, plight on!
Leap from yourselves into the light of gladness!
The light, the light! surely the light is sweet?
And, if descending from those ecstasies,
Ye touch the common earth with wavering feet,
Your life is at your will; whate'er betide,
We shall not check or chide.
The hand is dust that might restrain;
The voice whose warning should distress ye
By any augury of doubt or sadness,
Can never speak again.
The angel that so many woo in vain
Descends, descends! Ah, seize him ere he soar;

Ah, seize him by the skirt or by the wing;
What matter, so that, like the saint of yore,
Ye do not let him hence until he bless ye?
In our youth we had our madness,
In the grave ye may be wise.
Love on, love on, for Love is all in all!
Manners, that make us and are made of us,
Who with the self-will of an infant king
Do fashion them that have our fashioning,
And make the shape of our correction;
Virtue, that fruit whose substance ripens slow,
And in one semblance having past from crude
To sweet, rots slowly in the form of good;
Joy, the involuntary light and glow
Of this electric frame mysterious,
That, radiant from our best activities,
Complexion their fine colours by our own;
And Duty, the sun-flower of knowledge,—these
Change and may change with changing time and place:
But Love is for no planet and no race.
The summer of the heart is late or soon,
The fever in the blood is less or more;
But while the moons of time shall fill and wane,
While there is earth below and heaven above,
Wherever man is true and woman fair,
Through all the circling cycles Love is Love!
And when the stars have flower'd and fall'n away,
And of this earthly ball

A little dust upon eternity
Is all that shall remain,
Love shall be Love: in that transcendent whole
Clear Nature from the swift euthanasy
Of her last change, transfigured, shall arise;
And we, whose wonted eyes
Seek vainly the familiar universe,
Shall feel the living worlds in the immortal soul.
But nor of this,
Nor anything of Love except its bliss,
On that summer morning shalt thou know;
Nor, in that moment's apotheosis
When, like the sudden sun
That, rising round and rayless, bursts in rays,
And is himself and all the heavens in one,
Love in the sun-burst of our own delight
Makes us for an instant infinite,
Owning no first or last, before or after,
Child of Love, shalt thou divine
That, years and years before thy day,
In the little Arcady
And planted Eden of thy line,
On such mornings such a maid
Lived and loved as thou art living and loving,
Through the flowery fields where thou art roving,
And in the favourite bowers and by the wonted ways,
Stepped the morning music with thy grace;
Smiled the sunshine which thou with her face

Smilest ; so, with sweeter voice,
Helped the vernal birds rejoice,
Or, when passing envy stayed
Matins green and leafy virilays
Startled her sole self to hear,
Like a scared bird hushed for fear ;
Or, more frightened by my passionate praise,
Rippled the golden silence with shy laughter.
Yet I saw her standing there,
While my happy love I made,
Standing in her long fair hair,
And looking (so thou lookest now)
As when beneath an April bough
In an April meadow,
Light is netted into place
By a lesser light of shadow ;—
Standing by that tree where he
This morn of thine makes love to thee
Leaning to his half-embrace,
Leaning where, full well I know,
While slow day grows ripe to noon
Thou untired shalt still be leaning,
Still, entranced by Love's beguiling,
Listening, listening, smiling, smiling ;
Leaning by the tree—Ah me,
Leaning on the name I cut
In the bark which, while she tarried here,
Chased it with duteous silver year by year ;

But from the hour that heard her coffin shut
Blindly closed over the withered meaning,
Till argent vert and verdant argentrie
Encharged each simple letter to a rune.
Ah me, ah me! the very name
To which—another yet the same—
(The same, since all thy loveliness is she,
Another, since thou dost forget me)—
Thou answerest, as she answered me
When on summer morns she met me,
While the dews were deep,—
She whom earliest bird did rouse
From her maiden sleep,
From her bed in the old house,
Her white bed in the old house,—
She whom bird arouseth never
From that sleep upon the hill
Where we all lie still.

For what is, was, will be.   Suns rise and set
And rise: year after year, as when we met,
In one brief season the epiphany
Of perfect life is shown, and is withdrawn;
As maidens bloom and die : but Maidenhood for ever
Walks the eternal Spring in everlasting Dawn.

AN AUTUMN MOOD.

(1863.)

PILE the pyre, light the fire—there is fuel enough and to
    spare;
You have fire enough and to spare with your madness
    and gladness;
Burn the old year—it is dead, and dead, and done.
There is something under the sun that I cannot bear:
1 cannot bear this sadness under the sun,
I cannot bear this sun upon all this sadness.
Here on this prophecy, here on this leafless log,
Log upon log, and leafless on leafless, I sit.
Yes, Beauty, I see thee; yes, I see, but I will not rejoice.
Down, down, wild heart! down, down, thou hungry dog
That dost but leap and gaze with a want thou canst not
    utter!
Down, down! I know the ill, but where is the cure?
Moor and stubble and mist, stubble and mist and moor,
Here, on the turf that will feel the snows, a vanishing
    flutter
Of bells that are ringing farewells,
And overhead, from a branch that will soon be bare,

Is it a falling leaf that disturbs my blood like a voice?
Or is it an autumn bird that answers the evening light?
The evening light on stubble and moor and mist,
And pallid woods, and the pale sweet hamlets of dying
    men.
Oh, autumn bird! I also will speak as I list.
Oh, woods! oh, fields! oh, trees! oh, hill and glen!
You who have seen my glory, you who wist
How I have walked the mornings of delight—
Myself a morning, summer'd through and lit
With light and summer as the sunny dew
With sun: you saw me then—   ,
You see me now; oh, hear my heart and answer it.
Where is the Nevermore and the land of the Yesterdays?
    Aye,
Where are Youth and Joy, the dew and the honey-dew,
The day of the rose, and the night of the nightingale?
    Where—
Where are the sights and the sounds that shall ne'er and
    shall e'er
Come again?
Once more I have cried my cry, once more in vain
I have listen'd; once more, for a moment, the ancient
    pain
Is less, though I know that the year is dead and done.
Once more I hear
Under the sun the sadness, over the sadness the sun.
Bear? I have borne, I shall bear. But what is a man

That his soul should be seen and heard in the trees and
    flow'rs of the field?
Have I tinctured them mortal? or doth their mortality
    yield
Me like a fragrance of autumn? Ah! passion of Eve,
Ah! Eve of my passion,—which is it that aches to com-
    plain?
Oh, old old Minstrelsy, oh, wafty winds of Romaunt,
Blow me your harps. My sick soul cannot weave
These gossamers of feeling that remain
To any string whereon its ill may grieve.
Blow me your harps—harp, wind-harp, dulcimer,
Citerne, bataunt,
And mandolin, and each string'd woe
Of the sweet olden world, and let them blow
By me, as in sea-streams the sea-gods see
The streaming, streaming hair
Of drownèd girls, and every sorrowy sin
O' the sea.
And so let them blow out the din
Of daylight, and blow in,
With legendary song
Of buried maids,
The evening shades.
And when the thronging harps, and all
The murmurings of wild wind-harps,
Are still;
And shimmer of dim dulcimer,

And thrill of trill'd citerne,
And plaint of quaint bataunt, and throb of long
Long silent mandolin,
And every other sound that grieves,
Hath dropt into its colour on the leaves,
In the silence let me hear
The round and heavy tear
Of orchards fall.
And as I listen let the air unseen
Be stirr'd with words;
Let the ripe husk of what is gape open and shed
What has been;
Through click of gates and the games
Of the living village at play,
Let me hear forgotten names
Of ancient day.
Down like a drop of rain from the evening sky
Let somewhat be said;
Up from the pool, like a bubble, let something reply,
In the tongue of the dead.
Through the swallows that fly their last
Round the grey spire of the past,
In the faded elms by the height,
Let the last hour of light
Strike, and the yellow chimes
Forget and remember
A dream of other times. ·

And above let the rocks be warm with the mystical day
    that is not
To-day or to-morrow;
And from the nest in the rock let me hear the croon
Of orphan-doves that yearn
For the wings that will never return.
And below the rocks, on the grassy slopes and scarps,
Let the tender flowering flame of the exquisite crocus of
    sorrow
Sadden the green of the grass to the pathos of gentle
    September.
And below the slopes and scarps, where the strangled
    rill
Blackens to rot,
Let the unrest of the troublous hour
Blossom on through the night, and the running flow'r
O' the fatuous fire flicker, and flicker, and flare,
Through the aimless dark of disaster, the aimless light of
    despair.
And meantime, let the serious evening star
Contemplative, enlarge her slow pale-brow'd
Regard, until she shake
With tears, and sudden, snatch a hasty cloud
To hide whate'er in those pure realms afar
Is likest human sadness: and, full-soon,
Let night begin to slake
The west; and many-headed darkness peer
From every copse and brake;

While from a cottage nigh,
Where the poor candle of dull Poverty
May barely serve to show
Her stony privilege of woe,
Or if, like her, it try
To leave the cabin'd precincts of its lot,
Steals trembling forth to struggle and expire ;
A milkless babe that shall not see the morn
Starves to the fretted ear, ·
With lullaby and lullaby,
And rocking shadow to and fro
Athwart the lattice low ;
And from yon western ridge, black as the bier
Of day, let a faint, far-off horn,
Mourning across the ravish'd fields forlorn,
Sound like a streak of sunset seen through the grief of the
     moon.
And, further yet, from the slant of the seaward plain,
The bleating and lowing of many-voicèd flocks and herds,
Forced from their fields, mix on the morning breeze
With sob of seas,
Till the long-rising wind be high,
And, from the distant main,
A gale sweep up the vale, and on the gale a wail
Of shipwreck fill and fail,
Fail and fill, fill and fail, like a sinking, sinking sail
In the rain !
But ere all this to us let the dim smoke rise !

To us from the nearest field, from the nearest pyre
Of stubbled corn, let the dim smoke rise; and let
The fire that loosens the stubble corn
Loose the soul like smoke, and let tears in the eyes
Confuse the passionate sense till the heart forget
Whether we be the world, or whether the fading world be
We.

SONNETS

AND OTHER SHORT POEMS.

(Several among these existed only in MSS. and had not received the writer's finishing work.)

SONNETS AND OTHER SHORT POEMS.

TWO EPIGRAMS.

I.

ON A PORTRAIT PRESENTED TO J. Y. SIMPSON, M.D. (AFTERWARDS SIR JAMES SIMPSON).

UNTO myself my better self you gave.
I give yourself yourself : but ah, my friend,
In how inverse a ratio !   To amend
The unjust return these thanks are all I have,
Except a sigh, when that poor 'all' is o'er,
To feel, alas, no less your debtor than before.

II.

ON THE DEATH OF EDWARD FORBES.

Nature, a jealous mistress, laid him low.
He woo'd and won her; and, by love made bold,
She showed him more than mortal man should know,
Then slew him lest her secret should be told.

ON A RECENTLY FINISHED STATUE.

1854.

SAID Sculptor to immaculate marble—'Show
Thine essence; into necessary space
Most pure describe thine unshaped Purity!'
And lo this Image! As a bubble blown,
Swiftly her charms, dilating, went through all
The zones of sphered Perfection, till the stone
Smiled as to speak. Some coming thought half-shown
Forms on her parting lips, so that her face
Is as a white flow'r whence a drop of dew,
White with the fragrant flow'r, inclines to fall.
'Oh Everlasting Silence keep her so!
Immortalise this moment, lest she grow
To such a living substance as can die!'
He cried. Consent Eternal heard his cry.

THE CONVALESCENT TO HER PHYSICIAN.

FRIEND, by whose cancelling hand did Fate forgive
Her debtor, and rescribe her stern award,
Oh with that happier light wherein I live
May all thine after years be sunned and starred !
May God, to Whom my daily bliss I give
In tribute, add it to thy day's reward,
And mine uncurrent joy may'st thou receive
Celestial sterling ! Aye and thou shalt thrive
Even by my vanished woes : for as the sea
Renders its griefs to Heaven, which fall in rains
Of sweeter plenty on the happy plains,
So have my tears exhaled ; and may it be
That from the favouring skies my lifted pains
Descend, oh friend, in blessings upon thee !

SAMUEL BROWN.

(Died, on September 20, 1856, at Morningside, near Edinburgh, Dr.
Samuel Brown, well known and dear to the fit and few through-
out England and Scotland.   He was struck with mortal illness
when on the eve of completing the scientific labours to which his
splendid talents had been devoted ; and, after eight painful years
of patient and unconquered hope, was obliged to leave the demonstration of his discoveries to the good fortune of future times.)

HE came with us to thy great gates, oh Thou
Unopened Age.   Our noise was like the wind
Chafing the wordy Deep ; but broad and blind
They stood unmoved.   Then He,—we knew not how,—
Laid forth his hand upon them.   Lo, they grind
Revolving thunders ! Lo, on his dark brow
The unknown light ! Lo   *   *   *
        *   *   *   Azrael came behind
And touched him.   They clanged back, and all was Now.
We wondered and forgot; but He, unbent,
With eye still strained to the forbidden day,
Towered in the likeness of his great intent
As if his act should be his monument,
Till Azrael pitied such sublime dismay,
And led him onward by another way.

TO PROFESSOR AND MRS. J. S. BLACKIE.

IF Time that feeds love dies to die no more,
Immortal hours, dear friends, were yours and mine ;
For Morn that on the hills oped eyes divine,
And Eve that walked like Mary by the shore
Where that old Dreamer, as he built, of yore,
Saw her, and told his dream in such a shrine [1]
As was a kind of Mary, and the shine
Of Noon, and starry censers swinging o'er
With Night, all made ye dearer : thou whose soul,
Palimpsest of a dead and living world,
Taketh no dust from that nor stain from this,
And thou who with thyself hast so empearled
The writing—knowing well how rare it is—
That the scrolled jewels and the jewelled scroll
In total more than both complete a married whole.

[1] Tintern Abbey, dedicated to the Virgin.

TO THE AUTHORESS OF 'AURORA LEIGH.'

WERE Shakspeare born a twin, his lunar twin
(Not of the golden but the silver bow)
Should be like thee : so, with such eyes and brow,
Sweeten his looks, so, with her dear sex in
His voice, (a king's words writ out by the queen,)
Unman his bearded English, and, with flow
Of breastfull robes about her female snow,
Present the lordly brother.   Oh Last-of-kin,
There be ambitious women here on earth
Who will not thank thee to have sung so well !
Apollo and Diana are one birth,
Pollux and Helen break a single shell.
Who now may hope ?   While Adam was alone
Eve was to come.   She came ; God's work was done.

TO MRS. J. S. BLACKIE.

DEAR Friend, once, in a dream, I, looking o'er
The Past, saw the Four Seasons slow advance
Dancing, and, dancing, each her cognizance
So gave and took that neither dancer bore
Her sign, but in another's symbol wore
An amulet to lessen or enhance
Herself: till as they fast and faster dance
I see a dance and lose the dancing four.
Thus thy dear Poet, at his sportive will,
Commingling every seasonable mood
Of old and young, and the peculiar ill
Of each still healing with the other's good,
Bends to a circle life's proverbial span
Where childhood, youth, and age are unity in man.

DEDICATORY.

(This Sonnet, evidently intended as a dedication to his wife of the
poems published under the title of 'England in time of War,'
appears not to have satisfied the writer, as it existed, till now,
only in manuscript.)

BEAUTY is One.   But that so equal gold,
Run in the apt and kindly difference
Of each receptive and significant sense,
Configures to our many-minded mould.
Therefore, oh Love, though I no more behold
That sometime world where summer eloquence
I saw and spake, (adding nor time nor tense,
But singing forth the silent music old),
Yet walled in winter cities still sing I ;
For conscious of thy beauty mere and whole,
The perfect unit of thy face and soul
(Thy face thy soul confest to mortal eye,
Thy soul thy face by new perceptions known),
Thy One becomes my Many.   Take thine own.

SISTER TO SISTER,

ON RECEIVING A PORTRAIT IN A LOCKET.

'WHEN I received that love which is a face,
When I perceived that face which is a love,
Two voices, like those two old nations, strove
Within my heart, and the first-born gave place
And served the younger. " Ah this golden space
Doth cage the airy pinions of my dove!
And ah this value, which might prove and more
Another love, seems simony to the grace
Of ours!" Thus while one passion doth protest,
The other cries: "I care not how it be!
For, givest thou much or little, worst or best,
Nor. am I richer nor thou dispossest;
My fond subtraction is still thine in me,
And all thy dear remainder mine in thee!"'

ON THE DEATH OF MRS. BROWNING.

WHICH of the Angels sang so well in Heaven
That the approving Archon of the quire
Cried, ' Come up hither ! ' and he, going higher,
Carried a note out of the choral seven ;
Whereat that cherub to whom choice is given
Among the singers that on earth aspire
Beckoned thee from us, and thou, and thy lyre
Sudden ascended out of sight ? Yet even
In Heaven thou weepest ! Well, true wife, to weep !
Thy voice doth so betray that sweet offence
That no new call should more exalt thee hence
But for thy harp.   Ah lend it, and such grace
Shall still advance thy neighbour that thou keep
Thy seat, and at thy side a vacant place.

TWO SONNETS ON THE DEATH OF PRINCE ALBERT.

I.

In a great house by the wide Sea I sat,
And down slow fleets and waves that never cease
Looked back to the first keels of War and Peace;
I saw the Ark, what time the shoreless flat
Began to rock to rising Ararat;
Or Argo, surging home, with templed Greece
To leeward, while, mast-high, the lurching fleece
Swung morn from deep to deep.   Then in a plat
Of tamarisk a bird called me.   When again
My soul looked forth I ponder'd not the main
Of waters but of time; and from our fast
Sure Now, with Pagan joy, beheld the pain
Of tossing heroes on the triremed Past
Obtest the festive Gods and silent stars in vain.

II.

AND as I mused on all we call our own,
And (in the words their passionate hope had taught
Expressing this late world for which they fought
And prayed) said, lifting up my head to the sun,
' Ne quibus diis immortalibus,'—one
Ran with fear's feet, and lo ! a voice distraught
' The Prince ' and ' Dead.'   And at the sound methought
The bulwark of my great house thunder'd down.
And, for an instant,—as some spell were sapping
All place—the hilly billows and billowy hills
Heaved through my breast the lapping wave that kills
The heart ; around me the floor rises and falls
And jabbling stones of the unsteady walls
Ebb and flow together, lapping, lapping.

TO 1862.

(IN PROSPECT OF WAR WITH AMERICA.)

I.

OH worst of years, by what signs shall we know
So dire an advent? · Let thy New-Year's-day
Be night.   At the east gate let the sun lay
His crown : as thro' a temple hung with woe
Unkinged by mortal sorrow let him go
Down the black noon, whose wan astrology
Peoples the skyey windows with dismay,
To that dark charnel in the west where lo !
The mobled Moon !   For so, at the dread van
Of wars like ours, the great humanity
In things not human should be wrought and wrung
Into our sight, and creatures without tongue
By the dumb passion of a visible cry
Confess the coming agony of Man.

TO 1862.

II.

EVEN now, this spring in winter, like some young
Fair Babe of Empire, ere his birth-bells ring,
Shewn to the people by a hoary King,
Stirs me with omens.   What fine shock hath sprung
The fairy mines of buried life among
The clods?   Above spring flow'rs a bird of spring
Makes February of the winds that sing
Yule-chants: while March, thro' Christmas brows, rime-
    hung,
Looks violets: and on yon grave-like knoll
A girlish season sheds her April soul.
Ah is this day that strains the exquisite
Strung sense to finer fibres of delight
An aimless sport of Time?   Or do its show'rs,
Smiles, birds and blooms betray the heart of conscious
    Pow'rs?

TO 1862.

III.

METHINKS the innumerable eyes of ours
That must untimely close in endless night
Take in one sum their natural due of light:
Feather'd like summer birds their unlived hours
Sing to them: at their prison pitying flow'rs
Push thro' the bars a Future red and white,
Purple and gold: for them, for them, yon bright
Star, as an eye, exstils and fills, and pours
Its tear, and fills and weeps, to fill and weep:
For them that Moon from her wild couch on high
Now stretches arms that wooed Endymion,
Now swooning back against the sky stares down
Like some white mask of ancient tragedy
With orbless lids that neither wake nor sleep.

TO 1862.

IV.

HARK! a far gun, like all war's guns in one,
Booms.   At that sign, from the new monument
Of him who held the plough whereto he bent
His royal sword, and meekly laboured on,
Till when the verdict of mankind had gone
Against our peace, he, waiving our consent,
Carried the appeal to higher courts, and went
Himself to plead—She whom he loved and won,
The Queen of Earth and Sea,—her unrisen head
Bowed in a sorrowy cloud—takes her slow way
To her great throne, and, lifting up her day
Upon her land, and to that flag unfurl'd
Where wave the honour and the chastity
Of all our men and maidens living and dead,
Points westward, and thus breaks the silence of the
    world :—

TO 1862.

V.

(A QUEEN'S SPEECH.)

'Since it is War, my England, and nor I
On you nor you on me have drawn down one
Drop of this bloody guilt, God's Will be done,
Here upon earth in woe, in bliss on high!
Peace is but mortal and to live must die,
And, like that other creature of the sun,
Must die in fire.   Therefore, my English, on!
And burn it young again with victory!
For me, in all your joys I have been first
And in this woe my place I still shall keep,
I am the earliest widow that must weep,
My children the first orphans.   The divine
Event of all God knows: but come the worst
It cannot leave your homes more dark than mine.'

TO TÖCHTERCHEN, ON HER BIRTHDAY.

As one doth touch a flower wherein the dew
Trembles to fall, as one unplaits the ply
Of morning gossamer, so tenderly
My spirit touches thine.   Yet, daughter true
And fair, great Launcelot's mighty nerve and thew
Best clove a king or caught a butterfly,
(Since each extreme is perfect mastery
—Accurate cause repaid in the fine due
Of just effect—) and, child, it should be so
With Love.   The same that nicely plundereth
The honeyed zephyrs for thy cates and wine
Should train thee with the tasks of toil and woe,
Or hold thee against adverse life and death,
Or give thee from my breast to dearer arms than mine.

TO THE SAME.

TÖCHTERCHENLEIN, by whom the least became
The greatest title of dear Daughterhood,
Who hast not laid down life, nor spilled thy blood
For me, but throbbed them thro' the living frame
Of duteous days less different than the same,
Yet not too much the same to be construed
In number, that still multiplied thy good,
And, by the figure of a changing name
For changeless love, helped my weak utterance
Of thy desert; as step by step we climb
A height, or by a thousand measure one:
I verse this Poetry which thou hast done,
As he who gazing on a rhythmic dance
Finds even his common speech a little keep the time.

TO A FRIEND IN BEREAVEMENT.

No comfort, nay, no comfort.   Yet would I
In Sorrow's cause with Sorrow intercede.
Burst not the great heart,—this is all I plead—
Ah sentence it to suffer, not to die.
'Comfort?'   If Jesus wept at Bethany,
—That doze and nap of Death—how may we bleed
Who watch the long sleep that is sleep indeed !
Pointing to Heaven I but remind you why
On earth you still must mourn.   He who, being bold
For life-to-come, is false to the past sweet
Of Mortal life, hath killed the world above.
For why to live again if not to meet?
And why to meet if not to meet in love?
And why in love if not in that dear love of old?

AT THE GRAVE OF A SPANISH FRIEND.

HERE lies who of two mighty realms was free ;
The English-Spaniard, who lived England's good
With such a Spain of splendour in the blood
As, flaming through our cold utility,
Fired the north oak to the Hesperian tree,
And flower'd and fruited the unyielding wood
That stems the storms and seas.   Equal he stood
Between us, and so fell.   Twice happy he
On earth : and surely in new Paradise,
Ere we have learn'd the phrase of those abodes,
Twice happy he whom earthly use has given,
Of all the tongues our long confusion tries,
That noblest twain wherein the listening gods
Patient discern the primal speech of Heaven.

TO AN AMERICAN EMBASSY.

(WRITTEN AT FLORENCE, 1866.)

SINCE Sovereign Nature, at the happy best,
Is rightful and sole paragon of Art,
Who, tho' she but in part, and part by part,
Paints, carves, or sings the whole, is still possest
By thee, all thee, oh somewhere unconfest
Apollo! in the worlds of men who art
A man, and, with a human body and heart,
Lookest her visible truths, and livest the rest;
Surely that strategy was well design'd
Which, laying siege to Art's proud Capital,
Armed not, against her matchless pow'rs-that-be,
Music, Painting, Sculpture, Poetry,
But sent a living womanhood of all
To queen, by their own laws, the masters of mankind.

JOHN BOHUN MARTIN.

(CAPTAIN OF 'THE LONDON'.)

KEEPING his word, the promised Roman kept
Enough of worded breath to live till now.
Our Regulus was free of plighted vow
Or tacit debt : skies fell, seas leapt, storms swept ;
Death yawned : with a mere step he might have stept
To life.   But the House-master would know how
To do the master's honours ; and did know,
And did them to the hour of rest, and slept
The last of all his house.   Oh, thou heart's-core
Of Truth, how will the nations sentence thee ?
Hark ! as loud Europe cries ' Could man do more ? '
Great England lifts her head from her distress,
And answers ' But could Englishman do less ? '
Ah England ! goddess of the years to be !

FLORENCE : *February,* 1866.

DEPRECATING A GIFT.

(OF SOMETHING MADE BY THE GIVER.)

CHILD, your effectual hands create too much.
The things they fashion having, thenceforth, less
The type of matter than the preciousness
Of you, how can I serve myself of such?
The kindred in my being doth avouch
Your essence; in the very press and stress
Of action I am foiled to a caress.
Ah! give me something you but meant to touch!
Something your love has ripen'd till I'm 'ware
Of thoughts that came in light and stay'd in sweet,
Or th' apostolic shadow of your care,
Passing by, hath healed of malady,
Or wholed in use and grace: gifts rare and meet,
But not too rarely yours to be for me
Still meet, nor meetly mine to be still yours and rare.

PERHAPS.

TEN heads and twenty hearts! so that this me,
Having more room and verge, and striking less
The cage that galls us into consciousness,
Might drown the rings and ripples of to be
In the smooth deep of being : plenary
Round hours ; great days, as if two days should press
Together, and their wine-press'd night accresce
The next night to so dead a parody
Of death as cures such living : of these ordain
My years ; of those large years grant me not seven,
Nor seventy, no, nor only seventy sevens!
And then, perhaps, I might stand well in even
This rain of things ; down-rain, up-rain, side-rain ;
This rain from Earth and Ocean, air and heaven,
And from the Heaven within the Heaven of Heavens.

TO JAMES H.

WITHOUT Life's toil to win Life's earthly prize
What was thy mystery, oh, early Dead?
The careless world but counted thy young head
Among the multifarious heads that rise
And sink, forgot.   For thee, no watching eyes
Starred darkness; no torch led thee to the bed
Of clay.   Yet (if the Apostle justly said
Of all oblation) who or lives or dies
So well as to achieve a fairer fame
Than henceforth should be thine, oh, unknown youth,
Since on your votive marble, for once, Truth
Indites an Epitaph, and, 'neath thy name,
Transcends all laudatory verse in one,
' To him John Hunter raised this tributary stone.'

ON READING A DICTATED LETTER.

DEAR Friend, methinks when thus thy plenary soul
Speaks from yon pale default that lies so low,
The hale and stalwart by thy couch must know
Such fond intoleration to be whole
As he, who, where the storms of battle roll,
Himself unthrown beholds the cannon throw
His father at his feet, and, while a woe
Of splendid shame dements him to that sole
Passion, above the fallen field looks round
The red conversion of the baptized ground
For aught whereon to spend his sanguine wealth
And, seeking not the value but the cost,
Rushes to win whatever, won or lost,
May end this gross unwounded infamy of health.

UNDER ESPECIAL BLESSINGS.

(AUGUST 1869.)

LORD Christ, Lord Christ, ah for a little space
Turn hence.   Some day, when I again am low
In the new dust of whatsoever blow
Time hath in license, from Thy perfect place
Oh let the awful solace of thy face
Sun me, but not now! Lord, Thou seest me!   How
Can I, o'erborne by what Thy hands bestow,
Bear what Thine eyes?   Now, therefore, of Thy grace
I ask but that if ever, as of yore,
Thou lookest up and sigh'st, my kneeling thought
May kiss Thy skirt, and Thou, who know'st if aught
Touch Thee, mayst know, and through Thee, what no
      more
Is I, but, ne'ertheless, began in me,
May rise to Him Whom no man hath seen, nor can see.

ON RECEIVING A BOOK FROM 'X. H.'

OH, great-eyed contemplation whom I saw
Walk by the blue shores of the Northern Sea
Leaning upon a giant, who for thee
Seemed gentle, while black Night far west did gnaw
The jagged Eve, and, near, the flapping caw
Round Beatoun's shadowy Tower croaked down on me
More than the gloom of Night : ere thou couldst see
Beyond the inhuman ruin, or withdraw
Thy soul from eyes, which, as one tune can fill
Two voices, made the pathos of that soul
A double passion, standing dim and still
I saw and wondered.   Is this book thy scroll,
Ah Sybil?   Hast thou writ the unheard cry
I saw thee look that eve to Earth and Sea and Sky?

TO JAMES Y. SIMPSON.

Who, after inestimable benefits to mankind, died in mid-hope of
new achievements.

Oh teeming heart, that, for this once, in vain
Big with our good, didst undeliver'd die,
Had some god got thee with a progeny
O'er-great, that, born, might even dispute the reign
Of Death, as Death had seen the realms of Pain
Won by thine elder brood? We marvell'd why,
So seeming-careless of his sovereignty,
He spared and spared thee : doth this day explain
The Fabian greed that grudged a needless blow?
Knowing too well what deity possest
Thee, did the dead-eyed strategist foreknow
How the huge god must choke the mortal breast?
The mortal breast, deep under clod and sod,
Out of the half-saved world drag down the abortive god?

ON RECEIVING A BOOK FROM DANTE ROSSETTI.

SINCE he is Poet of whom gods ordain
Some most anthropic and perhuman act
Whereby his manhood shall so man his fact
That but his man of man is born again,
And since humanity is most humane,
Not at our pyramid's base, where we have tact
Of dust and supersurge the common tract
Of being, but up there, where form doth reign
To apex, let a Poet ask no fame
But that which, high o'er floods of Life and Death
From singing arks Ararat echoeth
To Ararat, and let him rather be,
Oh Poet, writ on yonder page by thee
Than hear what vulgar breath should make his world-wide
     name.

THREE SONNETS ON LOVE AND BEAUTY.

I.

TO A PROMESSA SPOSA.

Look on this flower, which, from its little tree
Of bodily stem and branches and leaves green,
Leans lovelier, being toucht, and smelt, and seen
A Rose, a Rose, a Rose! and, though thy three
Senses praise it triply unto thee,
And all their parlous difference intervene,
Yet unto thee, who knowest what they mean,
Thee who art one, and hast been, and shalt be,
Is one as thou; one Rose, one beauteous Rose,
One rosy Beauty.   Who shall reason why
The slow stem, on a sudden season, shows
It can be worm unto this butterfly?
We know but this, that when yon ecstasy
Transfigures the green tree, its time of fruit is nigh.

II.

TO THE SAME.

OH Soul! that this fair flower dost so mirrour,
Ask of thyself, saying—' Soul beautiful,
Oh Soul-in-love, oh happy, happy Soul,
That wert so dull and poor, and this sweet hour
Art so more floral even. than a flower,
That in thee it is better'd to a full,
Whereto each former rose is poor and dull,
Ah, what doth thus enlarge thee and empower,
That thou who, at thy most, wert a priesthood,
A vassal strength, a bliss feudàtory,
Hast grown a final joy, an absolute good,
A god that, for being god, believest in God
The more?'   Thou canst not clear this mystery,
Ah happy, happy soul, whose fruit of life is nigh.

III.

TO A FAIR WOMAN, UNSATISFIED WITH WOMAN'S WORK.

IF Beauty is a name for visible Love,
And Love for Beauty in the conscious soul,
Which when commoving to its highest whole,
Or making that whole part of wholes above
Itself, feels, like an eye, that it doth move,
But cannot see the motion visible
To others and in others; if the sole
Difference is ours who see the spirit a dove,
Or feel the dove a spirit; and if in
All worlds Love, Love, as song and text allege,
Sums the full good of life, who shall not bow
To Beauty? Thou, born in her shrine, if thou
Shouldst dare profane her, what would be thy sin?
The sacrilegious priest does more than sacrilege.

TO THE TIBER.

ON ITS LATE (in 1871) INUNDATION OF ROME.

WELL done, old Flood, that, hiding a clear eye
Beneath thy yellow veil, dost wend among
Those epic hills and dales of seven-topp'd song,
To keep watch on the stone eternity
Whereof the mortal tenants die and die;
One more is gone, the deadliest of the long
Line, the foul vast of whose unmeasured wrong
Twined to its summit in the triple Lie
Of that thrice-cursèd Crown.   And thou, brave flood,
Enterest a thousand years of carrion
To swill away the deeps of dung and blood,
And drown the garbaged tribes that stank thereon,
That so, at least, the new investiture
Be on clean threshold and a hearth-stone pure.

This Poem, on the death, in the Ashantee War, of Eardley Wilmot, 'who, early in the day, received a wound that entitled him to leave off fighting, but continued to lead his men till killed by a second wound'—is the last work of the writer, who, probably, intended to condense it into a Sonnet.

WHERE are you, Poets, that a Hero dies
Unsung? He who, when Duty brought too soon
His billet of rest toiled on till he had won
The countersign of Glory? There he lies,
And in the silence of your poesies
He looks a Poem; yea, so made and done
As if the Bardic Heavens had thrown him down
In model to your making. Close his eyes,
That yours may learn him. To fulfil the Law
In Gospel, force the seeds of use to flower
In Beauty, to enman invisible Truth
And then transfigure—this is Poetry.
And this the World and his dear Country saw
Hymned unawares in that unconquer'd youth
Who, scorning to give less than all his power,
Having bled for us, then aspired to die;
And, dying thus, left one more pledge behind
That England may again deserve to lead Mankind.

ENGLAND'S DAY:

A WAR-SAGA.

COMMENDED TO GORTSCHAKOFF, GRANT, AND BISMARCK.
AND DEDICATED TO THE BRITISH NAVY.

1871.

ENGLAND'S DAY.

Russian, Yankee, and Prussian,
Wherever you be,
That stand by the shores of our sea
And shake your fists over,
This is the Castle of Dover,
You knaves!
And yon's the flag unfurl'd,
That shall flog you over the waves
Of the world.
Ay, by the shores of our sea,
You knaves!
For wherever the breeze blows free,
And the hurling, swirling, up and down deeps go
    thundering under and over,
There the sea is our sea,
And there's a Castle of Dover,
Which carries a flag unfurl'd
That shall flog you off the waves
Of the world.

What are you trying to say,
You knaves?
Whatever it be, it so maddens the waves
That not a word comes this way.
Speak up! you've no need to be shy,
This is the land of charity,
Where we never regret the labours
We spend for the sake of our neighbours:
So no more thrimming and thrumming,
But mention whatever you want;
And if you can show us 'tis good for you,
We're just the People to grant.
Should you like, for instance, a drubbing or two?
We'll take neither fees nor thanks,
But do you the very best we can do:
Ay! and do it aboard your own planks,
And ask you nothing for coming!
Louder, my boy, ahoy!
Why what the fiends can you say
That makes such mountainous weather?
You look to be talking loud,
But I hear you no more than I see a feather
That a cyclone spouts to a cloud.
If you've got any breath, don't save it.
Well done! once more! I have it—
'England'—that's good for one's ears—
'England'—all right! and three cheers—
But unless that voice of your own

Can hoist up higher, I'm blest
If I'll catch a word of the rest!
For you no sooner open your jaws
Than there roars such a vast sea-shout
That I hear you no more than I'd hear the daws
If Dover cliffs tumbled down.
Now then, there's a lull, sing out!
Yo hoy! that's better.   Soho!
I've got it!   'England'—Yes—No—
'Has had her day.'   Oh, that's your say—
'England has had her day!'
O ye who bear, on every sea,
That flag of flags, so often sung,
Whose name, in every human tongue,
Is t'other word for Victory,
That banner of eternal youth
Your sires and grandsires, great and good,
Have colour'd with their mortal blood
And cross'd with their immortal truth,
A cheer, a cheer, and you shall hear
News that's worth a British cheer.
Do you see yon braggarts three,
Like three swash-bucklers in a play?
They've found it out for you and me,
So 'twon't be civil to say Nay.
And verse one of chapter A
In this great discovery
Is 'England'—what? ay, wait for that

And while you wait, my hearts, haul down
Your wind-blown pageant of renown,—
Yon glorious weed whose bayonets
The grasping tyrant ne'er forgets,—
Yon harp whose throbbing chords can beat
All sounds of battle but retreat,—
And let the keeper's hand lay low
The lions that ne'er fell to foe;—
Reef, reef the flapping toy away,
England, my hearts,—has had her day!
Now, true-blues, you've heard the news,
Hip hip hip, hurrah?
Not hip hip hip, hurrah, my boys,
But hip hip hip, aha!
From decks to shrouds, from shrouds to clouds,
Hip hip hip, aha!
The stays are taut, the sails are caught,
With ha, ha, ha, ha, ha!
Like woods at play, the big masts sway,
With ha, ha, ha, ha, ha!
The big ships ride from side to side,
With ha, ha, ha, ha, ha!
The north waves roll from pole to pole,
Ha, ha, ha, ha, ha!
From pole to pole the south winds troll,
Ha, ha, ha, ha, ha!
From air to sea, from sea to air,
The cross-clang clamours everywhere,

Ha, ha, ha, ha, ha!
From Baffin Bay, by Matapan,
Round Hindostan, and far Japan,
Back, back, to where it first began,
Ha, ha, ha, ha, ha!
Ha, ha, ha, ha, ha, my boys,
Ha, ha, ha, ha, ha!
The very globe shakes like a man,
With ha, ha, ha, ha!
Russians, Yankees, Prussians, all you
Who stand there scowling at Dover,
' England has had her day '—is that your cry?
Flood and earthquake! it's our cry too!
Had it, had it, a thousand times over!
Yea, and as sure as sky is sky,
And sea is sea, and shore is shore,
You shall see England have one day more!
And such a day shall England have,
That a thousand cities over the wave
Shall wring their bitter hands and say,
' England, England, has had her day!'
Some of us, when that day is done,
You knaves!
Shall go down with the battle sun
In the battle waves.
But as day by day
The sun goes round
Where'er yon flag's unfurled,

And still through dews of morn
Comes back to find Britannia crown'd,
And tell her of her world,
So sure with morrow
At sweet sunrise,
Like mourn of horn,
Like roll of drum,
Like boom of gun,
Like swell of bells,
Our name and our fame
Thro' England's tears shall come
Up the skies !
And, putting by the shades
From early window-pane
Of castled palace or white-cottaged lane,
Pass without rebuke,
And look
On what the sun sees :
Little children on their knees,
And pale dishevelled maids,
And ancient sires whose sorrow is not sorrow,
And mother sitting by the bed,
Where, years ago, was born
The face she shall not see again,
Who bows the passionate winter of the head
And sobs Amen.
And some of us shall come
In triumph home

Beneath yon flag unfurl'd!
Over the foam, over the foam,
Conquerors, conquerors, conquerors home,
Joyously sailing the lightsomest foam
That the gayest of gales ever curl'd.
On, on, over ocean and ocean,
To the goal of the patriot's devotion,
Once more, with heaving heart, to see
The Native-land of all the free,
The Mother-earth of Liberty,
The sacred soil that bears the tree
That sowed the world.
On, on, over ocean and ocean,
On, on, by shores that gaze and wonder,
Shores where friendly cities shout,
Shores where frantic foes blaze out
Their paffing wrath in vain.
On, on, like gods on living thrones of thunder,
Heclas and Ætnas smoking thro' the main;
On, on, like kings and kings,
In wingèd towns and tow'rs with wings;
On, on, town after town,
And, in their train,
Up ocean hill and down hollow,
Horn'd Leviathans that mount and wallow,
And all
The jubilant Elephant-herd of the sea,
That roar and roll and follow

Where the sea-shepherds call.
But some of those who come
In glory home
That day,
Shall envy us who sleep
In the Deep,
Far away !
When they see the eyes that weep,
When they hear the lips that pray,
Because we sleep
Far away !
Millions and millions of eyes that weep,
Millions of lips that cry
To God that day,
Because we sleep
Far away !—
Thousands and thousands of eyes that are dry
As they never were dry till that day,
Because we sleep
Far away !—
Thousands of lips that shall keep
Silence to God and Man that day,—
Silence, silence, deep,—
Deep, deep as the Deep
Where we sleep
Far away !

FRAGMENTS.

INTRODUCTORY NOTE.

THE following Fragments are by no means presented to the reader as compositions which have received, even so far as they go, that loving labour which only would have satisfied their Author. It is not even, in all cases, clear that he had decided to work them up for publication. They are to be viewed as purely tentative designs, including often mere suggestions for further development, mere memoranda of intentions, still to receive their ultimate form. The very hand-writing in which they were found has often been deciphered with so much difficulty (sometimes from partially obliterated pencillings) that, notwithstanding all pains, an erroneous word or phrase may unavoidably have crept into the text.

All these matters will doubtless be candidly borne in mind both by critics and the public.

Those who are responsible for this edition of Mr. Dobell's Poems (it may be stated here that the writer of the 'In Memoriam' is not to be held so responsible) felt it a duty to present this explanation rather than to suppress

the Fragments to which they refer.   Incomplete, rough
and unconnected first drafts though they be, the charac-
teristics of the Author's mind, especially of his psycho-
logical subtlety, are apparent in most of them.   In the
feeling in 'The Olive,' for instance, the sympathy of
Nature with the Divine Tragedy of the Cross, and the
lesson that the whole circumference throbs in affinity to
its Sacred centre, are not the less obvious because the
writer might have altered various details of his exposition.
Readers to whom the idiosyncracies of the Olive are
familiar, who hold in their memories the mystical sensi-
tiveness of its pallid grey-green foliage, sometimes limply
drooping, sometimes crisply uplifted, the resemblance to
drops of coagulated blood of its ripe fruit, the suppleness
of branch and twig, as of 'a lythe and pliant wythe,'
retained even when the trunks in ruggedness of venerable
girth rival our ancient oaks, will readily perceive the
accurate truth of physical feature given to the soul of this
lyric.

In like manner the feeling in 'Snowdrops,'—the only
passage which has been found of a poem that was to
have described what the eye hears and the ear sees in
the world of Spring,—of sympathy between the Poet
and external Nature so intense as to enable one observing
perception to include or to usurp the function of another,
is obvious enough, although of what might have been a
full season of birds and blooms (telling us, among other
things, the look of the soaring song of the lark), we have

only pale firstling blossoms thrown down for us. Of the same feeling many examples are to be found in Mr. Dobell's note-books : for instance of the Cuckoo is written—

> ' His voice the very colour of the cool
> And equal Dawn that like the sound of flutes
> Rose in the woody silence.'

Of the Night—

> ' To see the shining silence of the stars
> And the white quiet of the placid Moon
> Asleep upon the flowery fields of Heaven.'

Of the Sun—

> ' If yon meridian Sun
> Be but the golden clapper to this dome
> The Heaven, and on that mighty bell ring out
> The luminous clangor of a coloured world,
> A sight, a sense, a passion of the soul—'

Of the cry of the Bat—

> ' Well, who has ears to see
> May hear the bee sting, and with the same sense
> See the bat screet; for, by my holidame,
> I hold it conscience to call that a sound
> Whereby yon pricking flitter of the night
> Nettles the April silence.'

FRAGMENTS.

THE OLIVE.

I HAVE heard a friar say
That the Olive learned to pray
In Gethsemane,—
A holy man was he,
Jacopo by name,—
All upon his bended knees
From Jerusalem
He crossed Kedron brook
And to the garden came
Of Gethsemane,
And the very olive-trees
Are there to this day.
And I would have you know,
For I loved to hear him speak,
Good Friar Jacopo !—

That on an Easter-week,
In the time long ago
Of bloody Pilate 'King of Rome,'[1]
Lord Jesus
To the garden-gate did come
Of Gethsemane.
And as He came at the dear look
O' the Lord a sudden shudder shook
The wood, and wooden moans and groans
Allowed the silence of the stones.
(The stones that next day, as 'tis said,
Oped their mouths and spake the dead.)
And when He bent His sacred knees
The shame of limbs that could not bend
Suppled every bough's end
To a lythe
And pliant wythe.
But ere He spake a-silent stood
Every tree in all the wood,
And the silence began to fill
Inly, as the ears with blood
When the outer world is still.
And when He spake at the first
' Let this cup' did somewhat swell
Every twig and tip asunder,
Like the silence in the head

---

[1] Often, as doubtless the reader will remember, so called in old ballads and carols.

When the veins are nigh to burst;
And at the second was nothing seer
To stir, but all the swollen green
Blackened as a cloud with thunder;
But in the final agony,
When His anguish brake its bands
And the bloody sweat down-fell,
At the third ' Let this cup '
As He lifted up His hands
Black drops fell from every tree
And all the forest lifted up.

The Lord went to Calvary—
Well, perhaps, for you and me,
Brother, who being men are fain
To profit by the blessed loss
That quivers overhead while we
At the foot of the cross-mast
With the hereditary face
Reckon up our selfish gain,
Rend his sacred weeds and cast
Lots for the vesture of His grace,—
Aye, at the dabbled foot of the Cross
While that dear blood doth flow.
The Olive cannot chaffer so,
Not being a man, altho'
Since the pallors of that hour
It hath kept a human power

And is not quite a tree;
Now and then
Round the unbelief of men
It lifts up praying hands,
Because it is so much a tree
And cannot tell its tale
Nor reach
To clear its knowledge into speech.
And whether on that awful day
In Gethsemane
There was wind,
Or whether because day and night
And day again all winds that blew
From the City on the height
Shuddered with the things they knew
I know not, but you shall find
An Almighty Memory—
That yearly grows and flowers and fruits
And strikes the blindness of its roots
And suckers forth, but howsoe'er
It blindly beat itself beyond
Its planted first can do no more
Than stretch the measure of its bond
And shape as it had shaped before
The arborous passion that can ne'er
Be paroled into shriving air—
Sicken in the leafy blood
And turn it deadly pale.

And as when a strong malady
Of tertian and quatertian pain,
Turning the cause whence it began
Into the woe of man,
By loops and conduits else too fine
For an incarnadine,
Hath shaken, shaken it from the body into space,
When life and health again co-reign,
And all youth's rosy cheer
Tunes every nerve and summers every vein,
Some crucial habit of the brain
Sudden repeats the unforgotten throe—

SONG OF A MAD GIRL, WHOSE LOVER HAS DIED AT SEA.

(This Song was written, as also the Sleep-song which follows, in the
Isle of Wight, at a house almost overhanging the sea.)

UNDER the green white blue of this and that and the
other,
That and the other, and that and the other, for ever and
ever,
Under the up and down and the swaying ships swing-
swonging,
There they flung him to sleep who will never come back
to my longing.
The Father comes back to his child and the son comes
back to his Mother,
But neither by land or sea
Will he ever come back to me,
Never, never, never
Will he come back to me.
All day I run by the Cliff, all night I stand in the sand,
All day I furrow and burrow the holmes and the heights,
But whether by night or day

There's never a trace or a track,

Never a word or a breath,

In the swill and the swoop and the flash and the foam
    and the wind,

Never a fleck or a speck

Coming, coming my way.

The mew comes back to the strand and the ship comes
    back to the land,

But he will never come back

To all the prayers that I pray thro' the scorching black
    of the day

And the freezing black of the nights,

Never, never come back

To the ear that harks itself deaf and the eye that strains
    itself blind,

And the heart that is starving to death.

He was chill and they threw him to cold,

He was dead and they threw him to drown,

He was weary and wanted rest—

They should have laid him on my breast,

He would have slept on my breast,

But they threw him into the boiling boil and bubble,

The wheel and the whirl, the driff and the draff

Of the everlasting trouble.

I swear to you he was mine! I swear to you he was my
    own.

Madam, if I may make so bold,

Do you know what the dead men do

In the black and blue, in the green and brown?
Deep, deep, you think they sleep
Where the mermen moan and the mermaids weep?
Ah, ah, you make me laugh!
I'm not yet twenty years old,
But lean your ear
And you shall hear
A little thing that I know.
Up and up they come to the top,
Down and down they go down.
To and fro the finny fish go,
But slow and slow, and so and so,
Low over high, high under low,
Up and up they come to the top,
Down and down they go down:
When the sun comes up they come to the top,
When the sun sinks they go down.

FRAGMENT OF A SLEEP-SONG.

SISTER Simplicitie,
Sing, sing a song to me,
Sing me to sleep.
Some legend low and long,
Slow as the summer song
Of the dull Deep.

Some legend long and low,
Whose equal ebb and flow
To and fro creep
On the dim marge of grey
'Tween the soul's night and day,
Washing 'awake' away
Into 'asleep.'

Some legend low and long,
Never so weak or strong
As to let go

While it can hold this heart
Withouten sigh or smart,
Or as to hold this heart
When it sighs ' No.'

Some long low swaying song,
As the swayed shadow long
Sways to and fro
Where, thro' the crowing cocks,
And by the swinging clocks,
Some weary mother rocks
Some weary woe.

Sing up and down to me
Like a dream-boat at sea,
So, and still so,
Float through the 'then' and 'when,'
Rising from when to then,
Sinking from then to when
While the waves go.

Low and high, high and low,
Now and then, then and now,
Now, now;
And when the now is then and when the then is now,
And when the low is high and when the high is low,
Low, low;

Let me float, let the boat
Go, go;
Let me glide, let me slide
Slow, slow;
Gliding boat, sliding boat
Slow, slow;
Glide away, slide away
So, so.

BALLAD.

Oh Ladye fair, oh Ladye fair and mine,
Where'er thou be,
Canst thou divine
The Love that hungers thus in me?
The secret cell where lone I lie and sigh for thee?
Long, long I wait, but shall I wait in vain?
How long the Summer waited for the Rose!

Ah say, oh say I shall not wait in vain!
How long, ah fairest! must I keep
The vigil of unsleeping eyes?
Summer's sighs avail,
Summer that sang himself to sleep,
Summer that piping in a grove all day
Played out his lovelorn soul upon the nightingale,
Oh songs more blest than mine, ah happier sighs!

For at rich midnight all the bells
Of all the valley-lilies rang a tune

Like moonlight up and down the dells,
And June
As a naked maiden thro' the shades
Slipt thro' the woods and took her throne.

By this the east is red and white,
The queen of months is seen and known,
Like flocks of doves that soar and fall,
Like butterflies that hover and alight,
Like tears of ecstasy when tear on tear
From both wild eyes rains thro' the wreathèd hands,
The blush of morning drops upon the lands,
The Rose, the Rose is here!
And rapture, rapture crowns the passion of the year

Hark, hark,
Something stirs the arching green,
Thro' the verdurous aisles the doves are cooing,
And the birds of smaller quire,
As fairies that do run and sing
Before the bridal of their queen,
Flittering and fondly twittering,
Lead thro' the languid air the sick delight of wooing.

Sure thro' the distance dim I see the morn again!
Leaves that meet and part the hues of dawn disclose.
Has she heard my woes?
Has she pitied all my pain?

"Tis she ! 'tis she !

As Summer waited for the Rose

I shall not wait in vain !

As June soft slipping warms the purple Dark,

So thou slippest thro' the shades to me,

So throbs my throbbing heart its thickening throbs to thee.

LORD ROBERT.

Tall and young and light of tongue,
Gallantly riding by wood and lea,
He was ware of a maiden fair
And turned and whispered, 'Remember me.'
(Oh Lord Robert, Lord Robert, Lord Robert,
Oh Lord Robert, 'tis I, 'tis I;
Under their feet where the cross-roads meet
Dost thou think I can lie and lie,
Lord Robert, Lord Robert, Lord Robert?)

Day by day she walks that way
Never hoping by wood or lea
To be ware of the stranger gay
Who turned and whispered, 'Remember me.'
(Oh Lord Robert, Lord Robert, Lord Robert,
Oh Lord Robert, 'tis I, 'tis I;
Under their feet where the cross-roads meet
Dost thou think I can lie and lie,
Lord Robert, Lord Robert, Lord Robert?)

Chance for chance he rides that way,
And again by wood or by lea
He was ware of the maiden fair,
And again he whispered, ' Remember me.'
(Oh Lord Robert, Lord Robert, Lord Robert,
Oh Lord Robert, 'tis I, 'tis I ;
Under their feet where the cross-roads meet
Dost thou think I can lie and lie,
Lord Robert, Lord Robert, Lord Robert?)

Chance for chance that way rode he,
And again where he was ware,
Debonnair to that maiden fair
He turned and said, ' You remember me.'
(Oh Lord Robert, Lord Robert, Lord Robert,
Oh Lord Robert, 'tis I, 'tis I ;
Under their feet where the cross-roads meet
Dost thou think I can lie and lie,
Lord Robert, Lord Robert, Lord Robert?)

Chance for chance on a summer-day,
Meeting her still by wood and lea,
He leaped gay from his gallant grey
And said, ' I see you remember me.'
(Oh Lord Robert, Lord Robert, Lord Robert,
Oh Lord Robert, 'tis I, 'tis I ;
Under their feet where the cross-roads meet
Dost thou think I can lie and lie,
Lord Robert, Lord Robert, Lord Robert?)

Chance for chance when they hap'd to meet
He pressed on her lip, he breathed in her ear,
Dear dear words and kisses sweet,
Words and kisses too sweet, too dear.
(Oh Lord Robert, Lord Robert, Lord Robert,
Oh Lord Robert, 'tis I, 'tis I;
Under their feet where the cross-roads meet,
Dost thou think I can lie and lie,
Lord Robert, Lord Robert, Lord Robert?)

When the morn enchants the east,
When the south is dazed with noon,
When the eve weeps to the west,
When the night beguiles the moon,
The maid moon that sat so lowly,
Sat so lowly with bended head,
Sat so lowly and rose so slowly,
Rose so slowly and walked so lowly,
Ever, ever with bended head,
Till the black, black hour of the starless sky,
The black, black hour and the dark, dark bed,
And live maids weep as they turn in their sleep,
Weep in their sleep and know not why,
And the white owls shriek and the dead men croon.

Now all ye gentlemen, grand and gay,
When you meet a maid by wood or lea,
Sir Knight, I pray, ride on thy way,

Nor turn and whisper, ' Remember me.'
Lest you drink no wine so strong or fine
But out of the cup, like a shell of the sea,
Thou shalt learn how slaves from their wormy graves
Can do that bidding, ' Remember me.'
(Oh Lord Robert, Lord Robert, Lord Robert,
Oh Lord Robert, 'tis I, 'tis I ;
Under their feet where the cross-roads meet
Dost thou think I can lie and lie,
Lord Robert, Lord Robert, Lord Robert ?)

Lest never in hall when the knights stand tall
And the goblets flash and the ladies shine,
And thou risest up the king of them all,
To drink to wassail and woman and wine,
Risest up with thy jewelled cup,
But out of the cup, like the sea in a shell,
A voice thou hast known by hill and wood,
A voice, a voice thou hast known too well !
And the cold wine boils on the lip like blood,
And the blood streams cold to the heart like wine,
Cold and hot to the heart like wine.
(Oh Lord Robert, Lord Robert, Lord Robert,
Oh Lord Robert, 'tis I, 'tis I ;
Under their feet where the cross-roads meet
Dost thou think I can lie and lie,
Lord Robert, Lord Robert, Lord Robert ?)

FRAGMENT OF BALLAD.

How shall I sing? the thing I crave
To say is speechless as a Lover's·trance.
How shall I give to thee
What even now is all so wholly thine
That but by losing thee in me
Or me in thee it never can be mine?

As a sliding wave of sliding sea
Before my following hand doth dance
Ever and ever onward to the shore,
And breaks and is a thousand things at once,
And from the moment's multiplicity
Takes itself up again into a wave:

So all I feel and see
Breaks to the thousand-fold of Fate and Chance,
But from the moment's multiplicity
Takes itself up into the thought of thee.

FRAGMENTS OF POEMS FOUND SINCE THE WRITER'S DEATH.

BAYONET SONG.

(This song was only found on detached fragments of paper, as it had
been scribbled down during illness.   Some of the passages may,
therefore, have been misplaced.)

FIRE away, fire away, boys must have their play,
There 'll be hard work yet
Before sunset :
But what of the day when the boys have had their play ?
When the boys have played, why then,
Aha !
'Twill be time for the men,   •
Hurrah !
And the bayonet !
But, men, as we 've nothing to do till then,
And the match is on out there,
I think you and I may as well stand by
And see that the game goes fair.

No drummer ! no tambourettes,
The earth is our drum wherever we come,
Bayonets, bayonets, bayonets, bayonets,

Bayonets, bayonets, bayonets, bayonets,
Where's the drumstick that ever could beat,
Where's the drumhead that ever could drum,
Like the mighty foot of our thousand feet, •
And the earth that is dumb till we come and come?
Come and come and come and come
Bayonets, bayonets, bayonets, bayonets.

' Love your enemy '—yes, 'tis the Briton's grace !
I love him so well that I'd see his face.
Yon little ninepins all in a row,
How can I tell if I love 'em or no?
So hurrah, lads, up we go !
Here's to our nearer meeting,
And if when we come within greeting
I see my own special foe,
I'll leave him to Tom or John,
And find my work further on,
And perhaps he and I will shake hands by and bye
Side by side as we lie
(To-night on the gory slope of the hill
As the dew-tears drop from the sky above
At the silent thought
Of the friends whom we love
Better still),
And wait for the surgeon's cart
That's always coming and never comes, .
And when a couple of bearers pass

I'll give him my turn,
Tho' the flesh-wounds smart,
And the bone-wounds burn,
And the life-tide's running dry
Because he's my enemy.
But that's when I've spiked up John's and Tom's
And Rosie's and Poll's and Marjorie's
And little Jack's and todlin May's
And the victory's won and the bloody day's
Done, and of flesh that is grass
Along the braes the bloody hay's
Made, that is made, hurrah!
With the bayonet.

For till you show me the Sacred Word
I'm for Peter and his good sword,
Only I hope if we'd drilled him here
He'd not have missed the head for the ear.

Gods, I'd give a Life's delights
To have been there that night of nights,
With ten such men as I see here now,
When they spat their sin on the Sinless Brow
And struck Him without let,—
And have heard the ten steels clash at my call
And seen the ten steels flash in the hall
As we did them all up to the wall,
High Priest, low Priest, Romans and all,

Great and small up to the wall,
Up to the wall with the bayonet.
I would keep or lose my right hand
By the love of every man here
For the dear native land.
There is not a man here this day
Of whom come what come can
I could speak with an accent of scorn.

Who feels his courage grow colder
At sight of the foe,
Whose conscience is bolder
Because we are shoulder to shoulder,
Who goes up the hill because we are men
And not because he is man,
He shall serve his country yet
But not with the bayonet.

Well done—I like your eyes,
Neither sunrise
Nor sunset.
Well done—I know the grips
That will tell to barrel and stock
What the beard hides on the lips:
No strain on the rein, no tug on the slips.
No drummer! no tambourettes!
The earth is our drum wherever we come,
Bayonets, bayonets, bayonets, bayonets,

Bayonets, bayonets, bayonets, bayonets,
Where's the drumstick that ever could beat,
Where's the drumhead that ever could drum,
Like the mighty foot of our thousand feet,
And the earth that is dumb till we come and come?
Till we come and come and come and come,
Bayonets, bayonets, bayonets, bayonets!

You are not dogs but Lions, and who
Holds Lions in leash? Hurrah,
My Lions k with just such a pack
I'd hunt down the gods of Olympus! Alack,
This mount is all an Olympus. Up there
You see the bird-popping goddikins—ten
To one I'll warrant you—bah!
What then?
Who cares while theirs is the ten to the one
And ours is the one to the ten?
Were't one to twenty which of us would shirk
The odds or the glory? You see
How the land lies?
This fox-cover up the long rise,
Then fifty paces of open, and then the breast-work.
Scatter the pack in cover, make them cast wide,
From wood-side to wood-side.
Go in like hounds and come out
At the top like men and lions—full swing
Up the wood, but when it's grey-blue

Overhead come together like men.
A halt for breath,
Slow-time and still as death
To the covert-edge, and then
The rush and the roar and the spring!
Hunt's up, my Lions, hie in, hurrah!

MENTANA.

'Mentana ! Mentana! nome che rammenterà mai sempre tre cose : la prodezza dei pochi contro i molti, l'intervento francese, e l'immobilità forzata dell'esercito regio, testimonio quasi oculare del conflitto fra volontari italiani da una parte, e i soldati papalini e francesi. La confusione e lo scoraggiamento prodotti dalla dissolvente azione degli alleati moderati furono tali, che lo stesso Garibaldi non ebbe che vaghe e incerte informazioni sulla presenza dei Francesi a Mentana. Meglio informato, è certo ch'egli avrebbe preso altre disposizioni. Il valore dei volontari e del loro capo fu qual fu sempre : ma la sproporzione del numero e delle armi era troppa : Garibaldi si ritirò, e il suo campo rimase custodito da una gloriosa retroguardia di 500 prodi volontarii . . . *morti!*'— *Extract from* '*L'Emancipazione*' *of October* 31, 1874.

'MOTHER, I hear a word
In the air !'
Play on, play on, my son,
The word thou hast heard is some bright sweet bird
That singeth, why and where
Who knows?
As who knows why and whither
The little wind blows
That bloweth hither and thither
But hardly stirs thy hair,

Hardly stirs the gossamers
Or a film of thy golden hair.

'Oh Mother, Mother dear,
Bend down, bend down to me!
Ah Mother, what dost thou hear?'
Hush, hush, my son,
I hear a word in the air.
'Ah Mother, why is thy face so white?
Ah Mother, Mother, why,
Are thine eyes alight?
Ah Mother, why is thy face so red?
Mother, Mother, the hair of thine head—'

Silence, boy, we are near them,
Silence, boy, the dead, the dead,
I hear them, I hear them, I hear them!
They come, they come, they are here, they are gone,
And they cried, with a single cry,
'Mentana!'
The word is said, the night is fled,
Ere we knew it dawn 'tis day,
The graves are wide, the dead are up and away,
On the racing winds they race
To call the living land.
Boy, I am again a wife!
Boy, I saw thy father's face!
Round him rode the self-same band,

That went round him that great day
To Glory's latest Altar-place—
Went around and fell around,
When the red-legged assassin on the hill
With conjurations bloody and base
Jabbered the slanting sunset to his will,
And by such pests did so incriminate
The air with murder, that, when, weary and late,
Upon the well-won field the conqueror stood
Masters of all the eye could see,
The star-cracked and berotted victory [1]
Burst in each glorious hand
And tore the sacred limits of sweet life,
And sluiced the dear heart's blood.
Ah God! if such blood could sink into the ground!

Up, up, my son, up, up, my soldier-son!
On with thy white-cross cap, while I
Bind me around with tri-colour
And let us go.
Whither? Whither they have gone before!
Haste! The dead have fleeter feet than ours.
See, the answering vales already move!
What is that, that like a moving sea
Floods towards the citied lilies of the towers

[1] Allusions to facts as reported by some newspaper corre-
spondents' letters on Mentana.

That soon shall ring
' Mentana ! '

Well done, well done,
Thy little sword and gun,
Thou shalt wave the sword while I will cry
' Mentana ! '
See, as we run the hamlets run,
The little towns are waving in the sun,
' Mentana ! '
Hark the bells thunder, hark the trumpets blow
' Mentana ! '
The mountains hear, the mists divide,
Look, look, on high,
The great tops crowned with joy and pride
Clang to the clanging vales below,
' Mentana ! '
A thousand clarions blaze from side to side
' Mentana ! '

What, must we rest again the little feet?
Cub of the Lion is thy dam too fleet?
Yet thou hast proved thy kind,
For see the misty miles behind,
And lo, before us what was dim is clear.
The city-walls, the city-gate,
The towers, the towers
That from our mountain seemed like flowers,

But hence like Pedestals that wait
The Statue of our Italy divine.

.

That Italy who, tho' she hath been hewn
In pieces,—as when the demons hew
An angel, whose immortal substance true
To his Eternal Image is not slain,
But from a thousand falchions rears again
Still undivided by division
His everlasting beauty, whole and one—
When sounds the trump whereat the nations rise
Shall lift her unseamed body to the skies
And in her flesh see (God)—

SNOWDROPS.

Fragment of a Poem that was to have described what the *sight hears*
and the *hearing sees* in some of the natural facts of Spring. (Barton
End, 1874).

HAVE you heard the Snowdrops ringing
Their bells to themselves?
Smaller and whiter than the singing
Of any fairy elves
Who follow Mab their Queen
When she is winging
On a moth across the night
And calls them all
With a far-twinkling call
Like the tiniest ray of tiniest starlight
That ever was seen?

Far and near, high and low,
Don't you hear the little bells go?
Not in the big winds that blow
The roaring beeches to and fro,
Not in the lower rivers

Of the breeze
Below the trees,
When the stiff bracken shines,
And the thin bent quivers,
And the limp green waves to and fro,
You shall hear the little bells go,

But in the jets and rivulets
That sputter from the melting snows
When against the mighty bole
Of a beech they dash and swirl
And twist and twirl,
The licking leaves throw
A thousand airy drops invisible
Down the strong perpendicular
To where the snowdrops are;
Tiny drops that fall and meet,
And swift and sweet
Run dim viewless course of fitful force,
Like an airy waterfall
You shall hear the little bells go
All the tiny snowbells swinging,
Tiny chauntlets high and low.

NEW-YEAR'S EVE.

As when at twelve o'clock
Strong January opes the gates of Life
And we that were so cabined and so dark
Within the round tower of the rounded year
Feel the far Spring blown in on us and look
Straight to the primroses, and with the swallow
Skim thro' the dawns of daffodils and up
To bluebell skies, and from the bluebell skies,
Like a wild hawk upon a flight of doves,
Swoop upon June and Paradise, and on
Beyond the bounds of Eden to an Earth
Boss'd with great purples of new-clustered wine
Betwixt the tented harvests red and gold,
And so into a cloud, and know no more——

LONDON: PRINTED BY
SPOTTISWOODE AND CO., NEW-STREET SQUARE
AND PARLIAMENT STREET